The
POSEIDON
Network

ALSO BY KATHRYN GAUCI

The Embroiderer
Seraphina's Song
The Carpet Weaver of Uşak

WWII

Conspiracy of Lies
Code Name Camille

WEBSITE

www.kathryngauci.com

The POSEIDON *Network*

KATHRYN GAUCI

First published in 2020 by Ebony Publishing
ISBN:
Paperback: 978-0-6487144-0-8

For Charles

"Spy: Always in high society."

Gustave Flaubert,
Dictionary of Accepted Ideas (1850)

Greek Language Note on Names

When someone is addressed directly by name in Greek and their name ends with an "s", the "s" is omitted. Therefore Yiannis would become Yianni. For the sake of simplicity, I have retained the "s".

Contents

Chapter 1

"All war is deception"

Sun Tzu

Cairo. June 1942

One never knows where fate will take us. Cairo taught me that. Expect the unexpected. Little did I realise when I left London that I would walk out of one nightmare into another. In Cairo, the incessant noise of London's air-raids heralding the arrival of Goering's Luftwaffe was replaced by the jingling cacophony of Egyptian street-life: the call of the muezzin, the braying of donkeys, and the honking of a thousand horns from dilapidated vehicles, as tired and worn-out as the animals that sauntered through the streets at a leisurely pace. The city was an assault on the senses, a pungent mixture of incense, sweet-smelling sheesha, animal dung, and petrol fumes. Added to this was the ever-present musky odour of dust from the Western Desert — the smell of a long-buried civilisation.

While a short spell in war-time Cairo might have appeared preferable to the bombing of Europe, there was a heightened perception of danger. For men like myself, 1942 was a waiting game. I was living a double-life, newspaper correspondent by career who doubled up as an agent for Churchill's newly formed Special Operations Executive, otherwise known as SOE. The organisation that had started up to set Europe ablaze, was poised to set the Middle East ablaze too. Officially we did not exist, and along with pimps, gangsters, and black-marketeers, I had joined the ranks of the underworld. The shadowy souks and cocktail parties of Cairo's elite had become my haunts. At that moment I had no idea which way my life would go.

Throughout 1941/42, I found myself covering several successful expeditions by the British who dealt a demoralising blow against the Italians. That Christmas, the whole of Cairo celebrated. By spring, the euphoria had turned to despair. It wasn't only the Germans who were on our minds, but Greece as well.

When the Italians attacked Greece in 1940, the defence of Greece was seen as vital to the Allies in the Middle East, but the Greek Prime Minster refused the offer of help. Even so, morale was high amongst the Greeks in Egypt and they displayed a patriotic fervour for their homeland. In a matter of weeks, they raised more money than the whole of the Egyptian national defence budget, and several thousand Greeks decided to go back and fight with their fellow countrymen. I covered their departure from Alexandria. Spirits were high, especially after the defeat of the Italians. We seemed invincible.

Every evening, I followed the reports coming in from Greece. The Italians were soon pushed back into Albania. At first, early successes brought jubilation. Then things stalled. The harsh winter had taken its toll, and news soon reached us that the

Greek army was trapped in the Albanian mountains. It was not looking good. If Greece was not adequately secured, it would be vulnerable to a German attack. In January 1941, Hitler sent one of his best generals to North Africa to aid the Italians — General Erwin Rommel. When the new Prime Minister asked for help, thousands of Allied troops were sent to aid the Greeks. Three months later, on 6th April, Germany invaded Greece. The occupation of Greece created a supply line to Rommel's Afrika Corps which threatened to unravel our earlier successes. All of a sudden, our invincibility appeared short-lived.

I followed the hourly bulletins with a deep sense of foreboding. Once a week I made contact with SOE at their headquarters in a non-descript block of flats called Rustem Buildings. On other occasions I paid visits to various establishments for clandestine meetings with fellow contacts, some of whom I had never seen before and most likely would never see again. Since arriving in the city, I was aware that I would be sent on a special assignment, and although I was given no more information at that time, it became increasingly obvious to me that it might be Greece.

Throughout this period, Shepheard's Hotel was my home away from home. If I wasn't out of the city on an assignment, or at one of the many cocktail parties, charity events, or gambling at The Continental, I could be found in the Long Bar, a notoriously indiscreet place for picking up snippets of information covering everything from *affaires d'amour*, to plans of the next desert offensive. Joe Scialom, the Swiss barman, was probably one of the best-informed men in Cairo. I liked him immensely. With just one nod of the head, or a glance towards a corner of the room where a certain gentleman might be having an intimate conversation with another, I eavesdropped on a few important conversations which otherwise might have eluded me.

One particularly hot afternoon in mid-June, I happened to be sitting on the terrace, when a woman with dark dramatic looks, wearing a white cotton dress, caught my attention. I must confess to more than a mild curiosity. She was one of the most alluring women I'd ever laid eyes on and quite took my breath away. There were plenty of beautiful women in Cairo. I should know, I'd found myself in their arms on several occasions. This woman was different. She looked to be in her late twenties or early thirties and exuded an air of mystery that I couldn't quite put my finger on. I must have watched her for a full ten minutes. She was reading a book, quite oblivious to everything going on around her. Occasionally, she brushed her hair back or stroked the folds of her dress with her free hand. She wore red nail polish that appeared like droplets of blood as she moved her hand across her dress. I was mesmerized; drawn to her like a moth to a flame.

My thoughts were interrupted by a voice behind me.

'Ah, my dear Mr Hadley, there you are. I've been looking everywhere for you.'

It was Lady Georgiana, the wife of Sir Oswald Blythe Pickering, one of the top brass from the Foreign Office.

'I'm throwing a charity benefit party next week to raise funds for the military hospital. I think our boys are in need of it after our recent disaster at the Battle of Gazala. Can I interest you in a few raffle tickets?'

I stood up, pulled out a chair for her and called the waiter over.

'Can I offer you a drink?' I asked.

'That would be lovely. I could do with a gin and tonic,' she replied, fanning herself with a gloved hand. 'This weather is beginning to get me down.'

Lady Georgiana was in her early thirties with a slender figure and startlingly attractive looks. She was a Londoner who had spent much of her time in Paris before becoming the wife of Sir Oswald and was quite a glamour girl. Her parties at their villa on Gezira Island were legendary, and everyone who was anyone vied to be there. I was one of the lucky ones. She'd taken a shine to me from the moment I arrived. She said it was because I didn't pretend to be something I wasn't. What that meant, I was never quite sure. She pushed the book of raffle tickets across the table and gave me one of her charming smiles. I could never resist a beautiful smile and bought the lot.

'You're such a gentleman,' she said with a mischievous smile. 'I can always rely on you.'

As she put the money in her bag, I glanced in the direction of the woman in white. My heart dropped. She had gone.

'Are you alright?' Lady Georgiana asked. 'You seem far away.'

'I thought I saw an old friend,' I said casually. 'But I must have been mistaken.'

Inwardly, I cursed myself for not going over and introducing myself. Now it was too late. Instead, I contented myself with Lady Georgiana's chatter about her upcoming fund-raising event.

Chapter 2

I could not get the woman in white out of my mind. I made discreet enquiries to see if she was a guest at the hotel. Simply describing her as a ravishing, dark-haired beauty was like looking for a needle in a haystack, and without a name, it proved fruitless. I would just have to wait and see if she turned up again.

Fortunately, I didn't have to wait long. Two days later, I happened to be strolling past Khan Al-Khalili bazaar when I caught sight of her entering the Babal Ghuri gate. It was the flash of her white dress that caught my eye; only this time she was wearing a colourfully embroidered shawl that partially covered her dark hair. I decided to follow her. Navigating the bazaar's busy labyrinthine alleyways wasn't easy. They meandered in all directions and I almost lost sight of her when a line of donkeys passed, laden with copper and brass pots. When we reached the area of the cotton merchants, she disappeared into a small shop outside which stood several shabby mannequins displaying a few clothes. Their faces had been so amateurishly painted, they looked like gargoyles. The sign over the shop front told me the proprietor was Greek — Hadzigiannis — and I could see by the row of four men and two women busily working on sewing machines inside, that it was a tailor's. More suits and women's dresses filled the tiny window. I hung about for a while at a nearby fabric shop on the pretext of looking for a certain type of fabric, and at the same time keeping a lookout to see when she would leave.

Fifteen minutes later, she reappeared. I disentangled myself from the intense bartering taking place with the shop owner and set about following her again. We soon left the bazaar and were back in the main street. This time I followed her to a popular cafe, The Parisian, frequented by the European and Levantine communities. As she had no idea who I was, I went inside and sat at a table on the other side of the room, reading a newspaper. She ordered a coffee and looked at her watch. I could tell by the look on her face that she was agitated. After a while, she was joined by a chestnut-haired woman who appeared to be of a similar age. I wasn't close enough to hear their conversation, but the look on both their faces told me things weren't going too well. The second woman soon got up and left. The woman in white opened her purse, left a coin on the table, and walked out after her, leaving her coffee untouched. Naturally, I attempted to follow her, but by the time I got to the door, she was getting into the back of a taxi. I scanned the street desperately trying to hail another, but they were all full. I was back to square one.

*

Soft lights threaded through the trees and bushes surrounding the Blythe Pickering's villa could be seen flickering like fireflies from the mooring on the other side of the Nile. The felucca was already waiting for me. On board were three other guests, champagne in hand, eager to have a good time. I was looking forward to the evening. It would give me a chance to take my mind off our humiliating defeat at the Battle of Gazala, not to mention the woman in the white dress who, after less than a week, had become an unhealthy obsession. With no wind that evening to propel the sails, the boatman pushed the oar against the bank and we began to glide effortlessly across the water. Jazz music floated through the night air, mingling with the last calls of birdlife before they settled for the night amongst the reeds. Already my spirits were uplifted.

As we neared the island, the sounds of laughter rang out. A handful of intoxicated guests had decided to take a swim in the nude. Two Nubian servants in white gelibeyas and wearing turbans stood on the bank holding towels, looking on nervously. Sir Oswald and Lady Georgiana turned a blind eye to this sort of thing.

'Just letting off steam,' Sir Oswald was fond of saying. 'This damn war and the heat drive men crazy.'

The war had certainly thrown us into an unreal world. Who could blame them? We stepped out of the boat and were greeted by another servant holding a large tray of champagne. Helping ourselves thirstily, we headed along the pathway in the direction of the music. A jazz band was playing on the terrace and the makeshift dance floor in the centre of the lawn was filled with couples. The Blythe Pickerings certainly knew how to entertain and no war was going to prevent their guests from having a good time. Tables decorated with fragrant floral arrangements had been set-up all around the lawn and food was plentiful. I joined a group of friends and tucked into a platter of meat and pilaf. Lady Georgiana saw me and came over.

'My dear Larry,' she said, planting a kiss on my cheek, and pulling me up from my seat 'I have someone I'd like you meet.'

We threaded our way through the dance floor to the other side of the garden where a group of people were standing under a flame tree in a heated discussion about the recent events in Libya. I already knew most of them. One woman had her back to me. Lady Georgiana touched her arm.

'Alexis, allow me to introduce you to a friend of mine.'

When the woman turned around, my heart skipped a beat. It was the woman in white, only this time she was wearing a low-cut, emerald silk dress that showed off her exquisite Lalique diamond necklace to perfection. The ravishing creature in front of me was certainly a woman of grace and style.

'Alexis, this is Larry Hadley, a correspondent for the Daily News.'

The woman extended her hand. 'Good evening, Mr Hadley. Alexis Petrakis. It's a pleasure to meet you. Georgiana tells me you are an excellent reporter.'

You could have knocked me over with a feather. I had thought of nothing but her since I laid eyes on her, and now here we were, being introduced to each other. I had always been told that fate works in mysterious ways in the East. Perhaps they were right.

'Lady Georgiana flatters me,' I replied.

'She also tells me that you are familiar with the Balkans. Were you a reporter there too?'

Lady Georgiana laughed. 'Larry doesn't like to talk about himself. He's rather a dark horse.'

Alexis gave me the sort of penetrating smile that showed she saw straight through me. 'Is that so, Mr Hadley?'

'Let's say I spent a few years there, mainly Yugoslavia and Greece.'

'Where were you in Greece?' she asked.

'I was based in Athens, but I did manage to travel around quite a bit.'

'Then you would know the Church of the Virgin of the Swallow in Kato Kifissia?'

She asked me in Greek. Clearly, she was testing me.

'I believe that it was also a place of worship in ancient times, something to do with the nymphs of the Kifissios River,' I replied in my best Greek. 'I've never actually been there though.'

She smiled. 'Your Greek is very good. Did you pick it up in Greece?

'I studied both Latin and Classical Greek at school so it gave me a good grounding. It was in Greece that I was really able to polish it up.'

The band started to play a foxtrot and I asked if she would care to dance. Holding her in my arms, I pulled her closer and inhaled the scent of her perfume, a heady blend of rose, lily of the valley and something else — something exotic — maybe amber or sandalwood. Whatever it was, I wanted to devour her with kisses and I had a feeling she knew it.

'You dance well, Mr Hadley,' she said, when the music stopped.

In an effort not to make my feelings too obvious, I escorted her back to the group with the intention of joining my friends at the table.

'It was a pleasure to meet you, Miss Petrakis,' I said, as I took my leave. 'Hopefully there will be another occasion where we can dance together.'

Her eyes sparkled mischievously in the soft light. 'I shall look forward to it. And please do call me Alexis.'

Taking her words as a promising sign, I walked away. Her scent still lingered in the air. My God, she had definitely lit a flame in my heart and I prayed that the war would not take her away from me before I'd had time to get to know her better. All night I kept a watch on her out of the corner of my eye. Each time she danced with another man, I drank. Drink had steadily become my solace in times of stress. I'd seen too much. It dulled the pain. I had to watch myself. This was one woman I didn't want to see my vices.

At some time in the early hours of the morning, I said goodbye to my hosts and took my leave. Alexis had already left.

'A pretty little thing, isn't she?' Lady Georgiana said with a smile.

When I asked who, she burst out laughing.

'Oh, come, Larry. You can't fool me, and from what I saw, I don't think you fooled her either. Nothing like a Greek goddess to set the heart on fire, is there?'

For someone who had spent the last few years as an undercover agent, I thought I had perfected the art of not giving myself away. When it came to Miss Petrakis, clearly not! I had better lift my game. We were at war. Letting my guard down could spell danger.

Lady Georgiana looped her arm through mine.

'Come on, Larry darling. I'll walk you to the boat.'

As we neared the water, she informed me that they were going on a picnic in the desert the following weekend.

'Oswald wants to get a spot of shooting in too. We would love it if you would join us.'

I had plenty to keep me busy until then but the outing would be a welcome change and I accepted without hesitation.

'Fine. We'll pick you up in the lobby at Shepheard's 3:00 p.m. sharp. Don't be late. We don't want to miss the sunset.'

She stood on the bank and waved goodbye. 'And by the way,' she called out as an afterthought. 'Miss Petrakis will be joining us.'

As the boatman silently took me back across the Nile, I leaned back in the softly cushioned seat and smiled to myself. A week ago, all I had on my mind was the war. It had dulled my senses. Now my emotions were alive again. I had the woman in white to thank for that.

Chapter 3

The procession of three cars and Sir Oswald's jeep turned off the main road near the Great Pyramid at Giza and headed south towards Faiyoum. The road soon petered out into a featureless landscape of barren stony desert, seemingly devoid of all life. One of the cars was piled high with camping equipment and baskets of food and drink. The two Nubian servants, who had stood on the bank of the Nile with towels for the rowdy guests, and whose sole job now was to keep us replenished with food and drink, also rode with the luggage.

The rest of the party consisted of Sir Oswald, who drove in his jeep along with Brigadier Curzon, an old friend of the Blythe Pickerings' on his way to a posting in India, myself, a couple from Alexandria, two officials associated with the War Office, Lady Georgiana, Alexis Petrakis, and much to my surprise, the woman I had seen her arguing with that afternoon in The Parisian, who turned out to be another Greek by the name of Irini. Sir Oswald had also brought along his two hunting dogs who seated themselves excitedly in the jeep beside him. The heat was unbearable and except for Alexis, who wore a wide-brimmed straw bonnet under which her hair was pulled back and tied with a white scarf, we were grateful to be wearing safari hats. After travelling for almost an hour, we stopped for refreshments at an oasis village and consumed several small glasses of sweet tea in the village square before continuing on our journey. It never ceased to amaze me how crazy the British were in Africa. No sane Egyptian would be heading out for a picnic in such heat.

At some point, we turned left until the desert met a narrow strip of green in the Nile Delta. Here we set up camp — camp consisting of a tent under which the servants set up a long table covered with a white tablecloth, silverware, and one of Lady Georgiana's bone china dinner sets from Cairo's fashionable department store, *Le Salon Vert*. I was given the task of setting up the gramophone for the ladies. Leaving the women with the servants to unload the baskets of food, the men headed towards the bushes for a spot of shooting. Mohamed, Sir Oswald's man-servant, accompanied us as a beater.

This fertile area of palms, bushes and reeds proved to be a haven for water birds. We were all excellent shots and by the time the sun started to set, had managed to bag several dozen. When we returned to the campsite, the servants had a fire going and were sitting on their haunches baking freshly-made flat-bread. Sir Oswald handed them half a dozen birds. In no time at all, they were plucked, cleaned and roasting over the coals.

The sun was sinking fast, a blood-red fireball sliding towards the horizon, casting a magical glow over the desert landscape and becoming more intense by the minute. This is what we had driven so far to see. An ancient land bathed in a sea of shimmering reds.

'It's simply breath-taking,' Alexis said, handing me a glass of champagne. 'Even in war, the world can be a beautiful place.'

We all sat and watched the setting sun until finally, it slipped over the horizon and billowing waves of twinkling diamonds streaked the night sky. The warmth still lingered in the air. Someone put a record on the gramophone and the couple from Alexandria got up to dance. They were joined by Lady Georgiana and the Brigadier. Irini danced alone, swaying to the music with her eyes closed as if in a trance. Alexis leaned closer and whispered in my ear.

'Why were you following me the other day?'

Her question took be quite by surprise. I had to think quickly.

'I'm not sure what you mean?' I replied, rather unconvincingly.

She gave me a half smile and leaned back in the chair, studying me. 'Okay, Mr Hadley. Have it your own way.'

'I thought we'd agreed to do away with formalities,' I replied. 'Anyway, as we've become acquainted, I'm interested to know more about you. When did you arrive?'

'I came by naval boat from Crete almost a year ago. We were one of the last groups to escape.'

'What made you come here?' I asked. 'Why didn't you go back to Athens?'

She looked up at the night sky as if pondering her words carefully.

'Greece is no longer free. Let's leave it at that. What about you? You have the freedom to move about and report for your newspaper. How do you think things will turn out? Will we win or will Egypt be the next to fall?'

'If you ask me, the Germans have stretched themselves too far. This desert will be Rommel's undoing.'

She looked into my face, as if trying to read me. 'I hope

you're right — for all our sakes. We can't afford to lose. The consequences don't bear thinking about.'

It was almost time to depart. Irini put on another record while the servants packed everything away.

'And Irini?' I asked, still wondering where the other woman fitted into the picture. 'Did she arrive with you?'

'I met her here, in Cairo. She happens to be staying at the same hotel,' Alexis replied, curtly. 'I hardly know her.'

Her answer surprised me, especially after seeing them together in The Parisian. Clearly, she did not want to continue the conversation and I had the distinct feeling I'd touched a raw nerve.

'How about one last dance under the stars before we leave?' she asked, holding out her hand.

The heat of the day had well and truly gone by now and it was getting chilly. I held her close as we danced cheek to cheek. The words to the song echoed my feelings — *Stay as sweet as you are — don't let a thing ever change you — don't let a soul rearrange you...* How I wanted that moment to last. I knew nothing about her, but I knew I'd fallen in love. They always said war makes you do things you wouldn't normally do.

Heading back to Cairo, we made one more last stop at the oasis. The servants replenished our water while the village women brought us sweet tea and slices of fruit. Irini said she was going for a stroll. Some minutes later, we heard a cry. One of the villagers had found Irini lying on the ground near the well. By the time we got there, she was delirious, barely responding to our anxious cries.

'Get her inside,' someone called out in Arabic. 'Lay her on a bed.'

Soon the entire village gathered to see what was going on. An intense discussion ensued. Had she eaten something that disagreed with her? Did she drink too much? Was it sunstroke? The headman of the village called for the village healer. The old woman asked the men to step outside the room while she examined her. Irini's delirium was worsening by the minute, her heartbeat abnormally fast, and her vision blurred. Watched on by an anxious Lady Georgiana and Alexis, the old woman ran her hands over Irini's body.

'Fetch me some goat's milk,' she called out. 'Quickly!'

Minutes later, someone handed her a pitcher of fresh milk. In Arabic, she ordered the women to sit Irini up while she poured a little goat's milk into a cup. Irini's eyes were rolling upwards and her head was lolling on her chest. The woman forced her to take the goat's milk.

'Swirl it around your mouth and spit it out,' she cried, holding a small dish under her chin. 'Don't drink it.'

Not understanding Arabic, Mohamed and the headman entered the room to translate.

'She must spit it out,' Mohamed told the women. 'Whatever you do, don't let her swallow it.'

In her usual no-nonsense manner, Lady Georgiana slapped Irini's cheek, hard. 'Do as you're told, my girl. Swirl the milk around in your mouth and spit it into this dish.'

Irini spat the milk out and the woman whisked the dish away and examined it.

'The milk is curdling,' she called out. 'It's a snake bite. *Inshallah, in tamut*! God willing, she will not die.'

Fearful that they were too late to save her, the villagers started praying. The woman ordered someone to bring her certain medicines from her house while she returned to the bed and searched Irini's legs for the bite. It was at the back of her ankle — two tiny pin pricks, barely visible earlier by lantern light, but which were now red and swollen. She wrapped a piece of cloth around her calf in a tourniquet, bent over to suck away any venom from the wound, and spat it out on the ground. In the meantime, the men picked up sticks and began to trace Irini's footsteps. Next to the well was a pile of wood. Someone kicked at it. There lay the reason for Irini's illness — a horned viper, one of Africa's most venomous snakes. With one deft stroke, one of the men cut it in half with his machete.

Back inside the hut, the woman hurriedly pounded her medicinal concoction with cow's blood and forced Irini to drink it. She vomited it up straight away. The old woman was persistent, not giving up until she was satisfied Irini had swallowed the entire antidote. All we could do now was to wait and see. Drawing on a lifetime of tribal medicine, the woman was sure it would work. After a few hours, Irini developed a high fever. We were assured this was normal. By the time the sun rose, the woman declared the worst was over, but it would be touch and go if they didn't get her to a hospital straight away. Sir Oswald gave the village several hundred Egyptian Pounds for their trouble and we returned to Cairo, our high spirits somewhat dampened by the snake-bite incident.

Irini was taken to the hospital and put under supervision. Throughout all this, one thing caught my attention — Alexis's attitude to her. While Lady Georgiana had shown considerable concern, Alexis appeared unemotional and distant.

We dropped Alexis at her hotel before continuing to Shepheard's.

'Can I see you again?' I asked.

She shook my hand. 'I don't think that would be a good idea.'

If I am honest with myself, it wasn't quite the answer I was expecting. I was under the illusion that she rather enjoyed my company, however brief it had been. She saw the look of disappointment on my face.

'But who knows,' she added, with a smile. 'Maybe our paths will cross again.'

I watched her until she disappeared inside the hotel. A part of me wanted to run after her and take her in my arms, telling her that she couldn't escape from me that easily, but the other part — the cool-headed part that came with being a secret agent — told me to back off. I was licked.

Chapter 4

I spent the next few weeks in Alexandria. There was much to cover. After Rommel's recent win, Alexandrians were fearful the Germans would take over the city any day. Except for the military, most of the British had either left for Cairo or sent their families to Palestine or South Africa. Alexandria was normally a cosmopolitan place. Now it was silent — a ghost city. Those who were left hid behind locked doors, the German flag ready at hand to hang out of the window at any moment. Working undercover, it gave me a good chance to note those whose sympathies were not with the Allies. The Egyptian Nationalists despised us and there were several fifth columnists amongst the expatriate inhabitants ready to denounce the Allies. Each day, I reported back to my contacts in Intelligence. We had to turn the tide in this damn war or, as Alexis had pointed out all too clearly, we were done for.

In July, the first Battle of El Alamein was lost by Rommel. It was a stalemate. We were not out of the woods yet, but had dealt the Germans a bitter blow. I returned to Cairo in August amid scenes of jubilation. My first thought was to call by the hotel where Alexis was staying to see if she wanted to join me in celebrating our recent victory with a meal at *P'tit Coin de France*, but with HQ in Cairo and London eager for an update, I thought better of it. I did, however, make a phone call to the hospital to check on Irini. I was told she had been discharged after a week.

I finished my work and went downstairs to the Long Bar. A friend of mine who also stayed at the hotel was waiting for me. Jack Martins was an old friend from my days in the Balkans. He worked for MI6 and we'd spent many a night together getting drunk in less than salubrious establishments in the pursuit of women or a good story.

'I heard you were back and thought you might like some company,' said Jack, and suggested we go to a nightclub not too far away.

The streets were filled with late night revellers and off-duty soldiers making their way into the seedier parts of Cairo in the hope of having a good time before returning to the desert. We slipped into a nightclub in a side-street and were shown through the smoke-filled room to our regular table. A bottle of wine soon appeared on the table, along with a platter of finger food. The singer, accompanied by a pianist, sang a rendition of a Jerome Kerr song. After this, a belly dancer appeared. Her expertise in dancing was matched only by her expertise in persuading the soldiers to part with their money — Jack and I included. After we pressed a few notes into her jangling silver belt, placed provocatively so low on her hips that it looked as if it would slip off at any moment, she moved to the next table.

Jack asked me about Alexandria. He told me he was off to Turkey in a few days' time and hoped we might meet up there. I still had no idea where I would end up. My contacts were certainly keeping things close to the bone. I was just starting to enjoy myself when he dropped a bombshell.

'Two men came looking for you while you were away. Not sure who they were, but they had a whiff of the secret police about them.'

I stared at him for a moment, thinking he was playing one of his little jokes on me.

'I think it might have had something to do with the body they found.'

The look on his face told me this wasn't a joke.

'What body?'

'It's supposed to be hush-hush, but from what I gather, a young woman's body was found in the Nile. Turns out she was Greek, a friend of Lady Georgiana and Sir Oswald.'

I felt a sharp pain rise in my throat and struggled to breathe. *Alexis, God no! Surely not!*

'Are you alright?' Jack asked. 'You look as though you've seen a ghost.'

'Why didn't you tell me before? Do you know her name?'

'Steady on, old boy. You were away. I didn't think much of it. And to your second question, no, I don't know her name. There was nothing about it in the Egyptian Gazette.'

I downed my drink in one go and got up to leave. Jack asked if I knew who it was. I replied that I was as much in the dark as he was, but that there was someone I'd met recently from Greece and I hoped to God it wasn't her.

'I haven't seen her since our trip in the desert. If you don't mind, I'd like to check at the hotel where she's staying — just to put my mind at rest.'

Jack paid the waiter and we caught a taxi to Alexis's hotel. I asked him to wait outside as I would only be a few minutes, but he refused.

'Do you have a Miss Alexis Petrakis staying here?' I asked at the reception.

I drummed my fingers anxiously on the desk while the man looked at the guest list. Before he could reply, I felt a tap on my shoulder. I swung round and was confronted by two men in suits.

'Mr Hadley,' the taller one of the two said. 'We've been looking for you. If you wouldn't mind accompanying us back to HQ. We'd like to have a little chat with you.'

He took out a badge from his jacket, allowed me a cursory glance, and gestured towards the door. Jack looked on, dumbfounded. During our times together in the Balkans, we'd often found ourselves in a few sticky situations, most of them of our own making, but this episode had me baffled.

'Get on the phone to Sir Oswald,' I said to Jack, as they led me away. 'Be quick about it.'

*

There are times when it pays to have friends in high places. Sir Oswald came to my rescue within half an hour of me being bundled into a stifling hot room awaiting interrogation. After signing a document, I was allowed to leave. Sir Oswald said he was taking me for a bite to eat at the Gezira Sporting Club.

'They do a fine Nile Perch in aspic,' he said, as we drove away.

The last thing on my mind was food.

'We tried to call you when we found out,' Sir Oswald continued. 'But you were out of town.'

26

'For God's sake,' I said unable to contain myself any longer. 'Tell me what's going on. Who drowned? I heard she was Greek. Please don't tell me it was Alexis.'

'The woman was Irini,' Sir Oswald replied, matter-of-factly. 'Irini Vlachou.'

A part of me breathed a huge sigh of relief. The other part stirred up feelings of unease. 'But she'd only just come out of hospital.'

'It appears to have happened soon afterwards.'

'Perhaps she was released too early. Maybe she became disoriented and slipped. It's easily done.'

Sir Oswald picked up the menu. 'She was shot. It was murder,' he said, casting a glance over the dishes of the day.

'Shot!' I stammered.

'Clean through the heart. Whoever did this knew what they were doing.'

My mind jumped back to the argument in The Parisian.

'Why wasn't it reported in the newspapers, and what has this got to do with me?'

'The police are questioning everyone who is known to have been with her over the past few weeks. Naturally, as she accompanied us into the desert, I was alerted. I couldn't tell them anything as I'd only just met her myself. Georgie invited her because of Alexis.'

'So you knew nothing about her?'

'Afraid not, old chap. Georgie met Alexis at a garden party thrown by Mme Capsalis, wife of the Greek Prime Minister in exile. She took an instant liking to her. The first time I met Alexis was the night you came to our party. When Georgie asked if she would like to accompany us on the picnic in the desert, she asked if she could bring a friend along. That friend was Irini.'

Sir Oswald ordered the Nile perch accompanied by a Jerusalem artichoke mousse and a side dish of roast vegetables. My stomach still churned. I ordered salad and a cognac.

'This is where it gets rather murky,' Sir Oswald continued. 'I was called to look at the body to confirm it was the same woman. That's when I was told it was to be kept under wraps — although news does have a habit of travelling fast. The newspapers were forbidden to report it.'

'For what reason?'

'Security. It is thought she was following the Greek Royal family and members of the Greek government-in-exile. She was spotted on numerous occasions by their bodyguards. About ten days before we met, she was seen at Mena House, the residence of the King's mistress.'

'You mean Joyce Britten-Jones?'

Sir Oswald gave an uncomfortable cough. 'You see what I mean about news travelling fast.' He smiled.

I refrained from telling him that I probably knew more about the Greek Royal family and the Greek government-in-exile than he did. After all, I made it my business to know.

'Go on,' I said.

'It appears Irini was followed after being seen there. At first it all seemed innocent, until she was spotted in a cafe in a seedy part of the Arab Quarter, with a Greek.'

'That's hardly an indictable offence. After all, she is — *was* — Greek.'

'That man is known to be a Nazi sympathizer. Intelligence have had their eyes on him for a while. He runs a cotton exporting business — the Egyptian Cotton Co. Seems like his business interests soared when the Hitler came to power. He was a regular visitor to Germany and he does a lot of trade with Turkey and the Middle East.'

I wondered why he had never been drawn to my attention, especially as a part of my job was to spy on such people.

'Did they bring him in for questioning?'

The food arrived and despite the gloomy conversation, Sir Oswald tucked in with gusto.

'It really is good,' he said, referring to the fish. 'You should try it.'

I shook my head. 'This man,' I asked again. 'Did the police arrest him?'

'Mr Papaghiotis — Dimitris Papaghiotis,' Sir Oswald replied. 'Yes, but they couldn't pin anything on him and let him go. His excuse — he took a shine to her and wanted to strike up an affair.'

A smile crossed my face. If this wasn't so serious it would have been funny.

'Turns out he is in the habit of chatting up the new arrivals from Greece and was quite successful. He has a string of mistresses — some Greek, one Italian, and a few Egyptians. When the police showed me his photograph, I realised they fell for his money rather than his charms. He showered them with gifts. With so many leaving Greece because of the war, no doubt he affords them security when their funds run out.'

'So are you saying they still have no idea who shot Irini, or even a motive?'

'That's correct.'

'All the same, I can't see what her death has to do with me.'

'Mere formalities, that's all. They won't bother you again. I've seen to that.'

This sudden turn of events had thrown me. For one thing, it made me realise that Alexis was still very much in my thoughts.

'Tell me one thing, Sir Oswald,' I asked, after digesting the situation. 'What does Alexis have to say about all this?'

Sir Oswald put down his knife and fork and wiped the corner of his mouth with a white serviette, embroidered at the corner with an elaborate gold monogram of the Gezira Sporting Club.

'That is the question. I have no idea.'

I looked surprised. 'But both you and Georgie — I mean, Lady Georgiana — are well-acquainted with her now. And she was Irini's friend.'

Sir Oswald sighed heavily. 'Your guess is as good as mine. I'm afraid she's vanished.'

'Vanished!' I exclaimed, rather too loudly.

Sir Oswald asked the waiter to bring over a box of Cuban cigars. He took one, cut the end with a cigar-cutter and lit it with a match. 'Nowhere to be found, old boy.' He leaned back in his chair and drew on the cigar. 'I have personally looked into her disappearance. Wherever she is, she's not in Cairo.'

Chapter 5

The following evening, I met up with Jack Martins on the terrace at Shepheard's. I was exhausted and ordered a double scotch on the rocks.

'I've been looking for you all day,' Jack said. 'Glad to see you back safe and sound. Are you going to tell me what it was all about?

'You were right. There was a body found in the Nile. Thank God, she wasn't the woman I was worried about. However, I did know the deceased. She was a friend of hers by the name of Irini. I believe her surname is Vlachou. She joined us the day we went into the desert. No-one seems to know much about her, or if they do, they're not telling us.'

'And your friend, what does she have to say about this Irini?'

'That's just it, Jack. She's gone.'

'Gone where? Is she implicated?'

'Not as far as I know.'

I confess, Jack's blunt question about Alexis stirred up mixed feelings. I didn't want to tell him too much, yet I knew if I didn't, he would smell a rat and make discreet enquiries of his own. Jack was one of the few men I could trust. I decided to tell him everything — which wasn't much.

'I went back to her hotel this morning and was told that she checked out shortly after Irini's body was discovered. That's all I know. Even Sir Oswald doesn't know where she is.'

'Ah, that old dark horse,' Jack replied. 'Not much happens in Cairo that he doesn't know about. You sure he's not hiding something from you?'

'Why would he?'

'Just asking!'

I told Jack I'd spent much of the day re-tracing the same steps I took the day I followed Alexis.

'I can't do much about the mysterious Irini,' I said, 'but I am rather anxious about Alexis.'

'I can see that,' Jack replied. 'Where did you meet her?'

'I first saw her when she was sitting over there — behind where you're sitting now, three tables away. She was wearing a white dress and...'

Jack grinned at me. 'I've never seen you so concerned about any woman like this before. She must be one hell of a woman.'

'The thing is,' I continued, 'when I did see her again — on those two occasions, she struck me as a person who could handle herself. She was self-assured and, well, how shall I put it, not at all naïve. In fact, she was pretty cool. Maybe that's another reason I liked her — besides her beauty.'

'Why are you talking like this? Do you think she's dead too?'

'No. I think there's more to it than that, but I can't figure out what. Alexis and Irini had an argument in The Parisian. Irini walked out. And when I saw them together during our trip in the desert, Alexis all but ignored her. I am sure they didn't even like each other.'

Jack looked puzzled. 'An argument is not much to go on.

Why ask a friend along on an outing if you don't like her? Quite odd if you ask me. What about the tailor she visited — the one in the bazaar? Did you check him out?'

'You mean Hadzigiannis? Yes. I went in and asked to see the owner who turned out to be an old man who hardly has anything to do with the place. These days, his son, Stefanos Hadzigiannis, is in charge. When I asked him if he knew Alexis, he became anxious and said he'd never heard of her. I tried to describe her, including what she was wearing that day — the beautiful embroidered shawl — but he still insisted he had no idea who she was, adding that he has lots of beautiful Greek customers. I looked around the shop. None of the tailors met my gaze.'

'Hmm!' Jack said, puzzled. 'And what about the man Irini met in the cafe, the one who owns the cotton company? Dimitris Papaghiotis.'

I called the waiter over to get us another drink. 'Don't you find it odd that a man of his wealth with a string of mistresses, who he apparently is not afraid of flaunting in public, would meet up with another Greek woman, who I might also add, was quite attractive, in a seedy cafe? It seems out of character.'

'That had occurred to me,' Jack replied, thoughtfully.

We sat in silence for a while, pondering the next move. Jack said he would make some discreet enquiries of his own. Sometime around midnight, we bade each other goodnight. Working as an undercover agent can be a solitary life. I was used to keeping my feelings to myself, but this was different. Alexis had got under my skin, and for once, it was a relief to be able to talk to someone openly about it all. I was grateful to him for listening.

A week passed and I was still none the wiser about Irini's murder or Alexis's disappearance. In the end, I was forced to accept the status quo. Wherever she was, I was obviously not in her thoughts she was in mine. I had to move on.

In October, I left Cairo for Alexandria again. This time the Eighth Army had a new man at the helm in the shape of Montgomery. I liked him. He seemed to know his business. Holed up in my hotel room, which was so small I called it the foxhole, I reported back to HQ and SOE daily. Things were heating up. At precisely ten o'clock on the 23rd October, a thousand British guns opened fire. By the end of the first week in November, the Eighth Army had recaptured Tobruk. A few weeks later, I was summoned back to Cairo for a meeting with my SOE contact.

When I arrived back at Shepheard's, there was a note from Jack.

Larry,

Sorry to have missed you. Duty calls.

Jack

PS. Did a bit of sleuth work while you were away.

It seems that our Mr Papaghiotis has been passing on information to the Germans in Athens.

I hardly had time to digest this when the telephone rang. I was ordered to report to Rustem Buildings as soon as possible. When I arrived, the Colonel was sitting behind his desk with a file marked Most Secret. The assignment I had been waiting for almost a year was on. I was to leave Egypt that same night to help prepare the groundwork for the Allied landing in Greece. Using my alias — Kapetan Nikos Xenakis — my job would be to liaise with the White Rose, head of the largest Resistance group in Greece — the Poseidon Network.

The Colonel got up to shake my hand. 'Good luck, Hadley, and don't forget our motto — "Improvise and Dare".'

I would need all the luck I could get.

Chapter 6

Greece. December 1942.

It was two-thirty in the morning when the B-24 Liberator reached the Greek mainland. A voice called out from the cockpit to prepare ourselves. Within the next ten minutes, we would reach our drop zone somewhere in the mountainous region of Central Greece, north-west of Athens. We were informed from the outset that the weather in Greece had turned bad, but SOE deemed the mission too important to abort. I listened to the steady gentle sound of the engine and checked my equipment. As the plane neared the drop zone, it hit turbulence. I looked at the men's faces. No-one displayed the slightest sign of nervousness.

The hatch opened, and one by one we bailed out — right into a heavy snowstorm. I was the last. In the blackness, the whirling snow hit my face like a thousand sharp needles and I prayed we hadn't gone off course. Seconds later I saw the flicker of three fires below and landed in a clearing blanketed in snow. A handful of well-armed *andartes* rushed to my aid.

'Bravo, you made it,' a voice boomed out.

That man was my old friend, Loukas — or "*O Lykos*" as we were to know him by — "the Wolf".

'Kapetan Nikos,' he said, careful not to use my real name. 'Welcome back to Greece.'

I looked around. We were barely able to see more than a few metres in front of us. Thankfully, all my men had landed without incident, except one, who was missing.

'Let's get you all out of here,' Loukas said. 'My men will continue to search for him.'

We followed him up a steep embankment of rocks until we reached a cave where a handful of men had a fire going, roasting a sheep in celebration of our arrival. Shortly after we'd finished the meal we heard voices outside the cave. Loukas's men returned. It was not good news. They were carrying the crumpled body of the missing agent. His parachute had failed to open. The men crossed themselves.

'We have to bury him straight away,' Loukas said. He turned to one of his men. 'Father Papagrigoriadis, will you say a prayer for this brave *palikari*?'

The men took up pickaxes and shovels and went outside to dig a makeshift grave while I went through the agent's pockets and retrieved his papers. A cross of stones was placed on top of the grave as a marker. When the time was right, someone would dig up what was left of the body and take it to the village where it would be given a proper burial. With the snow still falling around us, and the temperature plummeting, Father Papagrigoriadis removed his gun and ammunition belt and laid them carefully against a boulder while he said a few prayers. Bob Cohen, aka Markos Boureli, had been one of my sappers and his skills would be sorely missed. It wasn't a good start.

Sometime later the men divided into groups and we left the cave. I headed north with Loukas to the mountain village of Ano Hora, some ten kilometres away. We arrived at a house just before daybreak. From here I would be heading back south to Athens where I would meet up with my men again. The house belonged to a widow whose husband was killed near Albania fighting the Italians. Loukas informed me she had a daughter who aided the Resistance.

The widow welcomed me like a member of the family. Food was scarce but she insisted on giving me a boiled egg, a plate of olives and a chunk of hard bread. I was still full from the lamb earlier, but to refuse her kind hospitality would have been unthinkable. She took our wet clothes, laid them in front of the fire and without uttering a word, tactfully left the house leaving Loukas and me alone. There was much to discuss. I handed him a package containing a quarter of a million drachmas.

'This should help ease the burden for a while. London is fully aware of the effects of the famine and the exorbitant black market costs. Use it as you see fit.'

'I wonder if London really does understand,' Loukas said, counting the money. 'Do you know how many died in the winter of 41/42? Hundreds of thousands! We don't even know the real figure ourselves. The British blockade threw us at the mercy of Charon. Even our old enemy, Turkey, sent food supplies via the Americans. The *Kurtuluş* made five voyages until it was sunk. It hardly made a dent in the situation.'

Loukas's steely eyes penetrated mine. I could barely look at him. I was aware of the British blockade during that harsh winter. It shamed me to the core. I also knew what it would do to the fabric of Greek society. It had already torn them apart.

'And now we are turning on each other,' Loukas continued. 'For the moment we have a common enemy — the Germans and Italians, but when they are defeated, all Hell will break loose. I know you, my friend. You are one of us, and we cannot help those who rule us, can we? At least not without bloodshed.'

A large part of why I had been chosen for this mission was not just because I spoke Greek, but because I had a good grasp of Balkan, especially Greek politics. In a nutshell, the country was divided into the Royalists, the Nationalists and the Communists. But it was never as simple as that. Each group had splinter groups. EAM — the National Liberation Front, together with its military arm, ELAS — the National People's Liberation Army, belonged to KKE — the Communist Party of Greece. Not all communists took their instruction from Moscow. Thankfully, the Soviet Union was now an ally in the war which made our dealings with the communists much easier. Even so, we trod a difficult line. It was an open secret that the British supported the King and were well aware he was not popular. Yet the thought of openly backing the communists was never on the cards. What would happen when the war ended was anyone's guess. I was in Cairo when a group of Greek guerrilla leaders were invited to talks with SOE and they made it clear that King George II should not return without a plebiscite. As an SOE operative I was advised to support whichever group could help us defeat the Germans. Now here I was, sitting with my old friend, Loukas, a communist and respected Kapetan of ELAS.

Loukas was one of those Greeks who looked as though he was born and bred in the mountains; a tall, muscular man in his early forties who sported a thick black beard and dark curly hair. In reality, he was a city man whose family had come from Smyrna in Asia Minor in 1922. I met him in Athens where he worked as a lawyer. He was married to a woman who had been his secretary. When the Italians attacked, he joined the *andartes* and went to fight in the mountains near Albania. He was still there when the Germans entered Greece. Rather than return to Athens, he found himself organising escape routes for Allied soldiers. By the time he returned to Athens, the Germans got wind of his activities and had his home and office staked out. He was unaware of this until he arrived back. It was early evening when he neared his street and instead of the usual activity, it was deserted. A car was parked several metres away from his apartment. In it were four plain-clothed men. Loukas smelt a rat and retreated to a friend's house in the next street. There he was told the Gestapo had taken his wife in for questioning and were refusing to let her go until she told them of his whereabouts. Naturally, his first thoughts were for his wife but when he told the friend he was going to give himself up, he was advised against it.

Instead, the friend arranged with a Resistance member known to be friendly with the Germans to tell the Gestapo Loukas had been seen near his home but was avoiding his apartment. Maybe it would be an idea if his wife was released under watch and she would lead them to him. The Gestapo took the bait. She was released from Headquarters and followed. Unbeknown to them, a woman passed her in the street and told her it was a trap. His wife headed for nearby Syntagma Square. On the other side of the road, she spotted Loukas in the crowd. For a few brief moments they stood and looked at each other. The Gestapo could tell by the look on her face she had seen him and closed in, hoping to recognise Loukas in the crowd. Then they saw her cross the road in his direction — straight into an oncoming tram. Onlookers rushed to her aid but it was too late. Loukas's wife had taken her own life rather than give him up to the Gestapo. That same night, Loukas fled for the safety of the mountains. Soon after that, he joined the Poseidon Network.

'I now have a price on my head.' He laughed. 'I never thought I'd see the day when I lived in the mountains, but this village has become my second home. When I am not in Athens, I operate from here to all points throughout these ranges and as far as Lamia.'

For a man on the run, the mountain air had certainly done my old friend the world of good. He looked in peak condition — fit and athletic.

'I need to meet up with my radio operator in Amfissa as soon as possible and contact Cairo,' I told him. 'After that I have to get to Athens. There's someone important I need to liaise with. He is to be my main contact here — the person who runs the Poseidon Network — the White Rose.'

Loukas smiled. 'A tough character, that one.'

'I gather you've met him.'

'Oh yes — several times in fact.'

He couldn't wipe the grin from his face, which I found rather unsettling.

We spent the rest of the morning drinking copious amounts of tsipouro, poring over maps, and talking about the recent joint operation between SOE and the Greek Resistance which saw the destruction of the Gorgopotamos viaduct. Operation Harling, as it was known, was meant to disrupt the flow of arms going to Rommel, but thankfully, the Battle at El Alamein had already reversed Rommel's fortunes. Loukas assured me that the successful operation had a positive effect on the Resistance. It gave them heart to think that the Germans and Italians would soon be defeated. Unfortunately, it still wasn't enough to bring all the Resistance groups together. Some had begun fighting each other again. I had my work cut out if we were to remain a united force.

The village of Ano Hora was a cluster of haphazardly built stone houses with tiled roofs set in a wooded area on the slope of the mountain. Towards midday, the blizzard eased and the sun peeked through the low clouds, adding a sparkling crispness to the undulating mounds of blindingly white snow. I heard voices and saw the old widow returning. This time she had a younger woman with her and two small children.

'It's fine,' Loukas said, seeing the anxious look on my face. 'It's only Anna, her daughter.'

'And the children?' I asked. 'Why are they bringing them here? Won't they talk?'

'Not these, Nikos. They are also on the run!'

I looked at him, waiting for an explanation.

'These children are Jewish — from Kastoria. They have lost their parents and were given to the *andartes* to take care of them. The Germans started closing down Jewish businesses and rounding up the men for labour gangs a while ago now. Eichmann has sent one of his top men to oversee all this. I have it on good authority that they are to make Salonika a Jew-free zone and this will spread until there are none left. At the moment, they are milking the Jews of their money — freedom for a reward. Some Jews have fled. Many are still here though, hanging on to the Greek government's pledge that nothing should happen to them. It's only a matter of months before the Germans move to expel them all.'

He stood up to warm himself in front of the fire. 'The *andartes* are hardly in a position to look after children. They are too busy fighting.'

'How many children are there?' I asked.

'Besides these two, perhaps another forty at least. It's hard to say. They're all hidden amongst the mountain villages. Not all Jews. Some are Christians whose families were wiped out for supporting the *andartes*. We are hoping to use our escape routes to get the Jews into Turkey and then on to Palestine. As for our own, who knows where the poor devils will end up?'

I couldn't stop myself from letting out a loud sigh. It was hard enough to get adults out of Greece, let alone children. The door opened and the children entered; a boy and a girl, barely five years old. They looked at me shyly and ran to Loukas, cowering behind his legs. He picked the girl up in his arms.

'No need to be frightened,' he said, giving her a kiss on her ruddy cheek. 'This is a good friend of mine. He won't harm you.'

The young woman was the last to enter. She wiped away the snow from her boots and introduced herself as she took the girl from Loukas.

'I've heard a lot about you,' she said, seating the children at the table and preparing them a bowl of fresh yoghurt. 'Loukas has told me all about you.'

'He has?' I asked, glancing at him.

'Yes. He said you are getting married soon and that we are to be invited to the wedding.'

Loukas grinned. I knew that was code for an operation that was to take place.

Anna finished preparing the children's food and came over to Loukas, touched his arm and looked into his eyes. It was a look filled with affection and concern. The old woman chose to ignore this tender moment.

'He said I was to take you to a place where you could find a good suit,' she continued.

Anna was a slightly-built woman who I judged to be barely out of her teenage years, yet it was plain to see she was a woman in every sense of the word. By the look in his eyes, I could tell that fact was not lost on Loukas either. He was smitten by her. Now I realised it was not only mountain life that gave him a healthy look, but Anna. I was happy for him. I only hoped the war would not tear them apart as it had done with his first wife.

It was decided that now the weather had cleared we should make a move. I had a full day's walk ahead of me if I wanted to reach Amfissa before nightfall. Loukas double-checked my ID. and travel papers.

'The dark hair suits you,' Loukas said, handing me back my papers. 'You could pass for a Greek. Let's hope when the roots start to show you can lay your hands on more hair dye.'

We laughed. My natural colour was chestnut with a tinge of red from my mother's side. When I was told I was returning to Greece, I had hurriedly dyed it in my bathroom at Shepheard's.

'If you get stuck for dye, you can always use shoe polish,' Anna added. 'The Turks were very fond of that.'

'I'll remember that.'

The children finished their meal and the old woman took them into another room out of earshot of our conversation.

Loukas handed me back my dry clothes, picked up his rifle

and slung it over his shoulder. 'I'll go with you as far as the bend in the river. From there, Anna will take you to Amfissa. She knows the area well. If all goes to plan, you should be in Athens in a couple of days. I will meet you there.'

Loukas saw the look of concern in my eyes and burst out laughing. 'I think you will find Anna a very capable woman. A match for even the best of us. Never underestimate Greek women,' he said, slapping me on the back. 'They are the equal of any man.'

'That I quite believe.' I smiled.

Anna lifted the top of a carved wooden chest, took out a pistol and put it in her inside coat pocket. She was such a slip of a woman I had a hard time imagining her using it.

We made our way across the mountain pass, avoiding the lower village of Kato Hora which Loukas told me belonged to another Resistance group who had been troublesome over the past few months due to heated political disagreements between the leaders. He assured me this would soon settle down. Knowing how long some of these mountain village feuds lasted, often for generations, I couldn't share his optimism. We needed everyone on side.

The snow blanketed the mountain in heavy drifts which slowed our journey down, and except for the crunching of snow and the occasional crack of a branch underfoot, it was eerily quiet. A few hours later, we reached the bend in the river.

'This is where we part company,' Loukas said. 'I will take a different route to Athens.'

He shook my hand and turned to Anna. 'Be careful. Don't take risks.'

In that brief moment I glimpsed that look in their eyes

again. They were in love. After what happened to his wife, I didn't know whether to be happy or sad for him.

I followed Anna for another few kilometres, at which point the mountain track joined a road leading to a wooden bridge spanning the river at its narrowest point. On the far side was a hut with a thin curl of smoke rising from a chimney. Anna told me the bridge was manned by the *carabinieri*, half a dozen Italian guards. Waiting in a clearing some metres before the bridge, was a man with three donkeys laden with panniers of firewood. I learnt that the man was one of Loukas's men who made this crossing regularly. He told me to take the reins of one of the donkeys and follow them. Anna walked ahead.

'Let us handle this,' she said, as we started to cross the bridge. 'They're used to us.'

We clattered noisily across the rickety bridge in a single file. Below us, the icy water, swollen by the heavy snows, thundered downstream in torrents, cascading against the rocks in foaming whirlpools. A soldier stepped out of the hut carrying a semi automatic and approached us.

'*Buon giorno*, Officer Mario,' Anna shouted out in Italian. 'What terrible weather we're having at the moment.'

The soldier walked over to us. 'Where are you going today?' he asked, observing the firewood. 'And who is your friend? I haven't seen him before.'

'My cousin, Nikos,' replied Anna chirpily. 'He's been staying with us for a cousin's wedding.'

The Italian came towards me and asked to see my papers. He slung his rifle over his shoulder while he examined them.

'Your name and address?' he asked in broken Greek, even though it was clearly written on the papers in front of him.

'Nikos.' I answered. 'Taking my hat off and bowing my head slightly in a somewhat subservient manner. 'Nikos Xenakis. 167 Patission St. Plateia Amerikis, Athens.'

'Apartment?'

'Apartment 3.'

The soldier looked at the photograph and then studied my face. I glanced at Anna and the old man. They looked nervous. Anna stepped forward.

'Officer Mario,' she said in an innocent voice. 'Surely you're not going to keep us hanging about in this cold weather. Look at the sky. There's going to be another blizzard.'

My senses told me things were not going to go as smoothly as anticipated. Anna assured me she had crossed this bridge numerous times without any trouble, but today was not going to be one of them. The soldier asked us to wait while he went inside to make a telephone call. We couldn't risk it. As soon as he passed Anna, she pulled her pistol out and brought it down hard on the back of his head. There was no option now but to kill him. I ran forward to help her. The Italian opened his eyes just in time to see me cut his throat.

'Sorry,' I said under my breath. 'You really should have let us through.'

The old man quickly pulled a submachine gun from a pannier and aimed it at the hut door while Anna and I pulled the man to the side of the bridge and hauled him over the railings. Luckily the noise from the river was too loud for anyone to hear him hit the water. We grabbed the donkey's reigns and ambled towards the hut as if nothing had happened.

'How many did you say usually man this place?' I asked.

'No more than six,' Anna whispered. 'There's not a village

around here for miles, so it's not deemed to be a high priority crossing.'

'We can't just pass as if nothing happened,' I replied. 'We have to catch them by surprise.'

When we neared the hut door, we heard laughter coming from inside. If we passed, someone would come out to see what was going on. There was no option but to attack first, but if we tried to storm in and take them by surprise, one of us could die. We decided to lure them out.

Anna approached the hut, leaving us with a clear view of the door. Cautiously peering through the window, she indicated to us that there were five more men inside. We aimed our guns at the door. With her finger on the trigger of her gun hidden in her coat pocket, she knocked on the door.

'Come quickly. Officer Mario has taken ill,' Anna called out. 'He's fainted on the bridge.'

She quickly jumped aside as the door flew open and the men poured out, right into a hail of bullets. The noise was so loud the donkeys brayed and bucked and almost took off in a stampede. I counted four dead. When I kicked the door open, the last one was cowering behind the door with his hands in the air, mumbling prayers in Italian. Seconds later he was dead.

'We have to get rid of these bodies also,' I said. 'If anyone finds out what's happened, there's likely to be reprisals.'

We stripped the men of their uniforms, dragged them to the bridge and threw them into the icy water. In all likelihood, their bodies would be recovered kilometres downstream and no one would be able to identify them. As for their bloodied uniforms, we wrapped them in a bundle and hid them in the pannier along with their guns and ammunition. Soldier's uniforms were hard to come by and when washed and repaired, our own men would use them. There was one more thing to do. Cut the telephone wires. All being well, we would out of here before anyone realised what had happened.

We were well and truly away from the bridge when Anna asked us to stop.

'Here,' she said, thrusting her hand into her coat pockets and bringing out three large salamis and a chunk of bread. 'They don't need this now.'

She threw us a salami each and then retrieved a small bottle of tsipouro from her inside pocket and took a long swig.

'All this has made me hungry.' She laughed, biting off a chunk of salami and passing us the bottle.

The weather was worsening again and the tsipouro trickled down my throat like nectar, warming me from the inside out.

Loukas was right when he said I should not underestimate Greek women. And this was one woman I was only too happy to have on my side.

When the plains of Amfissa were in sight, the old man left us, taking the guns and uniforms with him. Anna and I waited until midnight before we walked through the hundreds of olive groves to the town. There I was taken to a safe-house. She knocked on the door and we were greeted by a swarthy-looking man pointing a gun at us.

'This is where we part ways,' Anna said, her voice taking on a serious tone. 'I think you will find what you are looking for here. They make excellent suits. I am sure you will find one to your liking.'

Before leaving, she pressed something into my hand. It was

a tiny blue glass bead in the shape of an eye. They were every-where in Greece.

'Keep it with you. It will protect you from the evil eye.'

I knew then that no matter how many guns the Greeks had, they would still turn to their icons and charms in times of trouble.

Chapter 7

Athens. Three days later.

The Athens I returned to was not the one I had left. The hardships of war and famine had hit harder than even I expected. The city was heavily patrolled with army vehicles and well-fed soldiers scurrying to and fro amidst a sea of malnourished civilians. I passed long queues of emaciated, ghostlike figures lining up outside soup kitchens whilst others were simply too weak to queue and sat in doorways with begging bowls, staring into space with vacant expressions. These were the lucky ones. At least they were alive and with every breath there was hope. All around them, the bodies of those who had collapsed and died from starvation and cold were being loaded onto carts and taken away for mass burials. I pulled up the collar of my old, threadbare coat, purposely worn several sizes bigger to hide my well-fed body, and walked among them with a mixture of pity for my fellow man and immense hatred for the Germans.

The bad weather had also hit Athens. Snow lay in drifts against the side of buildings or had turned into grey slush along the pavements and roads. The trams had stopped and I walked to my destination, a pharmacy in Patission Street not far from the apartment that was to be my home for the next few months. A woman whom I judged to be in her mid-thirties stood behind the counter serving a customer when I entered and at the same time supervising a young girl who was washing an old man's badly bloodied arm. I waited by the door until the customer left.

'*Kali mera, Kyrie.* What can I do for you?' she asked, as she handed a bandage to the young girl.

'Maria Kouvaros,' I replied. 'I was told I could find her here.'

The woman narrowed her eyes. 'What is it you want?' she asked, guardedly. 'Who are you?'

'I'm here for the wedding. I've already been fitted for a new suit.'

The stern look on her face was suddenly broken by a big smile.

'*I* am Maria.' She laughed. 'And you must be Kapetan Nikos. Thank God, you made it safe and sound.'

I glanced at the old man who let out a sharp cry of pain as the girl cleaned his wound.

'It's alright,' Maria said, quickly putting me at ease. 'This is my father.'

She put her hand on the girl's shoulder. 'And this is my daughter, Chryssa.'

A skinny wisp of a girl, barely in her teens, with long black hair tied back into a long plait that almost reached her waist, threw me a shy glance and continued tending her grandfather's wounds. At the sound of our voices, a head popped around a curtain.

Maria gestured towards him proudly. 'This is my son, Yiannis.'

The teenage boy entered the room and shook my hand.

'Well. Don't just stand there,' his mother said to him. 'Get Kapetan Nikos something to eat and drink. He must be starving.'

Knowing the hardships the city folk suffered, I protested. It was useless.

'While you are with me, you will eat,' Maria said, sternly. 'When you are alone, you can do whatever you please.'

She put the closed sign up on the door and told me to follow her into the back room — a cramped space that doubled as their kitchen and dining area. Yiannis was in the process of making me a cup of Greek coffee over a rudimentary clay burner of hot coals. Coffee was a luxury and I knew it would have cost them a small fortune on the black market. Under normal circumstances, we would have taken this time-honoured coffee drinking ritual amongst friends for granted. Now it was reserved for special occasions. Today, I was that special occasion.

'What happened to your father?' I asked.

'He was beaten by the Germans,' Maria said, matter-of-factly, as she cleared the table. 'He happened to be in the wrong place at the wrong time and they gave him a good beating.'

She placed a handful of dried figs and apricots along with a thin sliver of hard cheese and dried rusks on a plate and pushed it towards me. A large flagon of retsina stood on the floor next to the sink. She picked it up and poured out three large glasses. I noticed her well manicured hands and wedding ring.

'Take this to your grandfather,' she said to Yiannis, handing him a full glass. 'He deserves a drink after what those bastards did to him.'

'*Stin yeia mas,*' she said, raising her glass. 'To our good health and a long life.'

She sat back in the chair, sizing me up. 'I hope you are going to tell us that the British are giving us more support. God knows, we could do with it.'

Her look was penetrating. This was one woman you could not fool. I reassured her we were committed in a common cause.

'We will see,' she replied. 'Talk is cheap, but the fact that you are here with your men, laying down your lives for us, says a lot. I have heard much about you, Kapetan Nikos. The men trust you. Don't let them down.'

I asked her about my apartment. Just how safe was it?

'Nowhere is completely safe and you are a new face in the neighbourhood,' she replied. 'But you don't have to worry, I own the apartment and I put the word out that you are my cousin from Larissa, here to look for work. Most importantly, the janitor and his wife hate the Germans as much as we do. They won't ask questions.'

'And the rest of the occupants; can we trust them also?'

'They have been there for years and mind their own business. If you keep a low profile, you will be fine.'

A hand pushed the curtain aside and her father and Chryssa entered. Chryssa emptied the bloodied bowl of water down the sink and washed her hands before joining us. Yiannis topped up our glasses. I savoured it even more than the brandy after the incident in the mountains with Anna. Retsina from Attica was the best. There was nothing like it. It always reminded me of happier times in Athens and I wondered if I would ever see those days again.

'It's good,' I said to Maria.

Her face beamed with pride. 'From my uncle's vineyard. Thankfully the Germans prefer other wine and haven't attempted to steal it all from us yet.'

I turned my attention to the old man. 'Why did they beat you up?' I asked.

'I was queuing for bread when a group of Germans passed and started to flirt with a pretty girl standing nearby. She turned her back on them but one of them pulled her aside. She struggled to free herself and they hit her. That's when I and a few onlookers started shouting at them. They levelled their guns at us and we feared someone would get shot. Then they set upon us and gave us a good beating. We were lucky; we could have been taken to Merlin Street.'

'And the girl?'

'She ran away.'

The old man looked across at Chryssa. 'She was not much older than her. Bastards!'

Maria spent some time telling me about several safe-houses in the area, one of which was a brothel run by a woman called Rosa. I looked at Chryssa and Yiannis to see what they made of this but their faces remained expressionless. The war had turned them into adults before their time.

'Now I think it's time for you to see your new home,' Maria said, as I finished my third glass of retsina. 'It's a block away.'

It took less than five minutes to reach my apartment on the corner of Patission Street and the tree-lined Plateia Amerikis. The kafenia were still open. Through the windows, dripping with condensation, I could see a couple of old men idly fingering their komboloia and playing backgammon. I was aware of their gaze following me as we slipped into the building. The janitor was sitting behind his desk reading a newspaper. Two paper flags had been placed on the desk where visitors could not fail to see them — the Hellenic and the German. Maria's wooden heels clattered noisily on the marbled floor.

'Good evening, Kyria Kouvaros,'

'Good evening, Vangelis. My cousin has made it, despite the bad weather.'

The man looked at me over wire-rimmed glasses, summing me up — a stranger who may not be who he was supposed to be.

Plateia Amerikis was a fairly busy residential area of Athens, yet already I felt everyone in the neighbourhood knew I'd arrived. News would travel fast. I had to be on my toes. Despite Maria's assurance that the man was on our side, I couldn't warm to him.

Maria did not want to linger any more than necessary. She ushered me towards the stairs. 'Come along, Nikos. Let's get you settled in.'

The apartment was exceptionally cold, but it was spacious and well appointed with a partial view across the Plateia.

'I'm sorry it's cold,' Maria said, blowing warm breath on her hands. 'Heating is something we have learnt to do without.' She switched the light on. It flickered intermittently as if at any moment we would be plunged into darkness. 'It's normal,' she laughed, when I flicked the switch off and on again. 'The electricity is not reliable so there's a box of candles in the kitchen.'

She opened the cupboard door in the bedroom and pointed to the top shelf. It was filled with heavy, hand-woven blankets of the type used in the villages. 'Extra blankets just in case you need them.'

My eyes fell on the clothes hanging on the rack below them;

suits, jackets, shirts and ties. Underneath these was a neat row of brown and black pairs of shoes.

'I took the liberty of supplying you with a change of clothes. I think you'll need them.' Maria eyed my threadbare coat with a mixture of disdain and amusement. 'There are several sizes to choose from. I'm sure you'll find something suitable.'

The kitchen had also been stocked; that is if you call a few jars of olives and dried rusks a larder. But there was milk — a luxury — and a bag of dried herbs the Greeks called mountain tea. Couldn't stand the stuff myself, although Greeks swore by it as a cure-all. A bottle of ouzo stood on the kitchen table. That suited me better.

'I'll try and bring you whatever food I can lay my hands on,' Maria said. 'And I expect you to eat with us from time to time. My door is always open. Remember that.'

Before she left, I handed her a wad of notes. The drachma was almost worthless these days, but it was still a large amount and I knew she would use it wisely. She pocketed it without counting it, saying it would go towards buying more bandages and medicines on the black market.

Chapter 8

The rendezvous with members of the Poseidon Network was to take place at 11:00 a.m. the following morning in Ermou Street, not far from Keramikos, the official cemetery of ancient Athens. I arrived early in order to survey the area. To get there I passed through Plateia Omonoias. German patrols and tanks were out in force and I was stopped several times to have my papers checked. From what I had been told, many of the Greeks who owned restaurants and kafenia in and around the Plateia were collaborators, which meant they could lay their hands on supplies that would otherwise have been prohibited to them. Maria told me most of these men "turned" during the great famine. They believed German and Italian propaganda that the Allies didn't care about them. "When bellies rumble, people sell their soul," she said. I could believe it. Who can fight on an empty stomach?

I reached Ermou and found a cafe within sight of the meeting place and sat inside at a table next to the window. From there, I was able to watch the comings and goings in the street, my antenna alert to anything amiss. One could never be sure. It only took a slip of the tongue and our cover would be blown.

The meeting place was on the first floor and the entrance was between two shops, a bric-a-brac shop selling everything from pots and pans to worn-out shoes and hats — most likely scavenged from the dead before the carts arrived to convey them to Charon — and a shabby-looking tailor's, outside which stood half-a-dozen wooden mannequins displaying simple dresses and suits. The mannequins had seen better days. Their painted and highly lacquered hair was in a style reminiscent of the Jazz Age, and the faces were badly chipped. I leaned across the table to get a better look at the sign. It read Hadzigiannis. Where had I seen that before? Then it hit me like a bolt of lightning. Cairo. The shop where I followed Alexis was also called Hadzigiannis. I slumped back in my seat. Memories of Alexis flooded my head making me feel quite dizzy. My God! How I'd fallen for her. She could have wrapped me around her little finger — and she knew it. I might even have considered giving up the Secret Service for her. Then again, maybe settling down would have killed the romance. I was never one for the conventional life and from the little I knew of Alexis, neither was she.

I checked the time. It was almost 11:00 a.m. The street was busy with people going about their business. During the last half an hour, I'd watched several men enter the premises, two of whom were SOE — Aris and Stelios — who were with me when we parachuted into the mountains. Exactly on the hour, a man stepped outside and stood in the doorway with a rolled-up newspaper. He opened it and appeared to be reading it. Once or twice, he glanced up and down the street. I paid the waiter and left. When he saw me approach, he quickly folded it, placed it under his arm, and stepped back inside. I followed him, but by the time I got there, he'd disappeared. At the top of the stairs a bare light bulb hung from a dilapidated ceiling that looked as if it would cave in at any moment. The light gave off an eerie yellowed glow, throwing my shadow along the wall. I felt like a character from a Raymond Chandler novel, but then that was something I had become used to in my line of work. Reality had blurred lines. When I reached the top of the stairs, someone flung open the door and there stood Loukas with a big grin on his face. Inside, the men started clapping as if I was the guest of honour at a surprise birthday party.

'Good to have you with us, Kapetan,' they said, shaking my hand. 'It's an honour for us to serve with you.'

After a round of introductions and the obligatory drink of ouzo, we got down to business.

There were ten of us, all crammed into this small room, which doubled as a store-room for the two shops below. Apart from my own men and Loukas, the others were commanders of their own individual groups from the Greek mainland and the Aegean Islands; the nucleus of a rag tag band of brothers in arms who were willing to lay down their lives for one common cause. All had been warned to leave their own political disputes behind. Discipline and a pledge of allegiance were vital. The one thing that did surprise me was that my main contact — the White Rose — was not there. The look on my face told Loukas I was not happy.

'Something unforeseen cropped up,' he said in a low voice. 'In the meantime, you are in charge.'

Over the course of the next few hours, we discussed everything from the homes and buildings requisitioned by the Germans and Italians, to vital infrastructure and communications. Collaboration and the escalation of reprisals were high on the list. The SD, who were given the task of controlling Greek and German police units, had taken to rounding off sections of the city in lightning sweeps known colloquially as *bloccos*. These round-ups struck fear into the hearts of the population and meant we had to be especially careful. No-one was immune and the guilty and innocent were caught up together. For the collaborators, it was an excuse to get back at someone they despised. Rarely was it because they had done anything wrong. Suspicion hovered over everyone like a black cloud.

'The Gestapo started rounding up enemies of the state the moment they entered Greece,' said Loukas. 'Sturmbannführer-und-Kriminalrat Geissler had a search-book. It was notorious. When he left Greece, we rejoiced and things went quiet for a while. Unfortunately, after Himmler paid us a visit over a year ago, he established offices and installed the State Secret Police and the SS Intelligence Service. We know it's run from Berlin. Our lawyers have defended several hundred Greeks accused of sabotage. The trouble is, the accusations are becoming more frequent.'

'Are we monitoring the headquarters?' I asked. 'Do we have men on the inside?'

One of the men reeled off a few names; everyone from minor clerks, translators, to cleaning ladies, delivery boys and drivers.

'Good work. Who are these people? Who's the most reliable?'

I fired a barrage of questions at them. It was important I got to know how much they knew and what was going on. The men discussed a few names among themselves.

'Manos,' one of the men replied, after a while. 'Manos

Kondoumaris. He is driver for the top brass of the Wehrmacht and occasionally, the SS.'

I wanted to know more. I'd met men who came into close contact with the enemy before. Some turned out to be double agents and met an untimely end.

I fired a barrage of questions. 'Where is he from? How did he get the job?' I wanted to know everything.

'He got the job as soon as the offices were opened,' replied the man called Kostas.

'These officials usually use their own men — even for minor jobs,' I answered, rather too quickly for it not to be noticed. 'Why did he get this job?'

Kostas bristled. Clearly he disliked having to explain all their moves to a foreigner, even if he was on their side.

'His wife was German and he speaks the language like a native.'

I raised an eyebrow. Loukas intervened.

'Kondoumaris worked in Berlin. He was there for years. That's where he met his wife, Lotte. They were only married a couple of years before she died, round about the time Poland was invaded. Seeing the worsening situation, he feared he would be called up for active service and decided to return to Athens. When the Germans arrived, they contacted all German nationals who had been living here. Greeks associated with Germany in any way were also on this list. Rather than wait for them to come knocking on his door, Manos went to their offices and offered his services. When they found out he could speak German, they gave him a job as a driver. We have him to thank for keeping us informed about those who were imprisoned and tortured. It was he who told us about the search-book.'

I digested this important piece of information. 'Fine. Such men are to be commended.'

The subject changed to maritime surveillance. SOE London wanted an immediate update on shipping and submarine movements. Keeping our finger on the pulse in the Aegean was not only vital for the escape routes to Turkey and Palestine, but to the Mediterranean as a whole. With the Germans losing ground in North Africa, there was an expectation that the Allies would try and launch an attack on Europe from the south. As yet none of us knew where that would be.

It was almost 3:00 p.m. when we brought the meeting to a close. I'd absorbed quite a bit over the course of the morning and I was exhausted and famished. I gave out the last of the money to the commanders and thanked everyone for coming. Everyone left except for my own men and Loukas. There was still much to discuss.

'Let's get a bite to eat,' Loukas said. 'I know a place not far from here that's still open.'

The shops either side the building were closed when we left. It was siesta time. While Loukas locked up, I tried to get a closer look inside the tailor's shop but I was too late. The ghoulish mannequins had all been taken inside and the shutters were down.

We were the only customers in Taverna Acropolis. Loukas told me the owner ran a soup kitchen next to the Tzisdaraki Mosque opposite the entrance to Monastiraki Metro station. He gave us a generous helping of delicious *revithia* soup and a plate of *horta*.

'Chickpea soup is his speciality, these days.' Loukas smiled. 'The Germans allow him to buy sacks at a time because he runs the soup kitchen. The *horta* arrives daily. The women collect it from the mountainside. They keep most of it for themselves, the rest they exchange with him for chickpeas or bones. Meat is a rarity, unless its dog or donkey.' He broke off a piece of bread and mopped it in the lemon-soaked juices of the *horta*.

'Delicious,' he said. 'It may be only grass and dandelions, but I'm quite full after all that.'

The men laughed. The truth was, we could have eaten a horse but our stomachs were shrinking. I thought of the delicious roast lamb on the mountainside the night we landed. It was likely to be sometime before I feasted like that again.

'The White Rose,' I said, bringing us back to earth again. 'I want a meeting as soon as possible.'

'Don't worry.' Loukas replied. 'It's arranged for the day after tomorrow. I just couldn't tell you in the meeting.'

'So there was no unforeseen circumstance?'

'No. One of the reasons Poseidon is effective is because we are one step ahead and operate on a need to know basis. Everyone of those men you met today take their orders in one way or another from the White Rose, but only a handful know his identity or whereabouts. What would have happened if the Germans got wind of that meeting? The entire network could have collapsed. Surely you must have realised that?'

'Smart. I like it.'

It was the only response I could give. Better to be safe than sorry.

'I am returning to Ano Hora tomorrow,' Loukas continued. 'I'll be back in a week's time. The White Rose will make contact with you. You don't have to worry.'

Loukas and I parted ways outside the taverna. Aris and

Stelios accompanied me to a safe-house to meet up with our radio operator, a man of Greek/English parentage brought up in Notting Hill for most of his life and who talked with a pronounced Cockney accent. His real name was Dimitris but we knew him as Jimmy the Greek. For the purpose of this assignment, SOE Cairo nick-named him Dancer, due to his agility in transmission work. We were lucky to have him. He knew the Balkans well.

Dancer was expecting us.

'Cairo is getting impatient,' he said, 'They want an update as soon as possible.'

We compared notes. Except for the incident with the Italians on the bridge, all had gone smoothly. He set up the radio/transmitter and started transmitting. The small light flashed as he tapped each letter over the airwaves — tac, tac, tac. Twenty-five words a minute.

'Anything else, sir?' Dancer asked. 'Better be quick before we're detected. We've only got thirty minutes.'

'Yes,' I replied. 'I want a background check on a man called Manos Kondoumaris — lived in Berlin — married to a German called Lotte — returned to Greece after she died — possibly between 1939 and 1940. Oh, and mark it urgent.'

Using his code, Dancer tapped for a few more seconds, signed off and took off his headphones.

'Let me know if you receive anything,' I said. 'In the meantime, I will see you again in a few days.'

Chapter 9

I found it hard to sleep that night. Too many things kept going through my mind. I was a stickler for details and it was not unusual for me to mull things over until I was sure all the pieces of the jigsaw fitted nicely into place. SOE called it my trademark. It was why they had entrusted me to lead so many missions. Only rarely had my hunches been wrong and I didn't want to dwell on that. Suffice to say that innocent people paid the price for my mistake. I was determined not to let that happen again.

The next morning I was still in bed when I heard a knock on the door. The lack of sleep was not helped by severe stomach pains from my new diet. All night long I was running to the toilet and all I wanted to do was sleep. I wrapped the blanket tightly around me and padded to the door, catching sight of myself in the mirror in the hall. I looked dreadful. I peered through the peephole and saw Chryssa standing there, swinging her arms to and fro in an unsuccessful attempt to warm herself up. She had a message from her mother.

'You are invited to eat with us this evening. Seven o'clock sharp. She says not to be late.'

I thanked her saying I would look forward to it. After she

left I took a wash. There was no hot water and the shock of the icy cold water brought me alive with a jolt. I spent the rest of the day trying to catch up on my sleep.

As requested, I arrived at the pharmacy in Patission Street at seven o'clock, and half expected to see the closed sign on the door. I was wrong. When I entered, the place was filled with sick customers and reeked of illness and poverty. With my queasy stomach, I wanted to retch. Maria was behind the counter, carefully weighing out white powder from an assortment of glass jars while Yiannis distributed small parcels of dried herbs along with detailed instructions on what to do with them. Chryssa was tending to a pregnant woman who could not stop vomiting.

Maria saw me and shrugged her shoulders. 'What can we do?' she said with a heavy sigh. 'Go and wait in the back room. I'll be with you as soon as possible.'

Her father stood by the stove stirring the contents of a large pot. The look on his face told me he was not coping well with the situation.

'This is normal,' he said, despondently. 'It's the lot of the Greeks. No sooner do we overcome one upheaval when another comes along. We must have done something to upset the Gods.'

I told him it was not only the Greeks who had upset the Gods this time. The rest of the world had too. Two hours passed before Maria closed the pharmacy, leaving Chryssa and Yiannis to clean the floor with disinfectant. In the meantime, her father and I occupied our time playing cards. She slumped down in the chair and wiped away beads of sweat from her forehead with her handkerchief.

'At least a room full of people heats the place up,' she said.

I thought of the infections that could be passed around. It was a wonder the family hadn't succumbed to illness themselves.

Maria tasted the stew and placed it in the centre of the table. She picked up our bowls and ladled it out — meat in a sauce of onions, thickened with tomato paste. I was surprised to see the meat and told her so.

All eyes were on me as I took my first mouthful.

'Do you like it?' she asked.

I wasn't sure if it was beef or lamb, but I complimented her. 'It's very good.'

They all laughed.

'*Aman*, Kapetan. It's donkey!'

If only she knew. I'd eaten this many times in the Middle East. Even the Blythe Pickerings had served it up on more than one occasion. In the hands of a good cook, I could never tell the difference between donkey and beef. I was just happy to eat meat for a change. I knew, however, the Greeks would only eat it as a last resort. Under normal circumstances, they would be ashamed to eat it at all, let alone serve it to guests. These were not normal circumstances though.

'Where did you get it?'

'I was out this morning when I saw a crowd gathering on the footpath. At first I thought another poor soul had died from cold and exhaustion. I was wrong. It was an itinerant vendor's donkey. The poor thing couldn't take any more and dropped dead. The onlookers were already hacking into it. A neighbour saw me and passed me a piece as a thank you for treating his wife and not charging.' She tucked into the stew with gusto. 'It pays to have good friends, you know.'

We finished the meal in silence, savouring every mouthful until our bowls were spotless.

Maria wiped her mouth on her napkin and rubbed her belly with exaggerated satisfaction.

'Now,' she said, turning her attention squarely on me. 'Let's get down to the real business of why I asked you here. I have some information for you. A car will pick you up tomorrow at midday on the corner of Patission and Imvrou. They will take you to a place on the outskirts of Athens. There you will have a rendezvous with someone important — the White Rose.'

The information was sparse, but it was vital. I didn't bother asking who relayed this to her, or if she knew the White Rose personally. She wouldn't have told me anyway. At least not until I knew her better. When it was time to leave, she saw me out. It was almost curfew and the streets were emptying fast. I thanked her for the meal. Her face looked tired and gaunt.

*

The car travelled northwards out of Athens and along the side of the valley of the River Kifissios in Kato Kifissia. The snow hung from the pine trees in white clumps, glistening in the winter sun. Kifissia was a summer resort for politicians and high society. Beautiful villas with a unique architectural ambiance graced the tree-lined streets. The Royal Family resided there before fleeing to Egypt. Now many of the villas had been requisitioned by the German and Italian High Commands. On seeing that I was heading into the lion's den, I was glad I'd chosen to wear one of the smart suits Maria had so thoughtfully provided me with.

My driver, a man with a humourless face and slicked-back hair, did not utter a word throughout our journey. The car veered of the main thoroughfare and along a narrow road. After crossing the river, the road wound upwards along the side of a ravine and came to a sudden dead end in a wooded area of pines, spruce and cypress. Two men with machine guns slung over their shoulder were waiting for us. The car came to standstill and one of them came forward and opened the passenger door.

'Follow us, Kyrie.'

We headed into the woods until we arrived at the long whitewashed stone wall of what used to be an old monastery. The entrance was through an archway topped with red tiles. The men gestured for me to continue alone. Inside the empty courtyard stood a tiny church which backed onto the rock at the side of the ravine. I walked cautiously across the courtyard towards the church with my hand firmly fixed on my gun. I had the feeling I'd been here before but for the life of me couldn't recall when. There were far too many small churches around here and for the most part, they all resembled this one. When I drew closer, the door opened and a priest came out, his black robes and chimney pot hat contrasting against the white-washed building and crisp white snow. He saw me and moved aside to let me pass.

'God be with you,' he said in a low voice, and walked away towards the gate.

The tiny church was aglow with the flicker of candles and a trickle of smoke emanated from an incense censor in a carved niche in the whitewashed wall. A woman, clad in a heavy black coat and wearing a woollen shawl, knelt in front of an icon, praying. Clearly there had been a mix-up or I was in the wrong place.

I left the church and stood in the courtyard, wondering what to do next. I heard the door open behind me. The old woman must be leaving.

'Hello, Larry. How good it is to see you again.'

I felt as if someone had winded me. That voice. I recognised it in an instance. I swung around thinking I was dreaming. This wasn't a dream. It was real.

'Alexis! My God! Is this some kind of joke?'

In that moment, it dawned on me where I was. It was the Church of the Virgin of the Swallow. The place she'd asked me about in Cairo. Alexis removed the shawl from her head and shook her glossy black hair letting it tumble around her shoulders freely. The memory of her sitting in the wicker chair on the terrace at Shepheard's was imprinted in my mind. Even dressed in the dull clothes of a grieving widow, she was still the most stunning woman I'd ever laid eyes on.

'White suits you better,' I said, with a coolness that belied my emotions.

She laughed. 'Still the same, Larry, I see.' She gave me a kiss on the cheek. 'Welcome to Greece. I'm glad they sent you.'

'Are *you* saying you are the White Rose?'

'Dear Larry, does it surprise you to find that a woman is heading Poseidon? You always struck me as the liberated type.'

If I am honest with myself, after the initial shock of seeing her again, it didn't surprise me at all. I wouldn't put anything past her. Alexis Petrakis struck me as a cool customer from the moment we met. It was one of the things that attracted me to her.

'So that's what you were doing in Cairo. Well, the boys in the office certainly kept that one to themselves.'

There was so much I wanted to ask her, but more than anything else I wanted to take her in my arms and kiss her. To hell with Poseidon, Kapetan Nikos and the White Rose, I wanted to recapture that night in the desert. I pulled myself together. Never let your guard down. It was a motto I'd learned to live with.

'Come on,' she said, wrapping the shawl tightly around her shoulders. 'Let's go somewhere warmer where we can talk. I'm beginning to freeze out here.'

*

The car dropped us off at a villa set amidst a lush garden in Kifissia. During my earlier stays in Athens there were times when I had taken long strolls through the village admiring the wonderful homes of the rich and well-connected. Money was attracted to Kifissia like bees to honey. In the summer, the gentle slopes of the mountainside with its pine woods and luxuriant gardens filled with all manner of fruits and vines provided a welcome respite from the oppressive heat in Athens. Now it was the middle of winter and snow covered the well-tended gardens with their fountains and urns like an enchanted winter wonderland.

A sturdy middle-aged woman with the countenance of a stern headmistress was waiting for us in the hallway. Alexis removed a gun from one of the pockets before handing her the coat and shawl.

'Will the Kyrie be dining with us tonight?' the woman asked.

'Something light — served early please, Rada. We will be dining out later.'

I was more than delighted to find a roaring fire in the drawing room. It served to remind me just how cold I'd been since arriving in Greece and how I'd got used to it.

Alexis placed the gun — a Beretta MI934 — on the coffee table, opened a drinks cabinet and pulled out a bottle of fine cognac. Clearly, she was not suffering as others were. I watched her as she poured the drink into a large, cut-glass, brandy balloon. With her beautifully slim figure, still clad from head to toe in black, albeit a simple slim-line wool dress, she reminded me of a panther — sleek and mysterious — full of danger.

'Your maid, the lady I just met in the hallway — Rada. Isn't that a Slavic name?'

'You are correct. It's short for Radostiina.' She handed me a glass and sat in the opposite chair, sliding her long legs to one side, one behind the other. 'I'm sure you must have known a few Radas in your time in the Balkans, Larry.'

I felt my cheeks redden. There had been one or two who I remembered with fondness.

Alexis smiled. 'I thought so.'

She took a sip of cognac and reached for her silver cigarette case lying on the coffee table next to the gun. I picked it up and flipped it open. She took a cigarette and held it near her mouth, waiting for me to light it. I obliged. Our eyes locked, both of us momentarily trying to read each other's mind; an intimate moment. I noticed she still wore the same red nail varnish. I also noticed the many expensive diamond rings that adorned her fingers. She sat back in the chair pursed her lips and blew out a steady stream of smoke.

'I have to say, Larry, at first I hardly recognised you. They've done a good job with your disguise. You could pass for a Greek.'

'How did you know it was me?'

'As soon as we knew SOE were sending over agents to help the network, I made a few discreet inquiries of my own. It wasn't Cairo who told me, it was Loukas. Apparently you and he go back quite a bit. I believe you both used the same aliases on another mission. When I realized Kapetan Nikos was none other than his old friend, Larry Hadley, frankly I wasn't surprised. Do you know how many newspaper correspondents I met in Cairo?' She smiled knowingly. 'Far too many. I always wondered exactly what your real work was.'

I thought back to my conversations with Loukas, recalling how he laughed when I asked if he knew the White Rose. The dark horse! He led me to believe it was a man in charge of the Poseidon Network.

'And now,' she said, matter-of-factly. 'I think it's time to get down to business, don't you?'

Business suited me fine. I had already been briefed about much of the situation, including the recent Harling mission to blow up the Gorgopotamos Bridge. We were given a brief outline of our mission — mainly to liaise with the Poseidon Network and cause disruptions for the Germans and Italians without getting caught. This being said, SOE was notorious for being short on details and my experience in working in foreign intelligence told me there was much I would uncover myself.

Alexis began to fill me in.

'The network was in its infancy when I left for Cairo. At that time, it didn't have a name or an official leader. When the Italians attacked, we were simply groups of *andartes* without any clear direction — a ship without a rudder.'

'What were you doing in Cairo?' I asked.

I was aware it was a blunt question, but I had never been one for subtlety — unless it came to women, and even then, I was not always subtle. No, go straight for the jugular suited me more.

'It's quite simple. I was already working with the Resistance when I left Crete.'

Hadzigiannis's tailors flashed through my mind. Was that what she was doing there? When I thought of that day, I thought of her arguing with Irini in the cafe.

'And the Blythe Pickerings, what do they have to do with all this? Were you using them for your own ends?'

'It was common knowledge that they are well connected in the upper-class Egyptian and expat community. I knew Lady Georgiana threw extravagant parties and I found a way to get an invitation to her garden party. We got on famously and she asked me to the party on Gezira Island.'

'Was it fruitful?' I asked, somewhat sarcastically.

She reached for the cognac as if biding time. 'Would you like another?'

She poured one without waiting for my answer.

'It was extremely fruitful. In fact your friend, Sir Oswald, was quite a dear. He was able to put in a good word for me with the Foreign Office.'

'Go on.'

'I won't bore you with the details. Suffice to say, things worked out better than expected. The thing was, I had to get back here without anyone knowing I'd been away. When I left Crete, I used a false name and passport. To all intents and purposes, I was still in Crete.'

'And Irini?' I asked. 'Where does she fit into all this?'

At the mention of Irini, Alexis looked decidedly uncomfortable.

'Larry, there are some things best left alone.'

She was guarded. Whatever it was that transpired between them was not going to be easy to uncover. I had met my match with her. But then again, she had met her match in me. She changed the subject.

'When you were given this mission, what did they tell you about the White Rose?' she asked.

I wasn't sure what she wanted to hear. Was her question to stop me delving more into Irini's death?

'The White Rose was to be my contact. We would meet up in Athens, and the rest you know.'

'And you are sure Loukas never said anything else?'

I was beginning to get a little irritated. She might have seduced me with her looks, but I wasn't one for playing games, especially when it came to my work.

'Spit it out. If you've got something to say, say it.'

'There is something you need to know. It's very important. The same evening you left Cairo, there was an incident at the checkpoint near Ekali. It's not far from here. The four occupants in the car were *andartes* returning from a rendezvous. When they arrived at the checkpoint, they were asked to get out of the car and their identity cards were checked. They were in order but the guard in charge smelt a rat and ordered the car to be thoroughly searched. They found guns and rounds of ammunition hidden in a secret compartment in the boot of the car. Knowing they were in deep trouble and would be taken to Gestapo headquarters, the men decided to make a run for it into the nearby woods. Only one of them made it. The others were killed.'

Alexis gauged my reaction before continuing. 'The thing is,' she said, 'one of those killed was my husband.'

My stomach turned over. I could feel the bile rise in my throat.

'I'm sorry,' I said.

It was a lame thing to say but I was in shock.

'No Larry, you don't understand. My husband was the White Rose.'

I felt as if my heart was hammering at my head. I handed her the glass.

'I think I need another drink.'

I had been blindsided. I didn't see that coming. A myriad thoughts tumbled through my mind. My eyes fell on the rings adorning her fingers. Sure enough, there was a narrow gold wedding ring which I had failed to see earlier because it was overshadowed by the brilliance of an even bigger and more opulent ring. Now it stood out like the brightest diamond.

'What happened?' I asked, quickly pulling myself together. 'Why didn't the Germans come looking for you? Why--?'

She put an upturned hand towards me. 'I know this is has come as a shock, but please let me continue.'

A part of me wanted her to stop there and then; that it was just a silly joke. Clearly, that was not going to happen. The other part of me wanted to know every detail. On that score, I would leave no stone unturned.

'Two of the *andartes* were shot dead. Theo was also shot but managed to escape into the woods with the other *andarte*. Unfortunately he was so badly wounded he died soon after. The *andarte* who survived knew the area well. He hid his body and came to tell me. The next day, he and I went to retrieve the body and we asked Father Haralambos — the priest you met at the church — to bury him.'

Alexis paused to light another cigarette before continuing with the rest of the story.

'My husband, Theo, took the name, the White Rose, at the time I was in Cairo. It was around that time that the organisation began to call itself the Poseidon Network. As his wife, I was privy to everything that took place. In a matter of months Poseidon went from strength to strength and, as you know, the network is like an octopus; it's tentacles reach all over Greece and into Turkey. It was Theo who made it what it is. Loukas was one of his right-hand men. They knew each other from his time in Athens. Of the men you met in Ermou, only a few, including Loukas, actually met Theo. To the rest he is just a name, albeit one to be revered and whom they swore allegiance to.

'When the accident happened, the *andarte* who escaped knew there would be trouble if they recognized Theo.' She made a sweeping gesture with her hand. 'Look around you, Larry. You see how we live. My husband was an important man. If the Germans discovered who he was, you can imagine what they would do.

'Only a handful of close confidants, including Loukas, know Theo is dead. To prevent chaos and fighting amongst the regional commanders of Poseidon, it was suggested that I take over Theo's role as I already knew the workings of the network and the contacts. Naturally, I agreed. We also thought it would be less likely for a woman leading a network to come to the attention of the Germans.'

She waited for me to respond.

'What happened to Theo's body?'

'We couldn't give him a formal burial. People would find out. Father Haralambos and the *andarte* gave him a makeshift burial. Only we know his whereabouts. It's better to keep it that way for a while.' She paused for a moment. 'So you see, when I arranged the meeting at the Church of the Virgin of the Swallow, I was killing two birds with one stone, as you English like to say — praying for the soul of my dead husband *and* meeting you.'

I studied her face carefully, still trying to take it all in. Throughout all this she had not shed a single tear. It was like looking at a mask. Only her mouth moved. I saw no sign of the grieving widow, but then, maybe she had seen too much already.

The maid, Rada, knocked on the door to announce dinner was served. We moved into the dining room where a light spread was waiting for us — cold meats and a few vegetable dishes. Prior to our conversation, I was ravenous. Now I'd lost my appetite. Not a word more was said about Theo. I had no option but to accept the status quo and carry on.

When the plates were cleared away, Rada appeared unamused that I had hardly touched the food.

'I'm not sure your maid approves of me,' I said after Rada left the room.

Alexis laughed. 'You mustn't take any notice. She's not bad when you get to know her.'

I found that hard to believe and I had no intention of getting to know her.

'Does she know about...?' I dropped my voice to a whisper.

'No. Let's keep it that way.'

'How did you get to know her?' I asked. 'I mean... where did you say she came from?'

Alexis looked at me sharply. 'I didn't, but as you're so keen to find out, I will tell you. She came looking for a job around the time Theo died. She was desperate and I took her on out of pity. She is more of a housekeeper than a maid. It's as simple as that. And before you ask, she is from Serbia. Her mother was Greek which is why she speaks Greek like a native. Her mother died during the famine.'

I was surprised and let slip that Rada looked too well-fed to have suffered in the famine. Alexis was not amused.

The clock on the mantelpiece chimed 7:00 p.m.

'There's a party at the Italian Ambassador's villa this evening. I've been invited. As I am alone, it would please me very much if you accompanied me. It will also give you a chance to mingle with some very important people. It's on occasions like this that one can pick up snippets of information valuable to our cause, but then I'm sure you already know that.'

The thought of suddenly turning up out of the blue at a function where I knew all eyes would be upon me, was not what I had anticipated at this point in the game, but it wasn't the first time I'd been thrown into such circumstances. At the moment, I was still coming to terms with what Alexis had just told me.

'I'm not sure I'm dressed for such a salubrious occasion,' I replied. 'Perhaps you should go on your own.'

'It's not becoming for a lady to turn up alone, Larry.' Alexis smiled. 'If you are worried about the right attire, I am sure we can fit you out in something more suitable.'

She took me upstairs to a bedroom overlooking the garden.

'This was Theo's room,' she said, seemingly oblivious to my discomfort.

I scanned the room. My eyes fell on a framed photograph which stood on a chest of drawers. It was of Theo and Alexis.

He was a handsome man. A pang of jealousy stabbed me. Alexis opened a large closet and pulled out an array of suits and placed them on the bed.

'You are about the same size so I'm sure you'll find something suitable here.' She picked up two dinner suits and held them against me, one at a time.

'How about this — or this?'

Both looked better than anything I'd ever owned. Some even looked brand new.

'I'll leave you to decide,' she said. 'And if you want to freshen yourself up, the bathroom is through that door. You have half an hour.'

After she left, I sat down heavily on the bed, surrounded by Theo's suits, and wondered if Cairo knew of this latest development. Probably not, but they would have to be told. I'd contact Dancer tomorrow and let them know. For the moment, I concentrated on choosing a suit and sprucing myself up. It didn't take long and I decided to have a quick look around the room before going downstairs. I wanted to know more about Theo. I picked up one of the photographs and looked closely at his face. He was a handsome man but he didn't strike me as a Greek. Maybe it was because of his light-coloured hair and light brown eyes, but then, I'd met many light-haired Greeks.

I rifled through a few drawers. Nothing of importance stood out; just a few personal items in a small velvet covered box; watches, cufflinks, handkerchiefs — that sort of stuff. I even checked the pockets of his suits. I tried the drawers to his writing cabinet but they were locked and there was nothing on top except a writing set. For a man who had just died, I expected to find more of his clutter around the place. Come to think of it, I hadn't even seen a photo of them in the drawing room either. Except for the suits, the room felt as though it was rarely used.

When I returned to the drawing room, the door was ajar. Alexis was talking with Rada and stopped suddenly when I entered. Rada hurriedly left the room but not before giving me a disapproving look. Clearly, she found the idea of me wearing the Master's clothes distasteful.

Alexis gave me a beaming smile. 'How handsome you look. That suits looks as if it was made for you.'

She had changed into a pale green satin dress and I repaid the compliment. She spun around in a graceful manner to reveal the low-cut back, resplendent with rhinestones. Her beauty and grace quite took my breath away. The black widow had morphed into a swan.

'Aren't you going to be rather cold in that?' I smiled. 'I believe it's starting to snow again.'

At that moment, Rada came in with a splendid sable coat. I took it from her.

'Allow me, Kyria Petrakis.'

She slipped into it with ease. I noticed her perfume. It was the same one she wore in Cairo. She picked up her black gloves, slid her jewelled fingers into them, and we left the house where her car was waiting for us. It was the same driver who had picked me up in the morning. If he knew of Theo's death, he certainly was playing along with this.

'You seem to have all this worked out,' I said to Alexis in a low voice, 'but haven't we forgotten something? How are you going to explain my presence? What is my cover?'

'Oh that's quite simple. You are my cousin from Larissa, here to see me for a few days.'

I couldn't help smiling to myself. It seemed that I was going to be everyone's cousin from Larissa.

Chapter 10

After showing our pass at the entrance to the Italian Ambassador's Kifissia residence, we drove along a sweeping driveway lined with snow-laden orange trees, towards the house. Luxurious black cars, covered with a light sprinkling of fresh snow, stood in the carpark outside a highly ornate villa designed in the Italianate style, known as Villa Aphrodite. The Italian Flag hung over the portico flanked on either side by the Hellenic and German. During the short drive, Alexis had already filled me in about the Ambassador. Apparently, he was man whose passion for Hellenic culture was second only to his passion for Italy, especially, Il Duce and the Fascist regime. I was also informed that the villa belonged to a cousin of the King's who went into exile at the same time as the rest of the Royal Family.

'Ambassador Marinetti has an eye for the good things in life,' Alexis said. 'He set his sights on this villa from the beginning. The King's cousin was an art collector, especially of ancient Greek statues. Unfortunately, he wasn't able to get all his collection out of the country in time. The Ambassador has now taken possession of it, along with his few priceless artefacts, although I am sure the wily cousin has secreted some of them away. Knowing that many of Occupied Europe's finest collections are being looted and taken to Germany by the Nazis, we must be grateful Marinetti has not seen fit to follow in their footsteps.'

The house was heavily guarded and we were obliged to show our pass at the door again. Alexis assured me there would be no trouble, even though the pass clearly stated Mr & Mrs Petrakis. She was right. Our names were ticked off a list and we were allowed inside. An enormous portrait of Il Duce took centre stage on the far wall in the hallway. Either side of the portrait were two marble statues of Aphrodite. To the left of these was a life-size portrait of Adolf Hitler. There was no mistaking we were in the lion's den.

Alexis deposited the sable in the cloakroom, looped her arm through mine, and as confidently as if we had secured an invitation from Il Duce himself, we made our way to the salon where a dance band was playing a tango, accompanied by a beautiful singer with a voice to match. A waiter stood by the door holding a large silver tray filled with champagne glasses. Following Alexis's lead, I took a glass.

She raised her glass towards me. 'To your health, cousin Nikos,' she said with a grin. '*Pame*, let's go.'

You need to be an actor, HQ had said when I joined the spy game, and they weren't referring to disguises. *If you are a good actor, you will go far. If not you could end up dead and we wouldn't be responsible for you.* Those words were ringing in my ears. This evening I would be guided by Alexis, and from the little I knew of her, she was the consummate actor.

I looked around the room. Most of the guests were wearing formal wear which made it easy to spot the uniformed, high-ranking Germans and Italians amongst them. The mixture of immaculate black, navy and grey uniforms with an array of shiny insignias served to remind everyone present that we were an occupied country. A tall, elegantly dressed gentleman spotted us through the crowd and made his way over. He welcomed Alexis with a polite bow and kissed the back of her hand. I noticed his shiny back hair was streaked at the temples with silver grey which gave him a distinguished look. He appeared to be in his mid-fifties.

'Kyria Alexis, your presence always brightens my soirées.'

'Giovanni. How kind of you.'

Giovanni! They are on first name terms.

He quickly turned his attention to me. 'I'm afraid we haven't met.'

Alexis introduced us. 'May I present my cousin, Nikos, Mr Ambassador. Nikos, this is Signor Marinetti.'

We shook hands, each of us summing the other up. He spoke Greek with a heavy Italian accent which added to his charm. He turned his attention back to Alexis.

'And Kyrie Theo, was he not able to come tonight?'

I watched Alexis's face.

'I'm afraid not. He went to Thessaloniki a week ago and has not returned. I'm expecting him back any day now. He may be delayed due to the heavy snowstorms.' She touched my arm. 'Rather than come alone, Nikos kindly offered to accompany me. I'm sorry I didn't telephone first to see if that was alright. I was hoping Theo would be back in time.'

'Well, my dear, let us hope he arrives home soon.'

Alexis commented on the music and the singer's charming voice. Marinetti took pleasure in telling us Carmela was a favourite of Il Duce's and had been flown out for the occasion. At that moment a distinguished looking man in a dark suit joined us.

'Signor Marinetti, aren't you going to introduce me to these delightful people?'

'Herr Doktor Franz Keller, may I present Kyria Alexis Petrakis and Kyrie Nikos...'

'Xenakis,' I answered quickly.

Like Marinetti, Keller kissed Alexis's hand.

'A pleasure to meet you, Kyria Petrakis.'

I noticed her face reddening.

He turned to Marinetti. 'This is what I always enjoy about your soirées, Herr Ambassador, the company is exceedingly delightful.'

Marinetti smiled politely at Keller's compliment but I recognised a look in his eyes that told me he disliked the intrusion. Clearly Marinetti was besotted with Alexis. She seemed to have him eating out of the palm of her hand — something I was all too familiar with.

The music stopped and the compère announced it was request time. Alexis seized the moment.

'Herr Keller, tell me, what is your favourite dance music?'

'Hmm, let me think.'

'I mean, if you were to choose one that reminded you of home, what would it be?

'*Shön ist der Nacht. Beautiful is the Night.* Yes, I would choose that. It reminds me of Berlin.'

I wondered where this conversation was leading. Alexis turned to Marinetti and asked if he could send someone over to play it. Marinetti offered to go himself.

'And if Carmela knows German, maybe she could sing in German?' Alexis added, careful to make sure Keller heard the comment.

We looked on as Marinetti approached the bandleader. After a huddled conversation involving Carmela, the band leader made a short announcement.

'Ladies and gentlemen, we have a special request for *Dark is the Night*. Carmela will sing it for you in German.' He swung around, nodded to Carmela, and raised his baton. The German guests, including Keller, listened approvingly. Alexis turned to me and winked.

'Would you care to dance, Herr Keller?' she asked. 'Maybe for a moment or two, you can imagine you are back in your beloved Berlin.'

By the time Marinetti returned, Alexis was whisking her way across the dance floor. All I could think of at that moment was how little she seemed to be the grieving widow.

Marinetti helped himself to another glass of champagne. Worried that he might start asking questions about why I was in Athens, I brought up the subject of art.

'Alexis tells me you are a connoisseur of Greek art?'

His face beamed. 'It is my passion. I cannot tell you how happy I was when Il Duce decided to send me here.' He leaned closer. 'Can you imagine if he had sent me to Ethiopia — or Libya, even — what a travesty?'

I wasn't sure if he was referring to the Axis forces losing ground, or the artworks. Knowing that artworks were being plundered, I treaded carefully. It was a fine line between asking too many questions and showing an interest.

'I confess to knowing very little about art,' I said. 'Alexis always says I must take the time to learn more. She thinks it's the mark of a civilized human being.'

Marinetti laughed. 'She is correct, Kyrie...'

'Xenakis,' I answered, happy that he could not remember my surname. Somehow I doubted Herr Keller would have that trouble

The music ended and everyone applauded. Alexis and Keller returned from the dance floor and Keller thanked Marinetti for a pleasurable evening, saying it was time for him to leave.

'I hope to have the pleasure of meeting you again, Kyria Petrakis,' he said. 'And you also, Kyrie Xenakis.'

I was right. He recalled my name with ease. Marinetti thanked him for taking time from his busy schedule to attend. Keller clicked his heels together and saluted. 'Heil Hitler.'

'Heil Hitler,' Marinetti and I repeated.

'I think we'd better be going too,' Alexis said. 'It's getting rather late.'

The guests all had curfew exemptions and I for one, didn't want to outstay my welcome. As we were leaving, a man approached us.

'Good evening, Kyria Alexis. I hope you've had a good evening.'

The man was Greek and apart from a brief nod of acknowl-edgement in my direction, he wasn't at all interested in me. I had the distinct feeling he had been standing around waiting for us.

Alexis asked if I wouldn't mind fetching her coat for her. While I waited at the desk for someone to retrieve it, I watched them both deep in conversation. The man was small and bald-ing and he wore heavy tortoise shell glasses, which on account of his round facial features, made him look quite unattractive. At one point, the man became quite animated and Alexis reached out to calm him down. When I returned with the coat, he gave another nod of acknowledgement and left.

'What a strange man,' I said, helping Alexis with the coat.

She didn't reply.

Outside, the snow had worsened. I dreaded the thought of going back to my freezing apartment. Thankfully that would not be possible tonight. It was well past curfew.

'Looks like you will have to stay the night,' Alexis said.

When we arrived back at her villa, any thoughts I might have had of comforting the grieving widow were quickly dispensed with. Rada was waiting for us.

'Did you have a good evening, Kyria?' she asked, taking the sable and shaking away a sprinkling of snow with her hand.

'Thank you, Rada. It was most enjoyable.'

Alexis turned to bid me goodnight. 'Thank you for a delightful evening, Nikos. Rada will see you to your room. Breakfast will be served at 7:OO a.m. in the morning room.'

It was a surprisingly formal end to a long and interesting day. I followed Rada to my room, which turned out to be Theo's. All his suits had been put away, the sheets on the bed were turned back, and a log fire blazed in the ceramic-tiled hearth.

Rada pointed to a bell on the wall at the side of the bed. 'If you need anything, push the button,' she said.

Ten minutes later I was fast asleep.

Chapter 11

I woke up the next day with a thumping headache; the result of too much cognac and champagne. I lay in bed for a while trying to get my head around yesterday's revelations. There were too many unanswered questions. It was certainly a shock to hear of the death of Theo, the White Rose, but these things happen and I could understand the need to keep his death a secret. Alexis would be the first one the Gestapo would haul in. What I couldn't understand was why Loukas didn't tell me. We had always been close. I wondered if Maria knew. The fact that Alexis and Theo were well connected didn't exactly come as a shock. High society agents are worth their weight in gold. Their ability to move amongst the enemy with ease is invaluable. Most speak several languages and have an excellent knowledge of other cultures. Obviously, Alexis and Theo Petrakis were two such people.

Neither did it surprise me that the new White Rose was a woman. Never underestimate a woman HQ had said, when they took me on. I could vouch for that. I'd known a couple of women leaders in my time and they were tough. One, a Romanian Princess — quite a beauty — was a dab hand with a stiletto. What did surprise me though, was Alexis herself. She was an enigma. She seemed to have that uncanny ability to lure you in to her web, and then, when you least expected it — wham — all was not as it appeared.

I surveyed the room. Apart from the odd photograph and a cupboard full of suits, I found it rather sterile. There was nothing to tell me what kind of a man Theo was. More importantly, there was nothing that gave me a hint of their relationship. Last night, Alexis had worn perfume. It lingered in the air. Yet there was not even the slightest whiff of her scent in this room. My stomach churned at the thought that I was lying in a bed where she had made love to another man.

My thoughts drifted back to Cairo. I was certain she had not worn a wedding ring and after what I knew now, I wasn't entirely certain my seeing her on the terrace at Shepheard's had been an accident after all. Maybe she had engineered it. The more I thought about it all, the more my head throbbed.

The clock chimed 6:30 a.m. and I took advantage of the hot water and luxuriated in a warm bath for a while before getting dressed. When I went downstairs to the morning room, there was no-one around and the table was set for one person. I helped myself to a selection of cold dishes from the buffet and sat down. As if on cue, Rada appeared with orange juice and coffee — real coffee — not the thick Greek coffee. For a brief moment, I was thankful for the Italian presence.

'Good morning,' I said, hoping she might warm to me a little more. 'Will Kyria Petrakis be joining me?'

'Good morning Kyrie,' she replied, her face as stern as ever. 'The Kyria apologises. She had to go out.' She reached into her pocket and pulled out a sealed envelope. 'She asked me to give you this.'

I waited until she left before I opened it.

Good morning, Nikos,
I hope you had a good night's sleep. The suit you are having
made for the wedding can be picked up at Hadzigiannis's tai-
lors, at midday in two days' time. I think you know where it is.
I am sure it will fit you well.
> *Alexis.*

P.S. Thank you for a delightful evening.

I re-read it, screwed it up and threw it into the embers of the fire.

Hadzigiannis's! Perhaps I would finally get to solve one of the missing links.

After breakfast, I was informed that the car was waiting to take me back to Athens. When we arrived at the same spot where I'd been picked up the day before, the driver handed me a small package and then drove away. Standing there on the street corner, the events of the previous day didn't seem real. But they were. The Poseidon Network was as real and as any other I'd worked for — and just as deadly.

I crossed the road into Plateia Amerikis and saw Aris waiting for me at the newspaper kiosk near my apartment.

'Have you forgotten we have a meeting with Stelios and Dancer?'

'Not at all. I got caught up in something. I'll tell you all about it later.'

I invited him inside while I unwrapped the package. It contained two packets of Greek coffee — a luxury.

Aris whistled. 'I am envious. All I get is herbal tea and a dark concoction that passes for coffee but tastes nothing like it.'

I put one packet aside for Maria and split the other between us.

Dancer was living a couple of kilometres further north of Plateia Amerikis. The area was filled with stone and marble cutting businesses for gravestones and houses. Occasionally the men got to work on something more artistic, like a piece of sculpture, but few could afford such art pieces these days. It was an unhealthy place to work. Marble dust filled the air and seeped into the lungs. Because of this, the Germans paid little attention to the area, which is why Dancer chose to set up his base to communicate with Cairo from here. A couple of the stonemasons belonged to the Resistance, which meant they kept an eye out for him.

The sun was shining by the time we arrived, and the men were busy at work fashioning chunks of marble into gravestones in the yard. Dancer's accommodation was little more than a shack but it did have a fire heater and a regular supply of wood given to him by the men who brought back marble from the mountainside. Outside, the dust filled our lungs. Inside, it was the smoke from the fire. Neither was good for the health.

'If the Germans don't get me, the dust will,' Dancer remarked jovially. 'The men tell me summer is the worst, the dust hangs in the air. So I have something to look forward to.'

I assured him we would not be in Greece by then — that is if we managed to stay alive. We had one hour before transmission time and I filled the men in about the White Rose. Naturally, I omitted the part about meeting Alexis in Cairo.

'She sounds a cool customer,' remarked Stelios, warming his hands in front of the fire.

Apart from that, they said very little. Nothing really surprised them.

Dancer prepared the radio and put on his earphones. Outside, the tac-tac-tac of the stonemason's hammers drowned out the tac-tac-tac of the transmitter. Dancer wrote down each message as he deciphered them and passed them to me. There was nothing out of the ordinary, just HQ checking all was in order. The last was the one I was waiting for.

Background check on Manos Kondoumaris — resident of Berlin from 1934 — minor clerk in the Greek Embassy — no evidence of a wife called Lotte — please advise.

Dancer saw my face drop. 'What do I tell them, sir?'

'Tell them to continue. Are they telling us he is still officially registered as a resident there? Maybe his marriage was registered in another city?'

Dancer tapped out the message and signed off with "Most Urgent".

'Anything else, sir? What about the White Rose?'

'No. Let's wait.'

'Is that wise?' Stelios asked. 'I mean, we *are* talking about the leader of Poseidon.'

'Give it a few more days, just to see what transpires.'

'Unless you believe he will rise from the dead, what can happen? His wife has taken over and if the network approves, who are we to rock the status quo? All the same, I think they should be informed.'

I couldn't really give him a reason as to why I wanted to delay updating HQ on this. Maybe I wanted to be sure Theo was really dead. Maybe I wanted to be sure of Alexis too.

*

It was exactly midday when I arrived at Hadzigiannis's tailors. The seamstresses and tailors were leaving for their siesta and a man was carrying the mannequins inside.

'Good morning. I've come about the suit for the wedding.'

After looking me up and down, he quickly scanned the street to check that I wasn't being followed and told me to go inside.

The place was empty. I waited until he locked the door and pulled down the blinds.

'Follow me,' he said.

We manoeuvred our way through to the cutting room at the back of the shop via a gloomy, narrow corridor filled with racks of suits and dresses. Thankfully, daylight streamed into the cutting room windows making it a more convivial place to work. Bolts of fabric lay on tables and the walls were lined with shelves filled with buttons and braids, and racks of paper patterns. He pulled out a seat for me and asked me to wait while he went outside via a back door. Minutes later, he returned with Alexis and a man I recognised as one of the two who took me to the Church of the Virgin of the Swallow.

I wasn't sure what to expect when I was told about this meeting and was pleasantly surprised to see Alexis herself turn up. Careful to address me as Nikos, she introduced the man as Leonidas, a close confidant. The tailor was not introduced at all but he was privy to the conversation. Both Leonidas and Alexis appeared on edge.

'Let's get down to business,' Alexis said. 'We have some information for you to send to Cairo as soon as possible.'

She asked Leonidas to continue. He moved a piece of cloth aside and laid a large map out on the cutting table.

'It concerns information on Axis shipping. We have it on good authority that one tanker and two cargo ships laden with ammunition are sailing towards Greece from Sicily. Another two are headed for Libya.' Working out the nautical miles, he pointed out where they were thought to be and how long it would take them to reach their destinations. 'On top of this, six new German submarines will be stationed at Piraeus in a week's time.'

I asked how he knew all this. All Leonidas would say was the information had been gathered by sources attached to the navy.

I glanced at Alexis. She gave nothing away but she sensed my apprehension.

'Rest assured, Nikos, this information is correct. Our sources have given us reliable information before and we acted on it ourselves. That was when the ships were in the Aegean and we were able to use the safety of the islands to get through the minefields. These ships are still in international waters and we don't have the means to put them out of action. The submarines are another story. We don't know where they are at the moment but you will be updated as soon as we know something.'

After a few more questions, I was satisfied.

'Well, if that's all,' I said. 'Then I'd better get a move on.'

I got up to leave.

Alexis caught my arm. 'There's something else.'

'Go on.'

Leonidas spoke. 'There are two more things we need to discuss. We're planning to sabotage the railway line between here and Thessaloniki. It's not a major operation, but it's vital because at a certain section, it intersects with another line and the Wehrmacht use it to aid the Italians fighting the Resistance in the area. We plan to do this at a point about ten kilometres from the nearest village.'

I raised an eyebrow. Sabotage always brought the risk of reprisals and Cairo preferred us to keep a low profile at the moment. Try and keep the dirty work till later, they told us. I also knew that if there were reprisals, it might spark trouble between the Resistance factions again. I couldn't help thinking the request was a test of our loyalty on their part, and if this was not a major operation, they were capable of doing it themselves. Leonidas's next sentence helped to sway me.

'We'd also like you to train the men in sabotage — you know, ready for when we put the bigger stuff into operation. Our men are experts when it comes to guns, but sabotage and explosions, well that's different. We've already had a few unfortunate accidents.'

'Fine. I will send Aris. He'll have the men trained in no time.'

There followed a brief discussion on how and where Aris would meet up with the men. Leonidas pointed out that he would be there himself as he knew the area well. He shook my hand and we moved on to the next point. This time Alexis spoke.

'This concerns the escape routes,' she said, pulling the map closer. 'We have extended the route for Allied soldiers and children into Turkey. We need to strengthen this operation immediately as the number of escapees is growing steadily by the day. We don't know how long the war is going to last and it's getting too dangerous to keep them secure. The Germans are stepping up their searches and they are far more thorough than the Italians.'

She pointed to the map, running her red-painted nails up and down the coastline in a fairly vague manner.

'From here, the route is via the islands to these points on the Turkish mainland.'

This time her red-nailed index finger stabbed at several islands in the Dodecanese, from Samos to Kastellorizio. They were all under Italian administration. A major part of my assignment was to help with the escape routes and make contacts to allow for landings in these islands when the time was right so I was more than interested to know who her contacts were in the area. Alexis's finger rested on a particular area on the Turkish mainland, not far from Izmir.

'Our men have established contact with the Turks along here. The villagers are helping us feed and protect the escapees. We've even got the Turkish military in the area on our side. It's not official and we need to pay them off. We cannot keep the escapees in this area. That means we need money — and more help on the Turkish side.' Alexis paused to gauge my reaction. 'Can you see what Cairo can do to help?'

Having given out most of the money that I'd brought to the resistance leaders, I wasn't sure how quickly I could lay my hands on more.

'Who's in charge of the operation in Turkey?' I asked, envisioning money slipping through my hands like water.

'No-one in particular. A few different people have been allocated an area to look after. I look after this route.' She pointed to the area around Samos. 'Once the people get to Turkey, each person relies on their own survival tactics. It's dangerous. If the Germans and Italians get wind of the Turks helping us, it could spark a diplomatic incident in Ankara and they might insist on the coastline being better patrolled, therefore we have to move them on to Palestine as quickly as possible.'

When I asked how many escapees were successfully reaching Turkey, she told me the figure was in the hundreds and rising. This included children.

'I would like your answer as soon as possible,' Alexis said. 'I am going to Samos myself soon and I'd like to give the men some good news.'

She was certainly forthright. I told her I would do my best. Leonidas looked at his watch and told Alexis they'd better get a move on.

'Something's come up,' she said. 'I'm sorry, but we have to go.'

She shook my hand and the meeting concluded. It was all very formal — as if we barely knew each other, which was probably right. We parted ways, she and Leonidas leaving the back way and I, the same way I entered, through the front. The tailor pulled up the shutters to let me out and after bidding me a good day, pulled them back down again. I walked towards the end of the street and looked back. The street was empty and I was alone. Not wanting to face returning to a cold apartment, I decided to go to the Taverna Acropolis for a bite to eat. It was closed. In fact the whole area seemed unusually empty, even for siesta time.

I walked in the direction of Tzisdaraki Mosque to see if the taverna owner's soup kitchen was still open. I was in luck. A line of starving people rugged up against the cold, were still waiting to be served. The owner recognised me and called me to the front of the queue. He handed me a bowl of steaming hot *revithia* soup.

'Have you heard the news?' he asked.

'What news?'

'There's been another *blocco* in the suburbs of Piraeus. It happened during the early hours of the morning. From what I gather the Germans have taken over a hundred men to Haidari. No doubt the poor bastards will be dead by morning.'

It flashed through my mind that Alexis and Leonidas must have known about it, which would account for the anxious look on their faces and them leaving so soon.

*

It was Maria who told me several members of the Resistance had been caught in the round-up.

'They also found guns,' she said, miserably. 'Word leaked out that there was to be an operation against the Germans sometime in the next few days. Now everyone is under suspicion, either from the Germans or the Greeks themselves.'

'Do they have any idea who it might be?' I asked.

She shrugged her shoulders. 'Who knows? I wouldn't like to be in their shoes when we find out.'

We spent the rest of the evening in small talk. In the short time I'd known her, Maria struck me as a strong woman, but that night she looked particularly weary and I had the feeling she was holding something back. I wondered if she'd heard anything about the White Rose, or more specifically about Theo's death. It couldn't be kept a secret for much longer.

Chapter 12

It was starting to get dark when I arrived at the stone-cutter's yard. A candle flickered in Dancer's window telling me it was safe to enter.

'What's wrong, sir?' he asked, pulling a second chair up next to the wood heater.

'You look as if you haven't slept a wink.'

'I haven't,' I replied. 'I need a drink.'

He looked at me with raised eyebrows and pulled out a bottle of ouzo and two glasses. It wasn't the first time he'd seen me like this.

'Things not going well?' he asked, pouring out a double shot.

What could I tell him? Nothing was wrong, yet everything was wrong.

'I won't rest until I've ticked off a few things that are preying on my mind.'

'And what would they be?'

Dancer was an even-tempered fellow. I'd never once seen him flustered or get angry, even when it came to eliminating anyone. Always as cool as a cucumber.

'Any news from Cairo?' I asked.

'If you mean Frau Lotte Kondoumaris — no. They're still looking into it.'

'Well let's hope they find something quick before the bombs obliterate the place.'

'Have you thought about checking Kondoumaris out here?' Dancer asked.

I stared at him for a few seconds and then burst out laughing. I had been too wrapped up in Alexis and it had clouded my judgement. *If you have stars in your eyes, you are no good to us,* HQ always said.

'You're a bloody genius,' I said, slapping him on the thigh, 'and I'm a bloody idiot.'

Dancer smiled. 'Thank you, sir. Coming from you, that's a compliment. Let's find out where he lives, that can't be too difficult. Poseidon must know.'

'No. I don't want them involved. They trust him, especially Kostas, and we don't want to worry them. In all probability, Kondoumaris may be quite genuine, but I think it better if we keep this to ourselves.'

We spent the next hour working out a plan. It was out of the question to use Aris. He would soon be on his assignment with Leonidas. I even thought of calling in one of the group who'd landed with us but for the moment they were far more useful in Northern Greece. In the end we decided that Dancer would do much of the sleuth work himself. As we had no idea what Kondoumaris looked like, he suggested hanging about in the vicinity of the SS Headquarters — a dangerous idea but then we were used to carrying out ideas that others would have steered clear of.

'I'll find a way, don't worry, sir. If I have anything to report, I'll let you know.'

Knowing that we had resolved to act, fired me up. I never was one for playing the waiting game, even though it was part of the job. We finished the evening with messages to Cairo about the ships from Sicily, the submarines arriving in Piraeus, and last but not least, a request for more money for the Aegean routes. I left in high spirits.

*

Two days passed before I saw anyone again. Two days is a long time when you have so much going through your mind and no-one to discuss it with. Dancer called by my apartment and informed me that Cairo had acted on the information about the ships leaving Sicily. In a swift bombing raid, the first three were sunk in the Ionian Sea and the other two, heading for Libya, were sunk south of Malta. It was good news, but not all news that day was positive. Over dinner later that evening, Maria told me that all the hostages had been shot, including several women. It was a bleak day for the Resistance.

A week later I received a message from Loukas to meet him at a safe-house in Athens. My package from Cairo had arrived safe and sound.

'The drop went as planned,' he informed me. 'The snow has eased and we had no trouble locating it. It came with three containers of ammunition and guns. They are safely hidden in the mountains.'

I counted the money and handed some to him. 'How about we go and celebrate somewhere decent. We need to talk.'

I could tell he knew what was uppermost on my mind.

'The only decent places are frequented by the Germans and Italians, but I know one place. It's near Omonoias. The owner knows me.'

'Does he know you are the Wolf?'

'No. He's an old school friend. I trust him.'

It was still early and the restaurant was almost empty when we arrived. The owner's face lit up when he saw Loukas.

'Good to see you again, my brother. It's been too long.'

'How's business? Loukas asked, glancing towards two uniformed Germans sitting at a table. 'Are they giving you any trouble?'

'Thank God, no. I keep my nose clean.'

He led us to a quiet table and handed us a menu. Most restaurants and tavernas no longer gave out menus; there was not much to put on them these days. My eyes fell on the lamb and immediately my mouth started to water. What a change from chickpeas and weeds.

'I'll have the baked lamb with orzo,' I said.

'Make that two,' Loukas added.

The owner disappeared into the kitchen. Minutes later, a young boy arrived with a carafe of wine.

Loukas informed me that because the Germans ate here, they made sure he had a good supply of whatever he wanted. I just hoped he didn't get strung up as a collaborator after the war.

'Does he ever pass on titbits of information?' I asked.

'Like he says, he keeps his nose clean.'

'But he knows you, and he must hear things.'

Loukas smiled. 'You're up to something. I know you too well.'

He poured out the wine and lifted his glass. 'To your health, my friend. And now I suppose you're going to ask me why I didn't say anything about the White Rose?'

'I'm sure you had your reasons,' I replied.

Loukas shifted uncomfortably in his chair. 'I did think about it. The truth is, I thought Theo's death might make you think Poseidon was compromised.'

'Did that thought cross *your* mind?' I asked.

'When I first heard of what took place at Ekali, I admit it did bother me. Apparently, the men made that journey quite often and knew the area well. Their papers were in order. They were also familiar with the soldiers manning those road-blocks. When I asked why they decided to search the car on that occasion, Alexis said the men in charge of the road block that night must have been replaced. '

'Do you know any of the *andartes* who were with him that night?' I asked.

'No. I am not familiar with that group. From what I heard, there were three. Two were killed outright, but Theo managed to escape. Alexis told me he was so badly injured, he died soon after. That's all I know.'

'How many know all this and whose idea was it for Alexis to take over Theo's name — the White Rose?'

'Only a few, and we all agreed Poseidon would be in danger of being torn apart if word got out. Theo was a strong leader and he held us together. He was not affiliated with any political side. His only aim was to free Greece.'

'You didn't answer my question. Whose idea was it for Alexis to take his code name?'

'It was hers. She knows everything about the network. As

his wife and a resistant herself, she knows his contacts, what operations he had planned, etc. Very few have that sort of knowledge.'

'And now she is the new leader of Poseidon,' I said matter-of-factly.

Loukas could see where I was heading.

'Don't you trust her, Nikos? Is it because she's a woman?'

'I don't care whether the head of Poseidon is a man or a woman, but this won't remain a close secret between a chosen few for long. You must know that. How will the other leaders react when they find out?'

'For the moment Alexis and I are working together. When the time is right, and I am hoping that will be soon, all the leaders will know. Then we will take a vote on the new leader.'

'What if Alexis wants to retain the role?'

Loukas sighed. 'We will see. It might be too much for her.'

I didn't want to bet on it.

'Fine,' I replied. 'What do I tell Cairo?'

'Tell them the truth. I'm sure they will understand.'

I was not so sure. Cairo was not too clever at reading the subtleties of life in the field. They would only want to deal with someone who was legitimately elected, even if they were *andartes*. There was too much at stake, not to mention money and guns.

We ate our lamb without uttering a word. The sensation of tasting meat — other than donkey — was utterly glorious. If there was one thing working as a spy taught me, it was never to take the simple things in life for granted. Meat was one of them. When we'd finished, I asked about the *blokko*.

'Maria told me everyone was executed. Does she know anyone caught up in it?'

'Yes. She was raised in that area and knows most of the families. Occasionally she supplies them with medicines.'

Loukas reached for his cigarette. 'Some bastard pointed them out as communist traitors. This sort of thing is on the rise. One thing's for sure. It's driving the people to join the Resistance. Many have already fled to the mountains.'

At that point, several Italian soldiers entered the restaurant with Greek women on their arms, laughing and talking loudly. Unlike the quiet Germans, the Italians were out to have a good time and they didn't care who saw them. The Germans gave them a dirty look.

'Come on,' I said to Loukas. 'It's time we made a move.'

Loukas laughed. 'What, and miss this!'

One of the Germans chastised the Italians for fraternising with the enemy and the Italians told him to get lost. For a moment it looked as if there would be a scuffle but the Germans would not be drawn further. They left, clearly disgusted with their allies.

'They're always having a go at each other.' Loukas smiled. 'If you ask me, it's a fragile friendship. The Germans might admire the Führer, but from what I can see, most of the Italians would like to see Mussolini dead for getting them into this mess in the first place.'

Before parting ways, I asked Loukas to make an arrangement for me to see Alexis. I wanted to give her the money personally and to discuss the escape routes in more detail. He told me I would hear from him in the next few days.

Two days later, Maria called by the apartment. It was short notice but I was to meet the White Rose at a kafenio near the ferry terminus in Piraeus later that afternoon.

'You are to make sure you have her "present" with you,' Maria added.

A few hours later, I boarded the train for Piraeus. When I arrived, gendarmes and German soldiers with machine guns patrolled the concourse, checking papers. Outside, ragged beggars were pestering the long queues of Greeks laden with bags and suitcases who snaked their way towards the Terminal entrance hoping to board the few ferries. Documents and travel passes were checked and rechecked. The distressed cries of those who had been turned away filled the air, oblivious in their misery to the angry shouts of German soldiers forcing them to move away.

The kafenio was a short walk along the seafront. I noticed Alexis's car standing nearby and walked towards it. Her driver sat inside along with three children; a boy and two girls who I judged to be between the ages of four and seven. The youngest girl clutched a porcelain doll and her eyes were red from crying. The older girl had a protective arm round her, but it was clear from the look on their faces that they were scared.

'She's waiting for you.' The driver said, gesturing across the road.

The kafenio was crowded with travellers and their luggage. Alexis was sitting at a table by the window, wearing her sable and a matching hat. She looked out of place — a kafenio was not her style. I was not quite sure how she would greet me. Would she be the formal Alexis, or the warm one? She was the warm one and greeted me with a peck on the cheek. She was wearing her perfume — the scent that instantly transported me back to Cairo.

'Thank you for coming at such short notice. We don't have

much time. The ferry to Samos leaves in an hour. Have you brought the gift?'

Blunt as ever! I handed over an envelope which she slipped into her handbag. I wondered if she had the Beretta in there too.

'Thank you, Nikos, you're a dear,' she said in a soft, almost seductive voice.

'Don't thank me, thank London,' I replied, 'I'm just doing my job. Who are they?' I asked, referring to the children in the car.

'Orphans on their way to freedom.'

'They look terrified,' I replied. 'Do they know where they are headed?'

'No. It's better that way. To say they are going far away to another land would only frighten them more. As it is, they keep asking for their parents.'

'Are they Jewish?' I asked.

'Yes. From Thessaloniki. Their parents were deported. They arrived in Athens via a woman who works with Loukas's network in the mountains. Because the children speak Yiddish at home, they have been told not to speak unless we are alone. I don't want anyone picking up their accent.'

I wondered if the woman she was referring to, was Anna. If so, I also wondered if she knew of her relationship with Loukas.

'Do you know who this woman is?' I asked innocently, trying to fish her out.

'Loukas is a clever man, Nikos. You know that. He has not divulged her name in case she gets caught. She must be important for him to do that.' She gave me a knowing smile. 'What do you think? You know him well?'

I told her if he chose not to reveal the name, it was for the best.

'So,' I said, offering her a cigarette. 'How long are you planning to be in Samos? More importantly, when will I see you again? HQ will want a full report on how their hard-earned cash has been spent.'

'Maybe three weeks. I have travel passes for myself and the children so I don't foresee any difficulties. We will be travelling as a family. The hard part is using the network to get us to the Turkish mainland. That happens at night and the fishermen have to be back before sunrise to avoid detection. I will stay in Turkey for a few days to make sure everything has gone smoothly. After that I return to Samos and then back here.'

When I asked her how she got the travel documents, she said her own was obtained from someone in Marinetti's office. Those for the children were obtained through a forger.

She looked at her watch. 'I'd better get a move on. I'll call you when I get back. Goodbye, Nikos,' she said, shaking my hand. 'Take good care of yourself.'

As I watched the car drive away, the children peered at me sadly through the back window. I fingered Anna's blue bead that I kept in my jacket pocket, hoping all would go well. A lot could happen in three weeks.

Chapter 13

The day after Alexis left for Samos, I left Athens for the mountains with Loukas. The ranks of the *andartes* were swelling and it was vital they remained organised. The foundations of village life were being torn apart and villages known to be supporting them were burnt to the ground. The route across the bridge that I'd taken that day with Anna and the old man had been strengthened. The bodies of the Italian guards had been discovered and buried by villagers further down the river and more solders were sent to the area. Now checkpoints had been erected on both sides of the bridge and they were manned at all times with soldiers with automatic machine guns.

Knowing this, forced us to change our journey and make the crossing at a point further up the river where the water was less treacherous. It was used by the *andartes* to distribute guns and ammunition to those groups hiding in the surrounding mountains. It may have been the best point to cross, but we then had to navigate a steep and densely wooded pass which took us several kilometres out of our way. The most dangerous part was not the terrain, but the group of ill-disciplined brigands and ruffians in charge of this area. Their leader was a man known as Thanassos, a tough character with a long black beard and eyes as dark as coal. He was never seen without his rifle and bullet filled bandolier slung sash-style across his chest. Thanassos was always spoiling for a fight and couldn't wait to get his hands on any German or Italian that strayed into his territory. Such behaviour was viewed by other groups as wild, and brought danger to the region. After several incidences of sheep stealing, which threatened to turn into a blood feud, Loukas managed to talk some sense into him. Against the wishes of other chieftains, Loukas promised him guns and a part of the action in exchange for unity.

When we reached the other side of the river, Thanassos and his men had already got wind of our arrival and were waiting for us. He greeted Loukas with a bear hug and lots of back-slapping, but when he saw me, he did not fail to hide a wariness I had come to associate with mountain Greeks when confronted with a stranger in their midst. Loukas explained that I was the one who saw to it that they would be supplied with guns and ammunition. On hearing this, his black eyes shone and he asked the men to bring tsipouro. I was not sure how I would navigate the steep climb after this.

We ended up staying the night with Thanassos's band. Gathered around a roaring fire, he regaled us with terrifying accounts of things he'd done to the Italians in the Albanian campaign. I was relieved to have him on side. He was definitely not a person to cross. The weather was still bitterly cold but thankfully the snow had melted. Protected from the elements in our warm, waterproof goat hair cloaks and sheepskin blankets, we slept like babies to the sound of rushing water and the smell of pine resin under an inky-blue, star-studded sky.

At dawn the next day, we set off for Ano Hora. The old widow was at home when we arrived. I could tell by the look on Loukas's face that he was looking forward to seeing Anna again but we were told she'd gone to Kato Hora on an errand. After dinner that night, we were left alone to talk. Loukas asked me if everything had gone smoothly with the White Rose.

'I met her just before she boarded the ferry for Samos,' I replied. 'She had three children with her.'

'It's easier for a woman to travel when she has children with her. It rarely occurs to the officials that children could be part of an escape route.'

'How many times has she made this trip?' I asked.

Loukas thought for a minute or two. 'I'm not sure.'

'Does she always go alone?'

'The first time was with Theo, sometime in October. They had two children with them on that occasion — Greek orphans from the north. The Poseidon Network had only just started and they wanted to check the escape routes out for themselves.'

'Why did they choose Samos?'

'Theo told me it was because they had connections with someone important in the Italian community in Athens and it was easy to get travel documents from them.'

'Did they ever tell you who that was?'

'No.'

'Do you think they could have come from the Italian Ambassador's office?'

Loukas studied me for a while. 'You mean Ambassador Giovanni Marinetti?'

'Yes.'

'It's possible. Theo and Alexis were always well connected,

even before the war. They have used those connections to our advantage. Why do you ask?'

'When I met up with Alexis in Kifissia, she asked me to accompany her to a party thrown by Marinetti at his villa. I got the feeling they knew each other well. In fact I'd go as far as to say he was smitten with her.'

Loukas laughed. 'That is hardly a surprise. Most men are smitten by her. She is beautiful and intelligent and she uses it to her advantage.'

His words stung and I couldn't help feeling she'd deliberately played me too. I felt a fool. Loukas saw my reaction.

'Ahhh, you too, I see,' he said with a huge grin. 'In all the time I've known you, you've always had an eye for beautiful women, but I am surprised to see you like this after only a couple of meetings.'

'I am not ashamed to say I do have a fondness for a pretty face,' I replied. 'They make my lonely life less lonely.'

The way the conversation was going, I felt the time was right for me to open up a little.

'Are you aware I've met her before?'

The smile on his face disappeared. 'No, I'm not.'

'We met in Cairo a few months ago. Before I was even given this assignment.'

This time it was Loukas who looked shocked.

'Cairo! Are you joking?'

'Would I joke about something so important?'

Loukas looked genuinely concerned which added to the general feeling of unease that had plagued me since reaching Athens.

'Something so important and you didn't know she was in

Cairo?' I was astounded. 'Surely Theo must have said something? Besides, I thought you may have known and that was one reason you didn't tell me she'd taken on the mantel of the White Rose when I arrived. I thought you wanted it to be a surprise.'

Loukas looked angry and swore under his breath.

'No. Absolutely not. When we knew Cairo was going to help us, Alexis asked me if I knew who they were sending. You were the only one of the group that I knew. I gave your name as Kapetan Nikos. The only thing I said was that we'd worked together before. She made no comment. Believe me, what you are telling me has come as a big surprise. As far as I knew, Alexis was in Crete when the Germans invaded. We all thought she stayed there until returning to Athens. Now you're telling me she was in Cairo. Why would Theo not tell me this? It doesn't make sense.'

Loukas was angry and he paced the room like a caged animal. I tried to calm him down. We had to get to the bottom of this before he confronted Alexis himself. I wasn't ready for that just yet.

'Loukas, do you know of a woman called Irini Vlachou?'

He thought for a few minutes. 'The name rings a bell, but I can't place her. Why do you ask?'

'Because her body was found in the Nile. The autopsy showed she had been murdered.'

He shook his head and sighed deeply. 'I think you'd better start from the beginning, don't you?'

Over the course of the next couple of hours, I told him everything that had transpired in Cairo. From the moment I laid eyes on Alexis; how I followed her through Khan Khalili market to a tailor's shop called Hadzigiannis — the same name as the tailor's in Ermou, the evening at the Blythe Pickering's villa, and the evening we spent in the desert. Eventually I got around to Irini's death and the sleuth work Jack Martins had done on my behalf which uncovered Irini being spotted with a Greek businessman called Dimitris Papaghiotis, who was supposedly a Nazi sympathizer. I wasn't surprised Loukas had a hard time taking this in; I was still having trouble myself.

'And all that time, you thought Alexis was in Crete?' I asked again, just to clarify the situation.

'I've already told you — yes. I saw Theo many times during that period. He never said a thing.'

'Do you think he may not have known himself?'

Loukas stared in disbelief and his temper flared up again. At first his abusive tirade was hurled at the Virgin Mary who often bore the brunt of things when Greeks got angry, then at the war and the Germans, and even me. Finally, he hurled abuse at SOE Cairo for trying to make trouble. Most of all he was angry with Theo and Alexis themselves.

I waited for his temper to subside. He angrily poked at the embers of the fire and added a few more logs while he digested this information.

'Loukas,' I said, treading carefully. 'How well did you know Theo?'

I saw he had tears in his eyes.

'We were like brothers. He built Poseidon from nothing. Before Theo, we were a rag tag of *andartes* with our own agenda. He was also the one who contacted Cairo for help.'

'Do you remember exactly when that was?' I asked.

'I know it was before Operation Harling. That was last

November, so maybe the month before. October, I think. About the same time that he and Alexis went to Samos.'

Loukas asked me to go over the time line of when Alexis was in Cairo.

'I met her in June 1942, which means that if she was evacuated from Crete on one of the last boats, she had been in Cairo for almost a year by that time. According to the friend who informed me of Irini's death, Alexis disappeared around the time the body was discovered — sometime in September.'

Thinking back on it, we only met a couple of times over a matter of a few weeks, yet it seems I knew her longer than that.

'When we met again in Kifissia, I distinctly recall her saying: "Things worked out better than expected. The thing was, I had to get back here without anyone knowing I'd been away. When I left Crete, I used a false name and passport. To all intents and purposes, I was still in Crete." That in itself tells me it was a secret mission, and by anyone's reckoning, that's a long time to be away from your husband without anyone noticing. Wouldn't you agree?'

Loukas nodded. 'If what you are saying is correct, then I would agree.'

'Which leads us to one of two conclusions; either Theo really did think his wife was in Crete all that time or, and I am leaning towards the second hypothesis, he knew of his wife's journey and was complicit in it.'

My thoughts flashed back to Cairo. Alexis had definitely flirted with me. I was experienced when it came to women and I knew her type of game-playing and foreplay when I saw it. I was convinced she wanted me as much as I wanted her. I thought of the night I spent in Theo's bedroom; how it was devoid of her presence, even her scent. Most of all, she did not fit the profile of a grieving widow.

'Would you say they had a happy marriage?' I asked.

He thought it over for a while before answering. 'I always thought so, but now you ask me, I can't say I saw them together too often. Theo was the one who stayed in contact with the *andartes* leaders. He always led me to believe she knew what was going on, which is why we agreed to let her take his name. Their high society contacts are vital to us having inside information.'

By the time we finished talking, it was dark. It had been a long day and we were both sorely in need of a good night's sleep. Loukas bid me goodnight. The widow had made up a bed for me on the floor next to the fire. As a guest, she had given me her best hand-loomed cotton blankets covered with a heavy kilim. I undressed and bathed myself with a bowl of fragrantly scented water sitting on the hearth and dried myself with a towel, skilfully embroidered along the hem in a repeating pattern of gold leaves. I had fond memories of these mountain village homes, with their ever-present smell of wood fires and home-cooked food. They may have been rudimentary dwellings but on occasions such as this, not even the luxury of Shepheard's Hotel could compare to the warmth I felt as I dried myself. I hung the towel over the chair to dry and slipped between the sheets, watching the red and blue embers dance in the hearth. Somewhere outside in the silence of the night, an owl hooted and not even thoughts of Alexis could keep me awake any longer.

Chapter 14

I awoke the next morning to find I was alone. The fire had long gone out and a chill was beginning to set in. On the table was my breakfast covered with a checkered cloth; a glass of fresh milk, a boiled egg, a handful of olives, and a dry rusk. I peered out of the window and saw the street was also deserted. Not a soul in sight. Except for the clucking of hens outside, I ate my breakfast in silence, going over the previous night's conversation in my mind.

I looked at my watch. It was almost ten o'clock and, as no-one had returned, I decided to take a stroll through the village. I was just about to leave when I heard the church bells ringing. They rang constantly. Something was wrong. I spotted a few old people scurrying towards the church and decided to follow them. Just as I was leaving the house, I saw the widow returning.

'Kapetan Nikos,' she called out frantically. 'Come quickly, something terrible has happened.'

'What is it? Where's Loukas?'

'He left for the mountains and he asked me to tell you to follow him. He said you'd know where.'

The only place I could think of was the cave, but I had no idea how to get back there. It was dark the night we left and there had been a blizzard. I would get lost in no time at all. The widow was so distraught, she could barely talk. I returned with her to the church where the villagers had gathered. The priest, Papagrigoriadis, was the same one who had buried Bob Cohen the night we arrived in Greece. He was doing his best to comfort the women whose shrieks and wails echoed through the tiny church like a banshee. I asked what was happening and was told that the village of Kato Hora was surrounded in the early morning by Germans.

'All the inhabitants have been rounded up,' he said, crossing himself. 'I fear the worst.'

'Is that where Loukas is heading?' I asked the widow.

'I don't know. Maybe.'

She started to wail and beat at her chest, beseeching the Virgin to save her daughter. 'Anna! Anna!' Her cry was heart-wrenching.

I pulled the priest aside. 'I have to meet Loukas at the cave but I will get lost if I go alone. Can you help me?'

'I can't leave here at the moment. These people need me, but I know someone who can take you there.'

He turned to a woman and whispered something in her ear. She hurriedly left the church and returned ten minutes later with a boy of about eight or nine.

'This is my son,' the priest said. 'He will take you there.'

I followed the young boy along a pathway north of the village until we came to a rocky ridge with an expansive view of the valley beyond. I could just make out Ano Hora, and further below, and what looked like speckled dots on the landscape, lay the village of Kato Hora. We moved further eastwards along the ridge until I came to the spot where we'd buried Bob Cohen. The cross of rocks still marked his grave. Now I knew where we were. The cave was nearby. I thanked the boy and gave him a few coins for his trouble. He said he would wait until he knew I was safe. I was to give him a whistle. I walked on further and spotted Loukas's men outside the entrance. I whistled back to the boy. He was nowhere to be seen but seconds later I heard him whistle in reply.

The men were in the process of loading guns and ammunition onto donkeys which alarmed me.

'Where's *O Lykos*?' I shouted.

'He's gone ahead,' someone replied. 'He'll meet us there.'

A man whom I did not recognise came towards me.

'You are to come with us. Make sure you have all the explosives you need. This could get messy.'

I went back into the cave with him. What I saw made my heart race. Scattered on the rock floor was an array of guns and ammunition, most of which I had brought with me the night I landed in Greece. Amongst all this were small packages and wooden crates containing explosives and grenades.

'Good God, man! What are you trying to do, blow us all up?' I asked angrily.

The man appeared unmoved by my outburst.

'We are going to Kato Hora to confront the Germans. Take what is necessary from these explosives and hurry. There's no time to waste.'

'Necessary for what?' I asked in disbelief.

An attack on the Germans on the scale these men appeared to have planned would bring untold disaster. Reprisals would not be limited to Kato Hora alone. It would ruin everything.

Another man appeared outside with a donkey and two empty panniers. 'This is for you,' he said. 'Take what you need and let's go.'

I carefully loaded the panniers with an assortment of explosives — plastic, wire, fuses and detonators, taking care to protect them against the movement made by the animal traversing the rocky ground. The rest I left, still in a mess, and prayed no-one would come snooping around. Even a wild animal could set those things off.

Loukas's band of *andartes* from Ano Hora and the nearby hamlets consisted of about twenty-five men. When the donkeys and horses were all loaded, we set off in a single file back down the mountainside. The road we took was barely a track and thickets of thorny bushes and rocks slowed us down. Fortunately, the men tackled the terrain well, steering the animals in and out of difficulties with the ease of mountain shepherds.

On the way down, I learnt what took place at Kato Hora. As a rule, the region was patrolled by the Italians who were, on the whole, much more amenable to the plight of the Greek villagers than the Germans. Every now and again, they stationed a customs officer in the area who soon became aware of foodstuffs being requisitioned from the shopkeepers and farmers by the *andartes* who came down from their mountain hide-outs. The village reached an understanding with him and rather than report these misdemeanours to his superiors, he turned a blind eye. Thinking that no-one would bother them, the *andartes* usually left their guns propped up against the kafenio wall while they went about collecting the food. The problem arose when a week ago, a two-man Wehrmacht reconnaissance team entered the village and saw them. To make matters worse, the Italian officer was not there that day to smooth things over. The Wehrmacht soldiers quickly turned around and left in the direction from which they came.

The frightened villagers raised the alarm by ringing the church bell. The *andartes* gathered their guns and fled the village as quickly as they'd arrived. The Wehrmacht rarely came into this area because it came under Italian jurisdiction, but the villagers all knew the Germans would not be as tolerant. Fearing a reprisal, they nominated a delegation of three men to leave for the main town in the area straight away and explain what happened to the Italian commander. In the meantime everyone fled their homes and slept in the surrounding fields and hills. The delegation arrived back with an assurance from the commander that he would smooth things over with the nearest German Division in his area. That was two days ago.

Yesterday the villagers had been preparing to celebrate the betrothal of one of their young women to a man from another village. A sheep had been slaughtered and was roasting over the coals in the plateia and most of the villagers were in the church giving thanks that they had been spared the wrath of the Germans. Unbeknown to them, a German division from Larissa had been assigned to teach the villagers of Kato Hora a lesson. A teenage boy was tending his father's sheep when he saw the trucks approach. He fired a warning shot but was too far away for anyone to hear.

The armoured division encircled the village and all the houses were searched. The boy raised the alarm across the mountains but it was early morning before the people of Ano Hora got to hear of it.

Before long we reached a clearing with a good vantage point of the village. Loukas and his men were waiting for us, checking their guns. With them were a band of *andartes* from Kato Hora.

'Anna's down there with them,' he said to me. 'She took yesterday of all days to visit a friend.'

Now I knew why the widow was calling her name in distress.

'What's happening?' I asked. 'Can you see what's going on?'

'They've separated the women and children from the men and taken them to the schoolhouse while they continue the search.' He pointed to a small building on the edge of the village where we could see half a dozen guards sitting outside. 'We can't see where the men are from here, but we think they've rounded them up in the plateia.'

'What are we going to do?' someone asked. 'If we attack, they'll kill them all.'

I could see Loukas was in a quandary. 'It's likely they'll do that anyway, otherwise they'd have let the Italians deal with it. If they were going to take them away for questioning, they would have done it before now. No. I fear they mean to send us all a message this time.'

'Somehow we have to divert their attention,' I said. 'There's only one road out of there and the Germans won't want to be cornered in a shoot-out they didn't see coming. Let me divert their attention by blowing up the furthest truck from the village. In the meantime, our men will have just minutes to try and save the villagers.'

Trying to divert their attention was the only option we had, and the men agreed. Loukas gave everyone specific orders. Two men were to go with me, a group to the school, and all the others were to fan out, ready to attack from all angles. We shook hands and set off in different directions.

Approaching the village along the road the Wehrmacht had driven along was not easy. Low-lying fields lay on either side and, because it was still winter, they afforded little cover. The men with me were the only two experienced in explosives. I gave each one all the parts to assemble and directed them to lay their explosives in hollowed out pieces of wood and place them along the road at regular intervals. I would go on alone which meant crawling through the muddy fields.

The Wehrmacht division consisted of at least fifteen trucks and not all could be manoeuvred into the village itself. Two had been parked on the road away from the rest and I saw the drivers sitting outside, smoking and chatting. Keeping as low as possible, I carefully started to assemble the explosives. When they were ready, I fixed the silencer on my gun. More than five minutes passed and every now and again I heard sporadic gunfire. Despite my lack of faith in any religion, I asked the *Panagia* to watch over me, kissed the blue glass bead Anna had given me for good luck, and slowly started to crawl towards the trucks. At that point, I smelt smoke and saw a dark cloud of smoke rising into the sky. The village had been set ablaze. Fortunately, the soldiers stopped talking and moved to the front of the trucks to see what was going on.

I managed to get behind the last truck and lay the explosives without being detected. With my body flattened against the truck, I moved towards the men. Neither of them heard me until it was too late. Both shots were clean, quick, and accurate. They had no idea what hit them. I hurried back into the field, hid behind a low wall, and lit the fuse. The first truck exploded, quickly followed by the second. Debris hurtled through the sky, falling not far in front of me, and a curling mass of flames from both vehicles rose in the air joining the dark clouds coming from the village. All of a sudden, machine guns opened fire, drowning out the screams of the villagers. Hidden behind a wall of smoke and fire from the trucks, I moved to the safety of the woods and made my way towards the village. My two accomplices were nowhere in sight but after earlier hearing a series of coded bird calls, I was confident their explosives were in place.

The scene that greeted me was like a nightmare. At that point I had no idea what was taking place but I knew it was not good. Dense smoke billowed towards the sky and all I could hear was the crackle of machine gun fire and screams. Most of the shooting seemed to be coming from the direction of the fields. I saw one of the *andartes* cornered in a group of buildings that had caught alight and went to his aid. Half a dozen Germans had him surrounded and were shooting at him, riddling the walls with bullet holes and sending chunks of stone flying into the air. I began to fire on them which gave the man chance to flee while they turned their guns in my direction.

In the midst of this mayhem I heard the sound of trucks revving their engines. The Germans were leaving. I positioned myself behind a stone wall and waited for them to pass, aiming carefully at the tyres, I fired my pistol. My shots were accurate. Two tyres burst, sending the first truck into a spin. As the other trucks slowed down to manoeuvre around it, I pulled the pin from a grenade and hurled it over the wall. It hit the next truck and exploded, damaging others. The rest drove on, leaving behind badly burned and wounded soldiers to the mercy of the *andartes*. I pressed myself against the wall and waited.

Minutes later I heard two loud explosions further down the road. My men had done a good job. Unfortunately, one truck got through. Whatever happened now, we would feel the full force of the Wehrmacht.

When I made my way into the village, the shooting had stopped but the devastation was all too evident. Bullet-ridden bodies lay strewn around the burning village reminiscent of a scene from the apocalypse. Most were German but there were many *andartes* amongst them. I headed towards the school. The door was wide open and flames were shooting out of the windows. All around lay the bodies of dead soldiers but there was no sign of the villagers. Amid the crackle of burning wood and collapsing walls, a shrill wail pierced the air. It came from the back of the school. A young woman was sobbing over the body of an older woman. The old woman had been mown down, her body covered in blood and torn flesh. Her eyes stared vacantly towards the heavens. I had lost count of the times I'd seen such a scene. One never forgets it.

Behind the school was an orange orchard and beyond that, the fields. Several *andartes* were scouring the fields for the wounded. I moved around checking that all the soldiers were dead. Those still living got a bullet in the head. I spotted Loukas coming from the fields. He was carrying a young woman in his arms — Anna.

'She's still alive,' he said, laying her down gently under an orange tree. 'She was hit in the chest but I think she will recover.'

Anna's head rolled to one side and blood was seeping from a wound above her right breast. Loukas leaned over and whispered words of encouragement in her ear.

'We have to stem the bleeding.'

He ran to the body of a dead woman and cut a part of her bodice with his knife. Folding it into a wad, he ripped Anna's jacket open, slit her blouse, and stuffed the wadding over the wound.

'Press on to this,' he said, and he removed his belt.

I sat Anna upright, still holding the wadding in place, while Loukas tied his belt over the fabric and around her chest. Her eyes flickered open and she let out a low moan. In a barely audible voice, she asked if she was going to die.

'No *agape mou*, you'll be fine, but you must lie still. I have to leave you for a moment while we see to the others.'

'The Germans...' she muttered.

'It's all over. Now shush. Lie still.'

Loukas stood up and picked up his gun. 'There's nothing more to be done except pray,' he said, his voice too low for Anna to hear. 'Come on, let's find the others.'

I don't know what came over me but I took the blue bead out of my pocket and pressed it into her hand. There was a glimmer of understanding in her eyes. She forced a smile and then closed her eyes again.

'Let's go, comrade,' said, Loukas. 'There's no time to lose.'

It was only a short distance from the orchard to the fields and it was strewn with dead bodies. Loukas told me the plan had been for his group of men to edge towards the school as quietly as possible. When they found it guarded, he gave instructions for each man to single out a German in order to finish them off before they could fire back. That was when they saw soldiers setting the houses alight. They had to act quickly. They killed the soldiers before they knew what was happening but when they unlocked the school house door, more Germans arrived.

'We kept them at bay for a few minutes,' Loukas said, 'while the women and children fled towards the fields. Unfortunately, there wasn't enough time and more soldiers turned up with machine guns and went after them. That's when we heard the trucks being blown up. It stopped them in their tracks. Thank God it did or none of us would be alive now.'

We stepped over a line of bodies — all women and young children — and moved further into the fields. Mercifully, a few had managed to escape and were still lying in the muddy ground, afraid to get up. Others had been wounded. When Loukas called out, traumatized faces started to appear from behind rocks, but there was no sign of the men from the village. Behind us, the village was still burning and we could see the rest of the *andartes* running about in a futile attempt to see if anyone was still alive. Then we heard a volley of fire and shouts for us to come over. They had found the men. Out of a village of 150 souls, less than half were men and they had been rounded up in the plateia and executed. We counted forty-five bodies, including the priest. The rest were unaccounted for.

After a few hours the fires began to burn themselves out. Fearful that the Germans who'd managed to escape would alert their compatriots and send out another division, all those still alive including the seriously wounded, retreated to the safety of the mountains. With the onset of nightfall, the temperatures plummeted and with no blankets, some of those with severe wounds died during the night.

In all, we managed to save at least thirty women and children, the youngest only six months old and found safe and well in his dead mother's arms. It was not good, but it was better than none at all. There were still a few unaccounted for and we hoped they'd managed to escape across the river which lay about two kilometres south of the fields. Most importantly for Loukas, Anna was still alive, although her wound did not look good. The cloth he'd used to help stem the blood needed cleaning and we had little water. He and I chose to forgo our water rations to clean the wound and we boiled the water in a beaker lent to us by one of the Kato Hora *andartes*. When it was ready, we borrowed a torch and moved her into the privacy of the bushes. We also had with us a small medicine bag which all the *andartes* groups carried.

'This is no time for modesty,' Loukas declared. 'You are a friend and I need your help.'

He peeled back her shirt to expose her chest and removed the wadding while I shone the light on her. Anna was fully conscious and moaned in pain as the cloth was pulled away. At the top of her breast was a gaping hole. The bullet was still lodged inside.

'*Christos kai Panagia*; Christ and the Virgin, we have to remove it,' Loukas said.

'Let me,' I replied. 'I've had training for these sorts of things and removed more bullets than I care to remember. Hold her still.'

With nothing to knock her out — not even tsipouro, Loukas held Anna in such a way that she couldn't fight us. I opened the medicine bag with its rudimentary instruments and took out a scalpel and tweezers. Loukas soothed Anna's forehead, telling her to relax while I dipped the instruments into the boiling water. I teased the tweezers gently into the wound until I came into contact with the bullet. Anna let out a terrifying scream and struggled. Thankfully Loukas was a strong man.

'I need to make an incision,' I whispered. 'Hold her tight.'

Anna passed out, allowing me to remove the bullet much faster. Finally I washed the wound again and sewed it up. When I looked at Loukas I saw he had tears streaming down his cheeks.

'I can't thank you enough, my friend. I couldn't bear to lose another woman I love in this damn war.'

I put a comforting hand on his shoulder. 'She was very lucky. She'll survive and hopefully, there'll be no serious damage to the breast.'

We had no sleep that night. There were others who needed our attention too. We knew some wouldn't pull through, but we still gave them hope. In the morning we moved the wounded to nearby villages. Anna was taken back to Ano Hora while Loukas and I discussed the ramifications of reprisals in the area. We both agreed that somehow, we needed to put pressure on the Italians to stop further unrest. The best option was to try and contact Alexis immediately and get her to use her influence with Ambassador Marinetti. The next day I headed back to Athens.

Chapter 15

Chryssa sat me down in front of the sink and wrapped a towel around my shoulders whilst her mother prepared the hair dye. Maria chastised me for not looking after myself.

'If you'd left it any longer, you'd have drawn attention to yourself,' she tutted. She tugged at the beard. 'And this needs a trim too. Athens is not the mountains you know.'

Chryssa giggled. Her mother might have said it in a playful tone but she was deadly serious. The Germans were constantly on the look-out for Allied soldiers masquerading as Greeks. It was common knowledge that the two main giveaways were the language and their colouring. After applying the hair dye, she told me to get rid of the beard, adding that I could keep the moustache, but it needed a good trim. I did as she ordered while she and Chryssa prepared dinner. When I'd finished, she inspected me like a small child, applied a touch of dye to the moustache, and returned to preparing the food. I asked her how things had been while I was away.

'Terrible,' she replied. 'More *bloccos*. More executions. Those bastards will pay.'

By that I assumed she meant the notorious Security Battalions and collaborators.

After a good five minutes had passed, she asked Chryssa to wash off the hair dye. When my hair was dry, she stood back to admire her handiwork.

'Now that is what I call a man,' she laughed. 'The women will come running.'

I wished that were true, but women were the last thing on my mind — except maybe for one and that wasn't wise. Maria told me she'd heard Theo was dead and Alexis was now in charge of Poseidon. I asked her how many knew. She shrugged her shoulders.

'I have no idea but news travels fast.'

'Did you know Theo well?' I asked. 'I mean the White Rose.'

'Not that well but we did meet on several occasions. It was he who helped get me medicines. I never asked where he got them from or who his contacts were, but packages used to arrive via special couriers. I was grateful for that. You get to be thankful for small mercies. Questions are avoided.'

I sensed she was quite moved to hear about Theo's death.

'And Alexis? How well do you know her?'

Maria looked at me for a second and smiled. 'You're fishing, Kapetan.'

'Maybe I am,' I answered, treading carefully to judge her response.

'Let's eat first and then you can get whatever it is off your chest.'

She ladled out fish soup which we ate in silence. When we'd finished, she looked at the list of medicines I'd given her for Loukas and handed it to Chryssa.

'Go and sort these out and wrap them up. Someone will call by for them tomorrow.'

'Now,' Maria said when we were alone. 'What do you want to know? I can't promise I can help, but I'll try.'

'The tailor's shop in Ermou — Hadzigiannis — what do you know about it?'

'I know it's been there for years. The old man who started it is a refugee from Asia Minor. His family were tailors in Smyrna. He's still alive but has little to do with the business. His son, Manos is the one who runs the business now.'

I thought back. The man would have been in his late forties. 'So you're saying he arrived from Asia Minor with his father?'

'That's correct.'

'And are there other family members in the business?'

'Quite a few I suppose. Why do you ask?'

It's now or never I thought to myself.

'There's a tailor's shop by the same name in Cairo — in the bazaar. Would they be related?'

Maria thought for a while. 'After the population exchange, not everyone came to Greece. They went to all corners of the world. Some to America, others to South Africa, and many went to Egypt, especially Cairo and Alexandria. Hadzigiannis is a common name but I did hear that they had an extended family in the same line of business. Maybe it was Cairo, I can't be sure. I know he had a brother in the business.'

I thought back to what Jack Martins told me. That Hadzigiannis was an old man and his son Stefanos ran the place now. My hunch appeared to be right; the two places were connected.

'Do you know if Alexis ever went to Egypt? Around the time the Germans attacked?'

'Not that I know of. I believe she was in Crete for a while though.'

I couldn't help thinking how everyone was supposed to think this.

'Have you ever heard of a man called Dimitris Papaghiotis?'

'I can't say I have. Who is he?'

'He runs a cotton exporting business in Egypt.'

Maria looked thoughtful. 'Theo made his money in the cotton business. Maybe he knew him?'

I sat back. It never occurred to me to ask how Theo made his money, and Alexis never volunteered to tell me. Maybe this was another connection.

'I thought Theo may have been an industrialist.' I said innocently.

'From what I know, Theo had his fingers in all sorts of pies. That's why they still live the way they do.' Maria paused for a moment. 'How much more are you going to ask? This is beginning to feel like a Gestapo interrogation.'

'Have you ever heard of a woman called Irini Vlachou?'

At the mention of Irini, her smile disappeared.

'What about her?'

'She was found murdered shortly before I arrived in Greece. Her body was recovered from the Nile. Apparently, she had been shot.'

Maria's face turned as white as a sheet.

'What's wrong?' I asked.

She got up to fetch a bottle of cheap wine. It was almost empty. She poured us both a drink and threw the bottle away.

'So that's where she ended up — Cairo! Well, well, what a surprise, although I am shocked to hear she's dead. Miss

Vlachou was Theo's secretary. Are you sure we're talking about the same Irini Vlachou?'

Now it was my turn to be shocked. I'd imagined lots of scenarios concerning Irini, but this certainly wasn't one of them. It did answer the question however, of how Alexis and Irini knew each other. Maria went on to describe her. It was definitely the same woman.

'I'm sorry this has come as a shock,' I replied. 'It's just that no-one seemed to know who she was.'

'I'm telling you this because I trust you Maria. There's more to this story. Alexis was also in Cairo.'

Maria shook her head in disbelief. 'This is turning into an evening of surprises for both us, wouldn't you say? First you tell me Irini Vlachou was there, now you say Alexis was there too. They certainly kept that quiet.'

I wasn't sure how much I wanted to tell Maria about the few times I'd met Alexis, so I stuck to the facts.

'I only met Irini once and that was when a group of us went for a sunset picnic into the desert. The men went to shoot water fowl by the Nile and the women listened to music and socialized. On the way back, we stopped at an oasis and Irini was bitten by a snake. Had it not been for the villagers, she would have died. On our return to Cairo, she was taken to hospital. I left the following day for work. When I returned, the police were looking for me. That's when I found out Irini's body had been found in the Nile. I never saw Alexis again either — until I arrived in Athens. It's all a bit of a mystery and I'm trying to fathom it out without letting Cairo know. If they think something is wrong, they will pull the plug on us co-operating with Poseidon.'

'Who else knows all this?' Maria asked.

'Just you and Loukas, and even he doesn't know much. I didn't tell him about Irini.'

Maria rubbed her head. She had enough on her plate without me adding to it. Our conversation was interrupted by someone crying in the pharmacy. Chryssa popped her head round the door to say a woman had brought her young son in. He had a broken arm.

'I'd better get going and leave you to it.'

'Stay a while longer,' she replied. 'Just let me see to this boy.'

I waited, all the time listening to the boy's harrowing screams as Maria tried to position the boy's bone back into place without it splintering. He was still wailing when he left.

'What happened?' I asked when she reappeared.

'He was caught stealing fruit by a German who cracked his arm with his rifle. The poor kid is so undernourished, his bone snapped like a twig. Unfortunately, it's a regular occurrence.'

We resumed our conversation.

'Did you know Irini well? I asked.

'No. Theo had an office in Athens. She used to work there. I only met her a couple of times, so I can't say I really knew her. When the Germans attacked, Alexis and Irini were in Crete. They had an apartment there because of his business interests. Theo thought it better that Alexis stayed there until things quietened down here, but from what you have just told me, they never did.'

'So what did he think happened to Irini? Why did he allow a secretary to stay there all that time with his wife? Wouldn't he want her back here to work?'

'I have no idea why. All I know is, we heard Alexis was safe and well, but the secretary went missing. I think everyone assumed she'd been killed in a bombing raid. So many disappeared, we didn't think any more of it. Now you've told me *both* she and Alexis were in Cairo, I don't know what to believe anymore. It doesn't make sense.'

I wholeheartedly agreed.

'Can I ask you another question and then we'll call it a night?'

Maria nodded. 'Fire away, although I don't know what else I can help you with. You seem to know more than I do.'

This was a long shot and I wasn't sure how she'd respond.

'Would you say Theo and Alexis had a happy marriage?'

'My God, Kapetan,' she exclaimed. 'What a strange question! I can't help you there. As I said, I didn't know them enough, at least not on that level. All I know is they were both well-respected in the Poseidon Network, especially, Theo.'

It was time to call it a night and I thanked her for her trust in me. My questions had raised more questions for both of us.

*

After a few days, I heard from Loukas that Anna was well on the road to recovery which was heartening. I also heard that Alexis had returned from Samos. I needed to see her with regards to her using her influence to stop further reprisals in the mountains. A message came via Chryssa that I was to wait in the usual spot for someone to pick me up the next day.

When I arrived at the villa, Alexis was walking along the driveway towards the house. She was dressed in her sable and wore a black veil over her head. Everything looked spick and span except for her boots, which were thick with mud. It had been a few weeks since we last met, and neither the terrible circumstances I'd been involved in or the growing unease of finding myself caught in a web of deceit that I still couldn't work out, had lessened my attraction to her. She simply took my breath away every time I laid my eyes on her.

'Nikos darling,' she cooed softly in my ear as she gave me her usual peck on the cheek. 'How lovely to see you again.'

I would have liked to think she was genuinely pleased to see me, but you could never tell with Alexis. She was such a good actress. And the fact that she called me Nikos and not Larry always served to remind me that I was here on an assignment. When we reached the portico, she removed her muddy boots and put on a pair of stylish flat shoes.

'I've been for a walk,' she said, seeing me eye the boots. 'I went to visit Theo's grave.'

'I thought he was given a makeshift burial,' I remarked, recalling that the grave was a secret the last time we spoke about it.

'We reburied him in the old cemetery next to the Church of the Virgin of the Swallow. It wouldn't be wise to tell anyone though. We can't draw unwanted attention to a well-known man who had recently been killed by the Germans. I'm sure you understand that. Besides, only a handful of people know what really happened.'

'You mean the full story of them returning back from a meeting and being searched at Ekali?' I asked.

Alexis gave me a long penetrating look. 'That's exactly what I mean.'

'Then what do people think happened to Theo? Those who don't know the real story, that is.'

'That he has disappeared. He went away on a business trip and we don't know what's happened to him. We can only conclude that somehow or another, he was killed. What else can people think? There can be no other explanation.'

I could see she was getting irritated with me. It all seemed too convenient. Theo goes missing, presumed dead. The only thing was, Theo wasn't just anybody. He was a prominent business man and the leader of the largest resistance network in Greece.

'I'm sorry I never got to know him,' I said. 'The leader of the Poseidon Network must have been some man. I think we would have got on well.'

'I am sure you would,' she replied. 'It was such an unfortunate and untimely accident. I'm still coming to terms with it myself. Now, if you don't mind, I've had an upsetting few hours, so can we please change the subject.'

We went inside where a light lunch had been prepared for us in the morning room. One could always guarantee eating well with Alexis — a feast in a world of famine.

'How was the trip?' I asked.

'Thankfully, all went well. I plan to make another one soon.'

'I would like to join you next time,' I said, helping myself to a slice of ham. 'Cairo would like more details about the escape route; the usual stuff — who our contacts are, etc., especially those in Turkey. We may be able to expand the network. What do you think?'

Alexis shook the napkin and placed it on her lap. I could see she was stalling for time.

'I think that's an excellent idea. I would enjoy the company.'

'Good, then I shall look forward to it. When exactly do you plan to go again?'

I cut the ham and popped it in my mouth, at the same time watching her reaction. I'd caught her off guard.

'Sometime early in summer.'

'Can you be more precise?'

She gave me a cool look. 'Not at the moment. It depends on a few things. Besides, you know we tend to take things a day at a time. Who knows what the future will be?'

She was right there.

'Well give me warning,' I said, pushing more food on to my fork. 'I may need other false documents.'

She wiped the corner of her mouth delicately with the serviette and poured out a glass of water.

'What's wrong with the ones you have? If I can pass you off as my cousin at the Ambassador's residence — in front of a German commandant as well — then there should be nothing to worry about.'

Ah, the "cousin" cover story, again. I wondered how long that story would hold up.

'I like to have all angles covered — in case of emergencies.'

'I can see that,' she replied coolly. 'Leave it to me. I will let you know in good time. You don't have to worry.'

'I'm not worried,' I replied. 'As I said, I just like to be prepared.'

I asked what happened to the children she had with her. She told me they were given over to our associates in Turkey. When I mentioned the Red Crescent and Red Cross, her reply was that she preferred to use Poseidon's own contacts. It resulted in them getting across the country to a refugee camp faster.

'The least we have to do with bureaucracy, the better,' she replied and changed the subject. 'I've heard about the massacre at Kato Hora. It's terrible. You could have been killed you know — and Loukas. He's a risk taker, but you, well...'

'I'm a risk taker too, in case you hadn't noticed,' I replied, with a smile. 'We did what we had to. If we hadn't acted when we did, everyone would have been killed.'

'I heard Loukas's woman was injured. I hope she'll be fine.'

'She's on the road to recovery, thank God.'

'Loukas told me you had something important to discuss with me,' she said. 'What is it?'

I came straight to the point. 'It's about the massacre. You know what will happen if we don't calm things down. It's already been a week since this took place and those still alive are afraid to go back. They're worried the Germans will return. Kato Hora lies in ruins and with spring around the corner, they need to get back to the fields. There's much to be done or they'll starve. Not even the inhabitants of the surrounding villages will go near the place for fear of being attacked. What we want you to do is to use your connections and have a word with the Ambassador to see if he can't use his influence with the Germans and persuade them that the Italians in the area have the situation under control. We all know the Italians are easier to deal with than the Germans. They don't want more trouble in the region.'

She thought it over for a few minutes. A skinny young maid with a sallow complexion came to clear away the plates and asked if we would be having desert — fruit compote.

'What happened to Rada?' I asked.

'It's her day off. This young girl is my cook and she helps out whenever I need her.'

I could only imagine what the poor girl thought when she

saw such excess. After we'd finished the meal, we retired to the drawing room for coffee.

'I will see what I can do,' Alexis said. 'But you do realise I have to be careful. Making a request to help someone in Athens is hard enough, but to ask a favour for mountain villages, that's quite another matter. The Germans will want to know more.'

'I will leave it in your capable hands. I'm sure you will find a way.'

She laughed. 'You can be so amusing, Larry. That's what I remembered about you in Cairo.'

'I would like to think I can be amusing,' I replied. 'The thing is, this is not an amusing situation. You did not witness the scene. You didn't see the terror in their eyes.'

Alexis looked uncomfortable.

'So when will I be able to give Loukas and the villagers some reassuring news?' I asked, pushing the point home.

She stood up, smoothed down her dress and asked me to wait while she made a telephone call.

She was gone about ten minutes. When she returned she looked happy with herself.

'I have a meeting with Giovanni at his office in Athens in the next few hours. I can't promise anything, but I'll let you know what happens.'

'Then I'd better get going to give you time to think of something to say.'

She offered to drop me off near my home on her way in, but I refused, telling her I had another meeting after this.

'It's a beautiful afternoon,' I said, looking out the window. 'I think I'll take advantage of such clement weather and catch the train.'

I left the villa and headed in the direction of the metro station. The tree-lined roads were empty and on any other occasion I would have enjoyed the walk. Today, however, I was consumed with other thoughts. Checking that I was not being followed, I slipped down another road and doubled back towards the Church of the Virgin of the Swallow. The door to the church was unlocked and I stepped inside. It was empty. A few lit candles crackled and flickered, their wax dripping into the sand, and a strong smell of incense pervaded the air.

I stepped back outside into the sunlight. Birdsong filled the air. I headed across the cobblestones and through the broken arch of the remains of what had once been the old monastery, towards the cemetery. It was rarely used these days and the grass had long grown over the old graves. The locals now preferred to bury their dead in one of the newer municipal cemeteries.

I scanned the scene in search of a freshly dug grave but the ground looked undisturbed. Then I saw what I was looking for. Next to an oleander tree and not far from the perimeter of the old monastery wall was a mound of brown earth and on top of it lay a simple wooden cross. I studied it for a while, wondering how long it had been there. Several footprints surrounded the grave. Some of them had hardened. Only two were fresh, and one set appeared consistent with the boots Alexis wore when I met her earlier. I knelt down and picked up a handful of earth, trying to make out just how fresh the grave was. At that moment I was conscious of someone standing behind me and reached inside my coat pocket for my gun.

'Kali spera, Kyrie. Good afternoon, sir. This is private property. You are trespassing.'

I spun around, dropping the earth in the process. It was the priest and he didn't look too happy to see me.

'Good afternoon, Father,' I replied, moving my hand away from the gun and pulling out a handkerchief to wipe my hands.

'What are you doing here?'

I racked my brains for a suitable answer. Anything I said sounded lame.

'I came to pray and as it is such a beautiful day, I thought I'd explore the old ruins. I didn't realise you still buried people here.'

His dark eyes shone with anger. 'Please leave now,' he said, standing aside to let me pass. 'This is consecrated ground.'

Clearly he did not want me hanging around so I bid him goodbye and left. He followed me at a distance until he was sure I'd left the place, locked the church door and hurriedly walked away. I wondered if Alexis would hear of this.

Chapter 16

I had arranged to meet my radioman in a bar in Athens at eight o'clock that evening. He had some important news for me. He was late, and I began to think something had gone amiss. I would give him five more minutes. After that I had to leave. Acting on instinct, fifteen minutes was the most we would ever wait for each other. Sometimes we didn't even wait at all. If the person was not there, we would often keep walking.

Relieved, I saw him cross the road. Aris and Stelios were with him.

'Good to see you,' I said to Aris, shaking his hand. 'How did the trip go?'

'Like clockwork. It couldn't have gone better. The men were quick learners. They'll put the training to good use.'

'Well it's good to hear something went right,' I replied. 'I suppose Dancer has filled you in with the Kato Hora massacre.'

The smile on his face dropped. 'Yes. Dreadful news. Let's hope it doesn't spark an all-out uprising. We could do without that at the moment.'

I turned to Dancer. 'What do you have for me? I hope it's something good.'

'It's about Kondoumaris, the driver. I've located where he lives.'

This was heartening news.

'He lives in Kaisariani.'

'I know it well. There are a lot of Asia Minor families there — and many of them are supporters of EAM/ELAS.'

'With all due respect, sir, do you think someone collaborating with the Germans would live in an area filled with families who are, for the most part, communist sympathisers whose sons, brothers and fathers who have joined the resistance? It strikes me as a bit odd.'

'We all know that time and time again, it's a tactic that works. Bury yourself in the heart of the lion's den and no-one suspects you.'

I couldn't help thinking that to some extent, that was what I was doing myself. Many would have thought going to a party thrown by the Italian Ambassador foolhardy. But we were actors. That's what we do.

'Still nothing from Cairo on the search for his wife, Lotte, then?' I asked.

Dancer shook his head.

'Sir, can I ask you a question? Why do you suspect him? What I mean is, the Germans are committing lots of crimes against the people on trumped up charges, reprisals and raids. Hasn't he given Poseidon valuable information of those brought in for questioning? Surely Poseidon knows him well, especially Kostas, and they don't seem worried about him.'

Between us, we had a rule that any of our SOE agents were free to voice concerns and opinions with each other, and I for one encouraged it. Yet in this case, I wasn't too sure I could give him an answer. In the short time we'd been in Greece, things had gone relatively smoothly for the Poseidon Network. If I was truthful with myself, there were far more unanswered questions about Alexis than about the driver. All the same, he worked for the Germans. I had to rule him out as a collaborator.

'I've learnt to trust no-one,' was all I could say. 'Especially someone who relays information from the enemy.'

Thankfully no-one brought up the issue of Theo's untimely death and the fact that we still had not told Cairo.

'So,' I continued, 'do you know his address?'

'Apartment 4, Chrisostomou Smirnis Street. There's something else. He doesn't ever go there with the car. He travels everyday to work and picks it up there. His hours are erratic so most of the time he walks home, even after curfew. He's obviously got a pass. Another thing, from what I can gather, he doesn't appear to mix with his neighbours. A bit of a loner who keeps to himself.

'Good work. Keep your eyes on him for another week. If no other information comes to light, we'll decide what to do then.'

After one or two more drinks we went our separate ways and I headed back to my apartment. Half way along Patission Street, I was aware of a car trailing me. For the second time that day, I reached inside my pocket for my gun. The car pulled up beside me and I breathed a sigh of relief when I saw who it was — Alexis's driver. He asked me to get in.

'Where are we going?'

He didn't answer. Reluctantly I did as he asked. The car made a U-turn and headed back towards the centre of Athens. Near Syntagma Square, we slowed down and for a brief moment I thought I was going to be dropped off at the illustrious Hotel Grande Bretagne, the preferred hotel of the Nazi elite. Thankfully, we drove past, turned into a side street and stopped at the smaller Hotel Apollo. Two large swastikas hung from the balconies.

The driver glanced at my face through the rear-view mirror and saw the look on my face.

'Room 314. Show them this and you'll be fine.'

He handed me a visitor's pass in the name of Konstantinos Valtos.

I got out of the car and watched him drive away, leaving me to my fate. The door swung open and two German officers stepped outside, each one accompanied by a beautiful Greek woman. The men were in high spirits, laughing and joking, although the women appeared embarrassed when they saw me and quickly turned their faces away. I'd lost count of the times I'd seen this; women out for a good time who were afraid of being accused as collaborators later. Their faces always remained seared in my memory.

I showed my pass to a man at the receptionist desk. He glanced at it and without uttering a word, discreetly gestured for me to take the lift. In the adjacent bar, several men and women sat around in plush armchairs, drinking and listening to a pianist. No-one seemed to notice me. When I reached the third floor the lift door opened and a man and woman stood arm in arm, waiting to go down. They stepped aside to let me pass. Again, the woman attempted to hide her face. I was in no doubt as to the type of hotel I was in. I walked along the quiet corridor until I reached room 314. With the gun in my hand, I knocked on the door.

A voice called out — Alexis's voice. 'Come in. It's open.'

Cautiously, I entered the softly lit room. Alexis stood by the window with her back to me. When she turned to face me, I saw that she'd been crying. Gone was her usual confidence, in its place a vulnerability that threw me off-guard.

'You can put that away,' she said, referring to the gun. 'You're quite safe.'

'What's happened?' I asked. 'Does this have something to do with the meeting you had earlier?'

'I suppose it does.'

'Then I take it, things didn't go too well?'

She asked if I would like a drink. 'I'm afraid I've only got whisky.'

She took two glasses from a shelf in the bathroom, poured us both a double shot and placed the bottle on the bedside table. She sat on the side of the bed, deliberating over what to say. I sat in the chair opposite and made myself as comfortable as I possibly could, given the circumstances. Waiting for her to speak, I was acutely aware of the sounds outside the room — the piano in the bar downstairs, a car passing by, and the occasional footsteps of someone walking across the floor in the room above us. The neon light of another, somewhat seedier hotel across the street, flashed erratically, missing one of its letters in the process. Hanging around in a place like this wasn't exactly my idea of fun and I began to get a little nervous.

'I haven't got all night,' I said testily. 'Have you got good news for Loukas or not?'

She took a lace-edged handkerchief out of her bag and dabbed the corner of her eyes.

'I did my best. Winning Giovanni over wasn't hard. It was Herr Keller who was the difficult one.'

I couldn't believe what I was hearing. 'Are you telling me you discussed this with the Germans?'

She gave a deep sigh. 'I had no choice.'

'I think you'd better start at the beginning, don't you?'

'I told Giovanni I had relatives in the area — an aunt to be exact — and that the family feared for their lives after hearing of what took place in Kato Hora. He asked if the relatives had any contact with the *andartes*, or were in any way antagonistic towards the Italians and Germans. Naturally, I said no, that was preposterous idea. I told him they were farmers who willingly gave produce to the German army to send back to Germany. He was sympathetic, especially when I made it clear that it would be best for the region if the Italians sorted the situation out themselves, rather than involving the Germans, as the Greeks generally got along better with the Italians.'

'"Naturally, I would like to help," he said, "but I have to clear it with the Germans first." I began to think I'd made a grave mistake and apologised for taking up his valuable time. I was about to leave but he stopped me.

'"Wait," he said, and left the room for a moment. When he returned, Keller was with him.'

At this point, Alexis nervously started to twist the corner of her handkerchief. Her eyes avoided mine.

'Giovanni then asked me to repeat my story. When I'd finished, Keller asked Giovanni if he'd mind if we discussed this in private. He obliged and left the room.'

I had the distinct feeling I wasn't going to like what came next.

'Keller pulled up a chair and sat next to me. He leaned over and took my hand. "Kyria Petrakis," he began, his voice as soft as velvet, "People often say, we Germans are harsh, that we have no regard for the countries we seek to befriend." He squeezed my hand tighter. "I can assure you this is untrue. You ask a favour of us — for a relative — and in turn, I ask a small favour of you."'

I felt my heart pound in my chest. 'What did you say?'

'I replied that if I could be of help, I would do my best.

'He asked me to give him the names of those I suspected were working to undermine them. I could only imagine he was talking about members of Poseidon, although he never mentioned the network. I told him I didn't know of anyone, but I could see he didn't believe me. He put his hand on my cheek and gently stroked it. I thought maybe he would just leave me alone, that his words were enough to scare me, but he didn't stop there.'

Alexis got up and moved to the window, staring at the flickering neon sign opposite. I couldn't bear it any longer.

'Did he want to fuck you?' I asked, matter-of-factly. 'Is that what he was really after?'

She turned to face me. 'Yes!'

I felt a cold chill run down my spine. I should shoot her and be done with it. Poseidon could manage without her.

'So you threw yourself at him, I suppose?' I replied, coldly.

She came over and slapped my face so hard, it stung.

'You bastard! You men are all the same. You fuck any woman who takes your fancy, just to get what you want, and when we do it, we are whores. Damn you! This is not about love.'

'I'm sorry,' I said, rubbing my cheek. 'I didn't mean...'

'You didn't mean what?' she shouted angrily.

'Tell me, how many women have you fucked just to get

information? The "honey trap" — isn't that what they call it? You are a hypocrite.'

I let her carry on. I deserved it. We'd put her in this situation by asking her to speak with the Ambassador. Maybe I had misjudged her.

I backed off. 'I'm sorry. It was wrong of me to judge you.'

'You didn't even let me finish,' she replied.

I apologised again and asked her to carry on, even though I didn't relish the idea of hearing more. She took a deep breath and continued.

'At that point I realised what he really wanted was me rather than information and if I didn't give him what he wanted, I ran the possibility of him alienating Giovanni's friendship with me, and worse still, risked him poking around in my affairs. I tried to play dumb but it didn't work. His hand moved from my cheek to my breast and he kissed me. I begged him to stop, telling him that Giovanni could walk into the room at any moment and my reputation would be ruined. He laughed.

'"Ambassador Marinetti and I have certain things in common," he replied. "We both like beautiful women."

'He pulled me into his arms. "Not here," I said, pushing him away. 'Let's go somewhere where we can really be alone."

'I was stalling for time, but at that point, it was all I could think of. He told me he knew of a hotel — this place — and that no-one would know of our little affair, as he called it. He asked me to meet him here at a certain time. That was just over two hours ago. When I arrived, he was waiting, sitting exactly where you are now. His jacket was hanging from the hook on the wall and he'd loosened his tie.'

My mind was racing. I reached for the whisky bottle and

poured us both another drink to stop myself visualizing them in bed together.

Alexis continued. 'He pulled the sheets back and asked me to take off my clothes. I did as he asked. All of a sudden, there was a knock on the door. It was his adjutant. Keller stepped outside the room for a moment and I tried to hear what they were saying but they were talking in such hushed tones, I couldn't hear a thing. When he returned, his demeanour had changed. Whatever they talked about had put him in an angry mood.

'He picked up my clothes and threw them at me. "Get dressed," he said. "Something important has come up and I have to leave."

'"Will you be back?" I asked, clutching my clothes. "I mean, do you want me to stay?'

'He put on his jacket, cast his eyes over my naked body and came over to kiss me. "No," he said, running his finger from my mouth to my breasts. "Maybe another time."'

I couldn't believe my ears. What a fool I'd been to jump to conclusions. So she didn't make love to him after all! When she saw the grin on my face, she came over and pulled me out of the chair by my tie.

'So you see, Larry darling, I am all yours if you want me.'

*

I'd lost count of the hours I'd fantasized about making love with Alexis, and if I am honest with myself, after Cairo, a part of me never thought it would happen. But never in my wildest dreams had I expected it to be like this. When she pulled me into her arms, all those fantasies resurfaced. It was as if I had been hit by a bolt of lightning from the Gods. How I wanted her! How I desired her! And how I wasted no time in reciprocating her insatiable lust. At that very moment, the whole of the German army could have walked into the hotel and I wouldn't have cared. If I was going to die, I was going to die happy, making love to the woman who had haunted my dreams from the moment I laid eyes on her.

Naked, she was even more beautiful than I had imagined. I savoured every part of her until there was not one inch of her that I had not explored. Her kisses were like wine, sending an explosion of desire through my body like volts of electricity. Her breasts were firm, her nipples taut and erect and she moaned with desire when I caressed them. At the same time, her hands were as adept at exploring my own body as mine were hers. When she spread her legs open and pushed my head between her thighs, my eyes lingered for a while on the profile of her dark black pubic hair. And then, like a man possessed, I devoured her with a hunger that was all consuming. I thought I would explode. She was a siren, luring me to my death and I didn't care. Eventually, I turned over and let her straddle me. With the soft light illuminating the glistening sweat on her flesh, it was like making love to a goddess with the temperament of a tigress. Finally, she threw her head back and arched her back, and together we reached the climax of our lovemaking.

I pulled her to me, running my hands through her hair, now damp with sweat. Her smell, the one I had always associated with her, had now become a part of me. I had made love to many women in my time — although love had nothing to do with it — but none compared to this.

We lay together for a while, neither one of us wanting to

break the spell of the moment with small talk. I caressed her back with my hand watching her body rise and fall with her breathing. In the street outside we could hear sounds of laughter coming from the hotel lobby. All of a sudden our moment of serenity was broken when a car screeched to a halt and a barrage of machine gun fire blasted the hotel, shattering the ground floor windows. This was quickly followed by a loud explosion from a hand grenade which rocked the building. Moments later, the car sped away. The neon sign opposite flashed as erratically as my heartbeat.

'My God!' I said, grabbing my clothes. 'We have to get out of here before we have the whole of the Wehrmacht and Gestapo breathing down our necks.'

In a matter of minutes, we were fully dressed and running down the stairs. People were already frantically gathering the lobby which was now a scene of chaos. The entrance was blocked by masonry from a first-floor balcony that had collapsed in the explosion. Shattered glass covered the floor. A group of men were in the process of moving the bullet-riddled bodies of a man and a woman who were leaving the hotel when the shooting occurred. Another man lay bleeding from an open wound on the glass-covered carpet. I had no idea how we were going to get out of the place. Armoured vehicles were already arriving and blocking off the street. Alexis grabbed my hand and pulled me towards the reception desk. The same man whom I'd shown the pass to earlier, was standing behind the desk shaking like a leaf.

'The Resistance,' he said in a low voice.

Alexis slipped him an envelope which he pocketed nervously while checking no-one was watching.

'That way,' he said, pointing to a door at the far end of the reception desk. 'It's the back entrance.'

Fortunately for us, everyone was too concerned about the man with the bullet wound who was fading fast, than to notice us slip away. We found ourselves in a narrow alleyway at the back of Perikleous Street. Sirens blared, more armoured vehicles arrived, and in the mayhem, more shots were fired.

Alexis took off her shoes and we ran as fast as we could, weaving and ducking our way through narrow back entrances, until we were well away from the hotel. We'd had a lucky escape and if it hadn't been for the receptionist, we would be being questioned by now. Alexis leaned back against a wall and ran her hand up and down her calf. She had scraped herself and was bleeding.

'Here, let me,' I said, crouching down and wiping the blood away with my handkerchief. I kissed her leg. 'It's only a graze. You'll live to fight another day.'

She laughed. The street was empty and I pulled her into a doorway and kissed her hard on the lips.

'I've a good mind to have you now, here in this doorway,' I whispered in her ear. My hand slid under her skirt, exciting me yet again. 'You temptress. You thrive on danger, don't you?'

She laughed. 'No more than you?'

She was right. I pulled my hand away. 'Come on. Let's get out of here.'

I asked where her driver had gone. She told me he was not too far away but with so much going on she suggested it would be better if we made our way to Hadzigiannis's tailors as it wasn't far.

'I have a key,' she said. 'It will be safe to hide there until curfew is over.'

I followed her through a wooden door that opened into the tiny yard at the back of the premises. Silently, she unlocked the door and we entered the empty premises. A beautiful silver moon hung in the night sky, casting an eerie glow through the window onto the mannequins. They appeared to be laughing at me.

'Don't put the light on,' she said, 'There are people living nearby.'

It was only eleven o'clock. The night was still young.

I wrapped my arms around her. 'We have all night, it's cold and I'm going to keep you warm.'

After a while my eyes became accustomed to the darkness and I noticed a piece of heavy cloth on a chair. I laid it on the floor as a makeshift bed.

'It's the best I can do,' I said, kissing the nape of her neck.

She took off her coat and made herself comfortable, pulling me to her.

'It's perfect,' she purred. 'Just perfect.'

In the morning I woke with a start. Someone was scratching on the door. I grabbed my gun lying on the floor nearby and peered through the window. Thankfully it was only a cat. Alexis stirred on the makeshift bed and pulled a woollen length of fabric tightly around her.

'You gave me a fright. What time is it?'

'Time we got going,' I answered. 'Curfew is almost over and someone will be here soon.'

She stretched out her arms and gave a long yawn. 'I suppose you're right.'

I passed her clothes to her. In doing so, her bag dropped off the table onto the floor. Along with her lipstick and powder compact was the Beretta. I picked it up and put it on the table.

'Were you intending to use it?' I asked.

She stood up, slipped into her panties and fastened her bra. 'Maybe,' maybe not. Were you intending to use yours?'

My reply was the same as hers although I did add that in light of the evening's unforeseen turn of events, I had more on my mind than murder.

'You and I are not so different after all, are we, Larry?' she smiled. 'We both know what we want and will stop at nothing to get it.'

Her words brought me down to earth with a thud. Was it what she said or the look in her eyes? Maybe both. I'd never been a romantic, but there were times when I came close to it. Alexis was one of those times. Now I understand how foolish I'd been. Me — Larry Hadley — known in MI6 and SOE as a cool customer with a track record for never letting his guard down. Well, I'd just blotted my copybook. I'd fallen for the oldest trick in the book — hook, line, and sinker. I didn't know whether to burst out laughing or shoot her. The latter was tempting, but messy. I went for the first option and laughed.

'What's the matter?' Alexis asked. 'Did I say something funny?'

'Let me kiss you one more time before we go our separate ways.' I pulled her into my arms and closed my mouth over her lips, my tongue tasting her saliva. She pressed her breasts against my chest. Then I pulled away, sharply.

'We have to get going,' I said,

I asked how she would get home and she told me her driver wasn't too far away.

'I'd offer you a lift,' she said, 'but maybe that's not wise. I mean, we really shouldn't be seen together, should we?'

I agreed and told her I'd make my own way back. After making sure everything was back in place, we left the building.

'Goodbye, Larry. Thank you for last night.'

I couldn't find the words to reply and pushed her through the door. 'Get going. I'll give you a few minutes before I follow.'

By the time I left, she had disappeared.

Chapter 17

A few days after the incident at the Hotel Apollo, the news of Theo's death was made public. As expected, the truth of what happened that night at Ekali was covered up and the official version of how the White Rose of the Poseidon Network met his death was completely different.

A formal meeting to discuss this was to be held in the room above Hadzigiannis's tailors and all the leaders of Poseidon were asked to attend. It promised to be an important event and I hoped it would end well and not disintegrate into old feuds on political grounds. I asked Dancer to transmit this information to Cairo straight away. Their reply was to keep them updated and play it by ear. Should events take a turn for the worst, we were to cease all communications with them. Knowing the Greeks, I had no idea how this would play out.

The day of the meeting, all those I'd met at my first meeting were there. There were also a couple of new faces. Last to arrive were Loukas, Leonidas, and Alexis herself. In order not to draw attention to herself, and befitting such a solemn occasion, Alexis wore a plain black coat and headscarf, and a pair of dark sunglasses. The men respectfully took turns in voicing their commiserations, me included.

'I'm sorry for you loss,' I said, when it was my turn.

'Thank you, Nikos. Your kind words mean a lot to me.'

Behind the veneer of the grieving woman, all I saw was her lying naked on the bed in the Hotel Apollo, giving in to her desires as if her life depended on it. Perhaps it did.

The story of Theo's death was that he had disappeared on a business trip to Thessaloniki. During the weeks he'd gone missing, she began to think the worst but with no sightings of him, no-one knew what to think. Then came the news that a car answering the description of Theo's had come under fire during an attack by a group of *andartes* about an hour's drive outside the city. Apparently, the car was thought to belong to the Germans. It exploded in a ball of flames and both the car and the occupants were burnt beyond recognition. The *andartes* all thought they'd got the right men and left the scene of the crime with a clear conscience. It was only recently that documents came to light near the scene which were proven to belong to Theo.

Two of the leaders from the area looked at each other. Thinking the finger of guilt might be pointed at them, they denied all knowledge of the event.

'This has nothing to do with us,' one of them exclaimed, angrily. 'We have no knowledge of such a thing taking place.'

The other agreed with him. 'Who found these documents?' the other asked.

'A local shepherd,' Alexis replied. 'It was his identity card. The shepherd had no idea who Theo was and rather than leave it there, decided took it to the police. They, in turn, contacted his office in Thessaloniki. I was officially told two days ago.'

This information was hard to digest and the room erupted into a noisy discussion about whose fault it was.

'Calm down, gentlemen,' Loukas said. 'Show some respect for Kyria Alexis. No-one here stands accused of this unfortunate event. We all know that there are bands of *andartes* who act alone. We must stand united against them or we'll have the Germans and Italians breathing down our necks.'

Alexis dabbed her eyes. 'Thank you Loukas.'

'Now, men,' Loukas continued. 'We must all try to put this behind us and move forward. The important issue is who will take Theo's place. I have already spoken with one or two of you and I propose Alexis takes on the mantle of the White Rose.' He glanced around the room to gauge everyone's reaction and then asked Alexis to speak.

'Gentlemen, some of you may or may not have worked with me in the past, and there are one or two here that barely know me. Let me assure you that as the wife of the White Rose, I know the workings of Poseidon better than most of you. I watched my late husband build up the network from nothing. In the early days we were just a few men — and women, I hasten to add — and none of us could foresee how big the network would become. During this time, I have been privy to my husband's contacts and in some cases carried out missions alone on his behalf. Unless anyone has any objections I would like to propose that I continue in his place as the new White Rose. Out of respect for my husband and to keep the continuity, I can't see any reason to change the name.'

The men listened and after a few brief discussions amongst themselves, one of them asked if anyone else proposed to became leader. After my conversation with Loukas, I wondered what he would say. Was he going to challenge her? It appeared not.

'Fine,' Leonidas said. 'I propose we take a vote on it. All those in favour of Kyria Alexis taking over the mantle of the White Rose, raise your hands.'

The vote was passed unanimously. I shook her hand.

'Congratulations.'

'Thank you, Kapetan Nikos,' she replied. 'I trust Cairo will look favourably on all this. We would hate to lose their support.'

'I can't see why not. It's in all our interests to work together.'

She smiled. 'That's true.'

I moved aside to let the men congratulate her. Loukas came over and stood by my side.

'It's for the best, Nikos. I can't take on the mantle at this point. I am needed in the mountains.'

'How is Anna?' I asked.

'She's recovering well. In a week or two, she'll be joining us in operations again.'

'Is that wise?'

'You try keeping someone like Anna at home when the Resistance needs us,' he grinned. 'She's a determined young woman, if you hadn't noticed.' He put his hand in his trouser pocket and pulled out the glass bead. 'She asked me to give it to you. She says you will need it more than she will.'

'Do you really believe in this superstitious blue bead, evil eye nonsense?' I asked.

He shrugged his shoulders. 'Who knows? Anyway, I am sure it will do just as much good as your prayers.'

We both laughed, even though there was little to laugh at. The war in Greece was worsening and we would need both the blue bead and prayers if we were to achieve liberation without anything going wrong.

After the issue of the new Poseidon leader had been sorted out, the discussions moved on to other things. Everyone complimented Cairo on sinking the ships coming from Sicily, but things were heating up everywhere. Psychologically, the Greeks were at breaking point. Inflation, hunger and the scarcity of all the basic necessities in life not only fuelled the ranks of the *andartes* but collaborators as well. There were far more raids and reprisals and everyone suspected their neighbour. Added to this, the *andartes* complained about the difficulties in communications. Telephone connections weren't safe and it meant the runners had to traverse the countryside on foot, frequently delaying urgent operations. Everyone looked at us for help and as usual, I promised to do what I could.

When the meeting drew to a close, I approached Kostas to see if he was still getting information from his contact. Aris, Stelios and Dancer were with me. Kostas said Kondoumaris was still forthcoming with names of those detained which had helped, although in many cases the people were executed before they could do anything about it. He also said he'd told them when there were operations taking place outside Athens. In those cases the men were able to warn the villagers or use acts of sabotage to scuttle the operations.

'In fact I have a meeting with him tonight at his apartment,' Kostas said. 'I was notified early this morning. Apparently he has something important he thinks I should know.'

My ears pricked up. Not wanting to sound too curious, I wished him luck and hoped the information proved useful.

When the meeting ended, I wasn't sure what I expected from Alexis, but if I was looking for a sign that she wanted to sleep with me again, then I was disappointed. She thanked me for my support and hoped we'd meet up again soon to discuss operations. There was no sign of acknowledgement of our brief romantic interlude. Not even a glint in her eyes.

Loukas asked if we would like to join him at the Taverna Acropolis. I couldn't face another plate of chickpeas and weeds and declined, arranging to meet him another time. The real reason, I declined was because I needed to talk with my men, especially Dancer. We went back to my apartment in Plateia Amerikis.

'What's the news from Cairo?' I asked.

'It seems that Kondoumaris was indeed married, but the woman was called Ursula and she was an actress. Lotte was her stage name. And she did die before he came here.'

I was lost for words. Perhaps he was the genuine thing after all.

I could see by the look in Dancer's eyes that they thought I was spending too much time on this.

'Now what? Do I stop tailing him?' he asked.

'Kostas said he had a meeting with him tonight at his apartment. Apparently he had something urgent to tell him.'

Aris and Stelios looked at me. I could tell they couldn't understand my obsession with the man either. I couldn't understand it myself.

'You said he usually arrives home well after curfew,' I said to Dancer. 'Around midnight or even later. Do you think we could manage to break into the apartment before then?'

'And do what?' Aris asked?'

'Have a look around.'

Dancer looked apprehensive. 'What if he arrives home earlier for the meeting with Kostas?'

'It's a chance we'll have to take.'

Dancer had mentioned on a previous occasion that the doors to the apartment block were locked shortly before curfew and by that time the janitor was not on duty. Anyone entering needed their own keys.

'We'll wait until curfew and then pick the locks,' I said. 'That shouldn't be difficult. If we don't find anything, I promise you that I will be the first to admit I was wrong and we were on a wild goose chase. I propose we arrive there fifteen minutes before curfew. Is there somewhere we can hide?'

'There's a small garden next to the church. It has quite a few trees and bushes. We can hide there,' Dancer replied.

The men left, leaving me alone with my thoughts. I lay on my bed and closed my eyes. Images of Alexis and our lovemaking tumbled through my mind. My thoughts were so vivid, I could even smell and taste her. It was as if she was right by my side. Before long, I drifted into a deep sleep, the best I'd had in ages. When I woke up, the reality of what we were about to do hit home and I cleaned and oiled my gun in readiness for the evening. Anna's blue bead was on the table. I kissed it and pocketed it. I was turning into a true Greek.

It took me just over an hour to get to Kaisariani. The evening was mild and the moon shone brightly in a cloudless night sky. Dancer, Aris and Stelios were already waiting and a rustle from the bushes near the church alerted me to our hiding place. The street was deserted and the few shops and kafenia in the area had long closed their doors, their shutters down in case of the odd vandalism, usually from some half starved person who deserved pity rather than chastisement.

Sometime around eleven o'clock, we decided to make a move. It was agreed that Dancer would keep watch as he was the only one who knew what Kondoumaris looked like. He would flash us a signal as soon as he saw him turn into the street. Aris, Stelios, and I had only just stepped out of the bushes when we saw a black car turn into the street. We immediately retreated back behind the bushes. The Gestapo and police regularly patrolled the streets on the lookout for anything suspicious and with the street so quiet we hoped whoever it was would drive on. Instead, it stopped right outside the apartment. Two men got out and the car moved away. Unfortunately it didn't leave altogether. The driver pulled up not far from where we were hiding and turned the engine off. All we could see were the silhouettes of two men in the front seat. Apart from that, there was nothing to tell us who they were. I strained to see if I could get the car number plate without being spotted. It was impossible. I did however note that the back bumper bar was bent, as if it had been in some sort of accident.

'I don't like the look of this,' I whispered. 'It's not Kostas. He's a big man. I would have known if it was him. Those two are much thinner. Besides, he would have come alone and he certainly wouldn't have come in a car.'

'Surely it can't be the Gestapo when Kondoumaris works for the Germans?' Aris said.

'We don't even know if they're going to his apartment? How many apartments are in the building?' I asked.

'Six,' Dancer replied. 'It could be the Gestapo targeting someone else.'

'Or they could be Greeks thinking Kondoumaris is a collaborator. Whether we like it or not, we're going to have to sit this out. Whoever they are, they were certainly able to get into the building easily.'

We waited until we saw a light flashing in first floor window.

Dancer nudged me. 'That's Kondoumaris's apartment!'

At that very moment, we noticed a man walking towards the apartment in the opposite direction.

'Oh no,' Dancer exclaimed. 'It's Kondoumaris. And from where I'm standing, he's walking straight into a trap.'

It was like watching a film in slow motion. After a few minutes which seemed like an hour, the light in the window flickered erratically. Then all went black. Minutes later, the two men appeared on the doorstep. The driver turned on the ignition and manoeuvred the car skilfully in the direction of the apartment. The men jumped in and the car sped away.

'What are we going to do now?' Stelios asked.

'You three stay here. I'll go alone. If I hear movement in the apartment, I will know he's fine and we can break in another day. If not, something is amiss and I want to know what. Keep a lookout. I'll signal you if I need you.'

I took out my gun and crossed the dark road into the building. Thankfully the outside door was ajar. Silently, I made my way up the staircase to his apartment. The door was closed. I put my ear to it and listened. There was no sound in the room at all. Slowly, I turned the door handle. That door too was unlocked. I pushed it open just enough to listen for any movement. Still nothing. I worked the gun's slide loud enough to warn anyone inside that I was armed and pushed the door open. My flesh turned as cold as ice at what I saw. The place had been ransacked and in the middle of the room was a body lying face down on the carpet in a pool of blood. I moved it over. The throat had been cut and there was a gunshot wound in his chest.'

I went to the window and flashed a signal to the men. When they arrived I closed the door and locked it.

'Jesus Christ!' Aris exclaimed, stepping through the mess. 'Looks like somebody's been having a party.'

'You're sure this is Kondoumaris?' I asked.

Dancer took one look and nodded. 'Poor bugger. They certainly had it in for him.'

'Whoever killed him, meant to send a message, but I'm not quite sure why. His murder was quick and unexpected so as not to alert the neighbours. He doesn't seem to have put up a struggle either.' I moved his hands with my foot. 'Look there's no defence wounds. If he was killed simply as a collaborator, they would have left a note pinned to his body, and I doubt they would have ransacked the place as well. From what I can see, he was shot at close range, and then they cut his throat afterwards. The fact that no one appears to have heard a shot suggests the killers used a silencer.'

I looked around the apartment. Drawers were opened and the contents scattered on the floor.

'Whoever it was, they were after something important.'

'Let's get out of here,' Aris whispered. 'If someone finds us they'll think we did it.'

'You go downstairs and I'll follow you. Give me a couple of minutes.'

When they'd gone, I shone my flashlight on the body and turned him over, careful not to step in the blood that was seeping into the carpet. The metallic smell of blood clung in my nostrils and the back of my throat making me retch. However many times I smelt blood, I could never get used to it. I knew it would linger in my throat for days. His jacket had two outside pockets, one was empty and the other contained a handkerchief and a few coins. Inside the jacket was another pocket. That too was empty. It was then that I noticed a strange angular protrusion in the fabric at the bottom of one of his trouser legs. I felt it and found it hard. When I pulled the trouser leg up, I saw that it covered up a small notebook hidden inside one of his socks. I recalled Kostas saying Kondoumaris kept a notebook in which he recorded the names of those taken in for questioning. This must be it. I hastily pocketed it and left, closing the door quietly behind me.

The men were anxiously waiting for me in the shadows of a shop doorway at the end of the street. I decided not tell them about the notebook until I'd had a good look at it. It was agreed we would part ways and make our own way back home. We arranged to meet at Dancer's the following afternoon.

*

In the privacy of my room, I made myself a coffee to rid myself of the nausea, and started to look through the notebook. At first glance it appeared to be almost indecipherable — a mishmash of untidy jottings, doodles, and old clippings. There was also a photograph in it — an attractive woman with short light-coloured hair wearing what looked to me like an extraordinary amount of eye make-up and deep lipstick. When I turned it over I saw it was signed *From Lotte, Berlin 1939.* So this was the mysterious Ursula/Lotte. Quite a stunning lady, by the looks of things. The clippings were in German and appeared to be from a theatrical magazine in which she appeared. I flicked through the pages. If this was the notebook Kostas referred to it didn't make much sense.

Dancer was preparing to make a transmission to Cairo when I arrived at his apartment later the next day. Aris sat near the wood fire with his feet up reading a newspaper whilst Stelios stirred coffee in the copper *briki*.

'Here,' I said to Stelios. 'Take a look at this. 'You're the master code-breaker. Tell me if there's a code somewhere. I can't make head or tails of it.'

'Where did you find it?' he asked. 'It smells terrible.'

'In Kondoumaris's sock last night. I didn't want to tell you until I'd had a good look through it. Kostas mentioned he kept a notebook with names in it. It might be this or it might be nothing at all.'

Aris looked at the photo of Lotte and whistled. 'Quite a showgirl by the look of her.'

Dancer peered over his shoulder whilst Stelios flicked through the book. 'Well, well! The elusive Lotte.'

'I'll see what I can do,' Stelios said. 'Give me a day or two? I'll get back to you as soon as I can. If there's a code, you can be sure I'll find it.'

'Bravo! I knew I could rely on you. Don't take too long though. The sooner the better.'

The conversation turned to Cairo. Dancer wanted to know what news we would give them.'

'Well, I suppose the time has come to let them know the White Rose is dead, long live the White Rose.'

'You don't strike me as a fan of Shakespeare,' Aris laughed.

'I am a man of many talents. Don't underestimate me.'

Dancer tapped out the message that Theo was dead and his wife had been nominated to step into his shoes as the White Rose. As all the leaders were in agreement, we would carry on as planned unless Cairo had any reason why we wouldn't. We also gave Cairo the official explanation of Theo's death.

'It will be interesting to hear what they have to say.' Dancer said when he took of his earphones.

I left the men soon after for my next meeting with Loukas at a safe house in the centre of Athens. The look on his face told me all was not well.

I have news that the Germans have moved into the mountains and are burning several villages. Thankfully Ano Hora has been spared but we don't know if they will return so the people have fled further into the mountain. It's estimated that in one village alone, all the men except those who had joined the *andartes*, perished. The countryside is bathed in blood.'

'Is Anna safe and well?' I asked.

'Give praise to the Virgin, yes, and she's back to her old fighting spirit. I only hope she stays strong. This is a setback for us and it's alerted the Germans to the area. We will have to lie low for a while until things quieten down.' He brought up Alexis. 'What happened? I thought you were going to ask her to speak with Marinetti.'

I wasn't sure how much I should say.

'I did. She told me she'd have a word with him. In fact, she made a call to his office while I was there. I know she went to see him about it soon after.'

'Well, either she didn't bring the subject up or if she did, it didn't do any good. My informants told me the Italians at the garrison heard nothing from him. Not a word.'

I was at a loss at what to say. I felt his despair yet I couldn't tell him about Keppler. Even so, I would have thought Marinetti would have tried to help her.

'I'm sorry,' I replied. 'I failed you.'

'Not you, Nikos. I know you did your best. Life stinks at the moment. The more we do, the more we get hammered.'

I changed the subject. 'How do you think the last meeting went? Didn't anyone query the official story of Theo's death?'

'Not to my knowledge. It made sense to me.' He looked at me questioningly. 'I can see by the look on your face, it bothers you?'

'Not really,' I lied. 'You know these people better than me.'

'There's to be an official memorial service at the church in Kifissia in a few days time. Apparently it's a small gathering. Just the immediate family and one or two of Theo's business associates. Alexis thought it best if members of Poseidon stayed away but I gather Maria is going. I'm surprised Alexis hasn't invited you, though'

'So am I,' I replied, feeling more than a pang of disappointment. 'Especially as I am supposed to be family. You know — the cousin from Larissa.'

Loukas laughed. 'Ah, that old ruse.'

Our discussions were interrupted by a knock at the door. A woman entered and called Loukas aside. When he came back he had Kostas with him. I didn't need to be a mind reader to know what he was about to say.

'One of our best informers has been found dead in his apartment,' he said. 'The driver, Manos Kondoumaris. Someone really had it in for him. He was shot and almost decapitated.'

Loukas shook his head in despair. '*Christos kai Panagia*, Christ and the Virgin. That's all we need.'

Kostas went on to say how Kondoumaris had something urgent to tell him and it was arranged that the pair would meet up at his apartment sometime around midnight.

'When I got there, the police were already searching the building and the occupants of the other apartments had been made to wait in the street whilst the search was underway. Seeing the commotion taking place, I made myself scarce in case someone queried why I was there at all, especially after curfew. It was only when I returned this morning, that I found out what had happened. What a bloody mess they made. I looked around for his notebook but found no trace of it. I just pray it doesn't end up in the wrong hands.'

'Who do they think did it?' Loukas asked.

'Probably Greeks. The neighbours told me everyone suspected him of being a collaborator. "He had it coming", one of them said. What I couldn't understand is that if they were out to kill him for that, why did they ransack the place?'

'Maybe they were looking for evidence,' I said. 'The fact that his pantry was stocked with more food than others, might have pointed to it — a favour for a favour. You know how people think.'

Kostas looked at me. His eyes narrowed. 'How did you know that?'

'I didn't,' I replied innocently, even though I had seen it for myself. 'We all know collaborators get something in return and food is one of them.'

'He wasn't a collaborator,' he shouted angrily. 'He was one of us. You've always had your suspicions about him from the

moment I mentioned him to you. What do you take us for
— idiots?'

'Calm down,' Loukas said. 'None of this is doing us any
good.'

In an effort to win him over, I apologised if I had given
him the wrong impression. 'Sorry,' I said, offering my hand in
a gesture of conciliation. 'I'm trained to be suspicious. No hard
feelings.'

Kostas calmed down and shook my hand.

'Now where does that leave us?' Loukas asked. 'Have we got
anyone else on the inside? What about the clerks; the cleaners
even?'

'I'm working on it,' replied Kostas. 'There's a few but they
aren't privy to the sort of information Kondoumaris had.'

Chapter 18

It didn't take long for Stelios to find a code within the scribbles of Kondoumaris's notebook.

'Most of what he's written is meaningless; meant to throw the Germans off the scent should they ever get their hands on it, but if you look closer,' he said, pointing at a few sentences excitedly, 'interspersed amongst the words are letters in Cyrillic. It's these that have a meaning.'

'Good God! You're absolutely right. The wily Greek wrote in code. Have you managed to work it out?'

'I'm coming to that,' Stelios replied, looking pleased with himself. He pulled out a small writing pad. 'If we look carefully, his code is not difficult at all. In fact, it's the most basic thing in the book. What makes this smart is that most Germans wouldn't be able to distinguish the Greek alphabet from Cyrillic. So at a quick glance, the letters look the same — all Greek. From what I can make out, the entries go back about to round about the time Poseidon was formed. The letters on this page, when formed together, say that certain men have been held for questioning at Gestapo headquarters. It lists the names. You can see there are a few women amongst them.'

He flicked the page over. 'The same goes for this. More names. This time it says they have been executed. And this one here mentions a *blocco* in Piraeus. It says around 50 men have been rounded up, some on suspicion of collaborating with the *andartes* and hiding weapons.'

I congratulated him on his excellent work, at the same time feeling a bit of a fool for thinking Kondoumaris might be a spy. He could tell what I was thinking and tried to ease my thoughts'

'Don't worry, sir. You were quite right to question him. You and I both know we've met more than our fair share of double agents.'

All the same, it didn't make it easier for me. I'd wasted valuable time on a wild goose chase. I looked at the notebook. 'What about the last few weeks? Was there anything out of the ordinary?'

Stelios smiled. 'I was coming to that. This is where it really starts to get interesting.'

'In what way?'

'About a month ago, there was an entry about someone called Franz Keller. It seems that he drove him to the Hotel Grande Bretagne as he often does, but this time it was to meet a lady. Apparently the woman in question must have been someone special as he notes he appeared particularly excited by the engagement. He doesn't give the name here, but later on he mentions him meeting a woman again.'

'That could be anyone,' I replied. 'He's a good looking man and from what I gather, he likes the women.'

'That may be so, but if you look here,' Stelios flicked over to another page, 'you see that he notes the woman is Greek. What's more she is married which appears to be the reason for his clandestine meetings. Keller must have let this slip. How and when, he doesn't say.'

All of a sudden, I felt a cold chill run down my spine.

'Kondoumaris doesn't know who this woman is. He just drops Keller off and returns when the meeting is over. But on this page, a few days ago, he happens to see her...'

'Go on,' I said, a little too eagerly.

'For some reason, mainly security, I would think, he doesn't actually name her, but on his last entry he's written these initials. See here, he's circled them. The 'A' is similar to Greek but the next letter is different. In cursive Cyrillic it looks like the letter 'M' which represents Te or "tau" in Greek. To the trained eye, it's A. T. What's more, he seems to have written it in a hurry.' Stelios pushed the notebook towards me, together with his deciphered jottings. There in front of me were the initials A.T.

'Kondoumaris occasionally notes the time Keller arrives and leaves his appointments.' he continued, 'but on the last entry he does not make a note of this. He just says he dropped him off at the Hotel Apollo. From what I've heard, it's a place where Italian and German officers have affairs. High class prostitutes work from here. Whether it's the same woman or not, he doesn't say.'

As I listened to all this, I had a sickening sensation in the pit of my stomach that Alexis might have been that woman, but on hearing that the woman's initials were A.T. I breathed a huge sigh of relief. A.T. did not equate to Alexis Petrakis. I was so nervous that beads of sweat appeared on my forehead. Stelios closed the notepad and asked if I was alright. I assured him it was probably the diet of chickpeas and weeds which were having an adverse affect on me.

'Do you think the urgent meeting he had with Kostas has anything to do with this woman?' he asked.

I shrugged my shoulders. 'We will never know will we?'

'What do we do now?' he asked. 'Do we tell Poseidon? More importantly, should we tell Kostas? He might have an idea who the woman is?'

I knew he was right, but I asked him to keep it quiet for the moment. I would think about it.

*

Several days later, I arrived back at the apartment to find a note pushed under the door. It was from Maria reminding me it was time for another "haircut" her euphemism for either having my hair dyed or because she had information to impart. I looked at myself in the mirror. The roots had grown out and I'd applied a touch of boot polish to cover it up. I thought I'd done a good job but I knew it wouldn't pass muster with Maria.

When I arrived, she scrutinised it carefully and tutted. 'You will be the death of us,' she exclaimed. 'Thank the Lord you didn't get caught in the rain.'

She told me she'd gone to Theo's memorial service. I asked her who was there.

'Not many at all. I was surprised, knowing what a well-to-do man he was. Possibly it was because people didn't want to show their faces knowing that the Italian Ambassador might be there.'

'Where there any Germans present?' I asked.

She narrowed her eyes, studying me in her usual way when she knew very I well I was fishing. Maria was one woman you couldn't pull the wool over her eyes easily. She was too shrewd.

'There were. A high-ranking official by the name of Herr Doktor Franz Keller. He was with his adjutant. I wasn't introduced, but I was told he was a close friend of the Ambassador. We all thought they were there to keep an eye on who turned up. After the service, everyone paid their respects to Kyria Alexis and left. You know, in Greece, when someone passes on, it is usual that the next of kin prepares a feast out of respect for the loss of the loved one. Everyone is invited back to the house. Kyria Alexis did no such thing. I was surprised, but the suffering she was going through was evident. There was no body to bury and for Greeks that means their soul will not find rest. She wept throughout the whole service.'

I didn't need to be there to imagine the scene. I was sure she put on a stellar performance of being the grieving widow.

'Theo was such a good man,' Maria continued. 'He always made sure I had a good supply of medicines for the pharmacy. Now it's getting harder and harder to get them. I have to turn people away that I know will die when they could be saved. That is a huge burden.'

I asked her to prepare a list of everything she needed and I would see what I could do to get them for her. She gave me a hug.

'You are a good man, Kapetan. May God protect you.' She gave me a sigh and wagged her finger at me. 'But even God cannot do miracles if you do not look after your hair.'

We both laughed. Thankfully it broke the despondent mood.

'Tell me,' I asked. 'What is happening with the *bloccos* in the suburbs? I heard you grew up near Kokkinia and still have relatives there.'

'It's a poor area; mostly made up of Asia Minor refugees.' she replied. 'Fortunately for me, I married well and was able to leave. My husband was from here. The pharmacy was his before he died almost ten years ago now. I took it over. Many of those who live in and around Piraeus have always been disadvantaged. Jobs are hard to come by and as a consequence, most of the inhabitants have communist sympathies. They are always being persecuted. It's nothing new. The thing is that now there are collaborators who are on the lookout for those aiding the *andartes*. The collaborators don't care who they point out. Some of my relatives have already been shot. If I ever find out who was responsible, I will kill them with my own hands.'

'Do you really think you could do that, Maria? Kill someone in cold blood I mean.'

'My ancestors died for freedom. I will do the same. You don't know me, Kapetan.' She laughed. 'I could kill these people just like that.'

She clicked her fingers to stress the point. I believed her. She changed the subject.

'I have been thinking over our last conversation — the one where you asked me if Kyria Alexis and Theo were happy.'

My ears pricked up. She wanted to talk.

'I did hear a rumour — it's only a rumour, mind you — that Theo was having an affair with his secretary.'

All of a sudden, I felt the truth was slowly rising to the surface.

'I made a few discreet enquires,' she said in a low voice as if someone might overhear us which was impossible in her cramped kitchen. 'It turns out that Theo was a bit of a ladies' man. He had a few secretaries and some travelled on business with him.'

'Did Kyria Alexis know this?' I asked.

'I presume so. It's hard to hide that sort of thing isn't it? My sources told me that there was one in particular that he'd taken quite a shine to. I think it might be the woman you asked me about? Irini Vlachou?'

I was lost for words.

'So if what you are saying is true, Alexis must have known. If she meant so much to him, do you think he sent her to Crete with Alexis in the hope that she would be safer there?'

Maria shrugged her shoulders. 'It could be. After the Germans attacked Crete, they lost contact. That's all I know.'

Little by little the pieces of the jigsaw were coming together. The fact that they did know each other before Cairo fitted one piece of the puzzle, and the animosity Alexis showed towards Irini that day in the Cafe in Cairo fitted another. I was getting somewhere, but still had no idea how this would play out.

I thanked her for the information, whilst at the same time being careful not to let her think anything was wrong — if indeed anything was and all this wasn't just a set of circumstances that looked odd but with no real basis.

Our conversation came to an abrupt end when we heard a loud banging on the pharmacy door. We were in no doubt as to who it was. No-one else but the Germans would make such a noise at that time of night. Maria's father had long retired to bed and Chryssa and Yiannis had been in the pharmacy all evening preparing medicines for the following day. Chryssa poked her head round the door. She looked terrified.

'Stall them for a minute,' Maria said and then ordered her

son and myself to help her move the heavy dresser away from the wall. Within a matter of seconds, the three of us had managed to slide it far enough away to reveal a hole in the wall.

'Get in,' Maria ordered. 'Quickly.'

This was easier said than done. I barely fitted and was still wriggling into position when they slid the dresser back in place. My knees were bunched up under my chin and my right foot was jutting out of the hole, wedged in such a way that I could barely move it. The hammering grew louder and Chryssa managed to open the door only moments before it would have been broken down.

In a matter of minutes, the place was filled with Germans who wasted no time in conducting a thorough search. Whilst Maria's father was being hauled from his bed and bundled down the stairs, I heard a voice demanding to see her books and papers for her medical supplies. It was the Gestapo. In spite of their intimidating behaviour, Maria kept her cool. She showed them her 'official' books and calmly accounted for everything, telling them that these days most of what she dispensed was for malnourishment and the prevention of fleas. Throughout it all, I could hear the muffled sounds of the place being searched.

From my pitch back hideout, the pain was excruciating and I hoped they wouldn't be hauled away leaving me stranded. Outside, I heard the sporadic sound of machine gun fire and screams, followed by more gunfire. Even though the men could find no fault with Maria's books, she was asked to accompany them back to Headquarters. Her father, Chryssa and Yiannis were also ordered to go. Eventually, everything went quiet. I couldn't have pushed the dresser away even if

I'd wanted to. It was impossible. My back was racked with pain and I could barely feel my legs due to lack of circulation. I was wedged in the hole so tightly that I had no option but to stay put.

The hours slipped by slowly until eventually I heard voices. Maria and the family had returned. The first thing they did was push the dresser away. By this time I was in a bad way and couldn't budge. Maria grabbed my shoulder whilst Yiannis grabbed a leg, and together they pulled me out like a sack of potatoes. I lay there on the floor in severe pain, swearing my head off in Greek. Maria couldn't stop laughing.

'Kapetan! What a sight you look.' And as if to add insult to injury, added 'but at least your hair looks good.'

She told me I would be surprised to know how many people she'd hidden in that hole, especially children waiting to be smuggled out of the country. I couldn't even begin to imagine the terror they must have experienced. After a few painkillers washed down by a large glass of ouzo, I began to feel better.

'Thank God you returned when you did. What the hell was all that about anyway?'

Maria's joviality disappeared. 'That,' she said angrily, 'is what happens when someone rats. Someone informed the Gestapo that enemy soldiers were being hidden in this street. If you go outside, you will see the results of their work. One whole family has been executed. Their bodies are still lying against the wall. We are forbidden to go near them. The Germans want to make an example of them.'

'Did they find what they were looking for? Any escaped soldiers I mean?'

Maria nodded. 'I'm afraid this time they couldn't get away

in time. The only good thing about that — if there is a good thing — is that it stopped them searching other houses.'

My aches and pains paled into comparison compared to the fate of the escaped soldiers.

Chapter 19

Not long after the discovery of Kondoumaris's code, Dancer moved to another safe house. The Germans were particularly adept at picking up radio locations and his transmissions had attracted attention. The last transmission almost cost not only his life, but that of the stonemasons as well. A radio-van located the position of the transmission to the stonemason's yard. If it had not been for the quick thinking of the stonemasons and marble cutters loyal to the Resistance, Dancer would have ended up at Gestapo Headquarters. As it was, he managed to evade the raid by hiding amongst slabs of marble with his wireless and few belongings. It was far too dangerous to return and he moved to a safe-house in nearby Kato Patissia.

So far all the men who had landed with me, apart from Bob Cohen, were still alive and active, which was remarkable by SOE's standards, although I was not to fully realise this till after the war. We were careful. Even so, a large dose of luck was needed during these operations.

Dancer's new safe house was next to a church. The priest belonged to the Resistance and as a consequence, allowed him to use the church for his transmissions. The space allowed him to manoeuvre the twenty feet of wire into position needed to make the necessary transmissions, which was always a problem. He was also able to keep the radio hidden in a niche originally used to hold votive offerings but which had been covered up securely with a silver icon that could be opened like a door with a key. The priest had two keys. He kept one for himself and the other he gave to Dancer. The church also hid a cache of guns behind the iconostasis. The priest slid back a weighty slab of marble to reveal a large hole in the ground which made the normally calm Dancer break out in a sweat when he saw just how much was stored there.

'We will go down fighting,' the priest said. He smiled. 'God is on the side of the righteous.'

I hoped he was right.

*

During the first few months of 1943, we had done a good job of deceiving the Germans in convincing them of an imminent invasion of the Balkans and Hitler defined the 'South-East" of Europe as an operational and strategic theatre of war. Under his command, there had been an impressive build-up of troops and weapons, most deployed from Yugoslavia. Only the Italians appeared to be suffering. For the most part, they despised the Germans. Things were made worse when reinforcements failed to arrive from Rome and they assumed they were being forgotten. To make matters worse, thousands of Italian soldiers were ill with malaria. The Resistance took advantage of this. They had their spies everywhere. Most Italians liked to socialise and get drunk and when they did they cursed the war. The *andartes* kept their eyes and ears open should anyone decide to lay down their arms. Many had already defected to join them. In the central mountains, Anna had a group of women who played up to these men and reported back to her. Morale was very low indeed.

I spent most of the following weeks out of Athens with Loukas organizing sleeper cells, raiding German and Italian supplies for weapons, and obtaining medical supplies for Maria and others like her. Throughout this time, my thoughts kept drifting back to Alexis and my last conversation with Maria.

Having convinced myself that Herr Keller was a womaniser and as a man of position could have almost any woman he desired, I began to shake off the fear that Alexis might be involved with him. Their meetings were purely coincidental. What was preying on my mind now was why Irini died in the way she did, and most of all, why was she following the King's mistress at Mena House and others in the Greek government in exile. And why did she meet with a known German sympathizer? If she was Theo's mistress, one would have thought she was looking out for him. Perhaps he'd told her sometime before she left Crete that the relationship was over and he was going back to his wife? Perhaps she had it in for Alexis and wanted to prove to Theo, she was more loyal than his wife. Who knows what went on in those last few months between the German occupation of Crete and the time I met them? One thing was for sure, if Theo had other women, it would account for Alexis's coolness with regards to her husband — at any rate, the side I saw. To most people brought up in the ways of the upper classes, one was forced to look the other way at indiscretions. Life was all about keeping face. What was good for the goose was good for the gander. It certainly answered why Alexis was a woman who acted as flirtatiously as she did.

When I returned to Athens, there was an urgent message from Cairo. I was to leave Greece immediately for Turkey. This latest assignment was so secretive I could not even tell my men. Dancer passed on the message to me in a code that only I knew. He knew it was something important but as far as they were concerned, I was going on another adventure which was nothing new to them anyway. Stelios was to take charge whilst I was away. Only one other person knew of my mission, and she was the woman I would be travelling with. She went by the code name, Stella. I was to make my way to the Island of Evia where she would meet me at an allocated spot on a remote stretch of the coastline. From there, a fishing boat would take us to the island of Skyros and on to the Turkish mainland. It was a circuitous route and given that all went to plan, we would arrive at our destination within a couple of weeks at the very latest. Once I landed safely, I would be met by another SOE operative. At this point in time I had no idea who that would be. All I knew was that, should I reach Turkey safe and sound, the importance of the new assignment would be revealed.

The idea of a dangerous mission didn't bother me, but the idea of leaving without seeing Alexis was not something I relished, yet I knew that was what I had to do. I thought of her constantly; she was in my blood — a disease that you know could kill you if not checked. If I was going to see her, then I only had a few hours in which to do it. I thought about catching the train to Kifissia but in the end, reason prevailed. She had made no attempt to see me again after our night of passion, and as far as Poseidon was concerned, all had been going well. Reluctantly,

I turned my attention to the job in hand, packed a light suitcase, and left Athens just before curfew. I was now Giorgios Liakos, an elderly man who walked with the aid of a walking stick. Avoiding the numerous checkpoints, even though I had a new set of travel documents and ID, I arrived at my allocated meeting point on the island of Evia the following evening.

Stella turned out be an old friend but because of my disguise and alias, she didn't recognise me. Fooling someone I knew with a new disguise never failed to give me great satisfaction but it occasionally had its downside which in this case included being thoroughly searched whilst staring down the barrel of a Mauser. When she realized who I was, her demeanour softened considerably and she threw her arms around me in an embrace more reminiscent of a burly mountain fighter than the feminine woman I knew her to be.

I first met Stella in Belgrade when we both worked for MI6, and like me, she had been recruited to SOE because of her knowledge of the Balkans and her fluency in languages — Greek, Serbian, Russian, English, German, and Turkish. Her parents were Greeks from Istanbul who now lived in England. She was also an expert sharp-shooter. Throughout the time I'd known her, she'd had several aliases. Stella was the latest one.

'Giorgaiki mou!! Little George,' she exclaimed, affectionately, even though I was a good few inches taller than her. 'How glad I am to see you. It's been a while since we were together. When was it?'

'March 1939,' I replied. 'When the Germans took Prague. That was when we made our way out of the Balkans. And if I remember correctly, you were still with that Polish lover of yours, the Szlacta, Count Borkowski. What happened to him?'

Stella smiled. 'You mean Jan. He saw the writing on the wall and went back to Poland. The last I heard, he ended up in England and joined the RAF. The war spoilt it all but it was good while it lasted.'

I knew exactly what she meant.

'Anyway, *Giorgaiki mou*, what about you? I must say, I didn't recognise you in that disguise. You look at least thirty years older. You always did have a talent for theatrics.'

'All the world's a stage,' I replied. 'You're not too bad yourself.'

We laughed. It was good to see her again. The times we'd shared together were good and bad. Mostly good I'm happy to say, and the bad we didn't talk about.

'So,' she said, after the pleasantries were over. 'I'm to accompany you all the way to Turkey. It's not going to be easy. The Germans patrol these waters like sharks, and several members of the network, mainly fishermen, have been executed for operating without the right documents or at night. With each death, we have to find someone else and that's getting harder.'

One of the men with us brought our happy reunion back to earth. We had less than an hour at the most to get away before the patrols were back with their searchlights. I was taken to a cove where two men were loading heavy wooden crates of contraband on board a small caique. It looked as if it would capsize at any moment. There was no such thing as a plimsoll line and if there had been, it would have been well under water by now. Stella and I stepped aboard and we were pushed out into the open sea. A wind started to whip up and fearing we'd be caught in a storm, I fingered Anna's blue bead in my pocket and prayed to Saint Nicholas to keep us safe which Stella thought was hilarious. Thankfully the storm stayed away that night and we reached the safety of a series of caves in the cliff face of a normally uninhabited island, but which was now home to several *andartes*.

With the boat safely hidden inside the mouth of a cave, the andartes prepared us a feast of grilled fish. Afterwards, I was shown to my bed — a precarious looking ledge a few metres above the water. Tucked up under a coarsely woven blanket, I fell asleep to the sound of water lapping against the rocks. In the morning we finished off the rest of the fish but because of German patrol boats, waited until nightfall before moving on to our next destination. This was repeated until we reached Skyros at which point, the contraband was unloaded. A week later, we reached the island of Psara next to the German held island of Chios, not far from Samos. The Turkish mainland was only a few miles away.

Chapter 20

Didim-Aydin, Turkey. June 1943

We arrived at a deserted beach on the Turkish mainland sometime around midnight on a moonless night. As soon as we landed, three men with machine guns appeared out of the scrub to greet us. They were Turks. One of them welcomed me in Greek. Stella informed me she would not be accompanying me further and wished me the best of luck. Her job was done.

'Goodbye, *Giorgaiki mou*. This is where we part ways.' She gave me a hug and a kiss on the cheek. 'Take good care of yourself. Let's hope our paths cross again.'

I was sad to see her go. Stella had always been good company. 'I owe you,' I said,

'You can buy me a drink at one of those swanky hotels you like to stay in,' she laughed. 'After this damn war has ended.'

'It's a date. Stay safe.'

I watched her get in the boat and head back out to sea. With no moon, the boat was soon swallowed up in the darkness. I followed the Turks along the rocky coastal pathway until we came to a large olive orchard guarded by several men. I was searched and ushered on. The path meandered through groves of ancient olive trees until it opened out into a clearing. In the middle stood a stone house. More guards sat around on a veranda over which trailed bougainvillaea, grape vines and dried gourds. One of the guards knocked on the door and I heard a voice call out for me to enter.

The house had no electricity and the room was lit with candlelight throwing long sinister shadows against the white-washed walls and illuminating several men's faces sitting around a wooden table like the chiaroscuro of a Rembrandt painting. The men stood up to greet me, except for one who stood half-hidden in the shadows.

'You made it,' he said in English.'

I recognized the voice instantly. It was my old friend, Jack Martins, from Cairo.

He emerged out of the shadows with a big grin on his face. 'Good to see you, old boy,' he said, shaking my hand. 'I suppose I'm the last person you expected to see?'

'So this is where you ended up?' I replied.

One of the men brought out a large bottle of tsipouro, filled the tulip-shaped Turkish tea glasses and handed them around. We raised a toast, commenting on how good it was to still be alive.

'You know I can't tell you what I've been up to,' Jack said, 'suffice to say, I've been on the move as have you.'

He introduced me to the other men; a few Greeks, another Englishman, a Palestinian and two Turks, one of whom was Ali who owned the house and the olive groves in the area. Except for Ali, all of them had an alias. Recognising we had much to discuss, they left us alone and went to sit outside. The only other to stay was the Englishman who turned out to be a Scot and was introduced as Bill.

'So what's all this about?' I asked, making myself comfortable for what I knew would be a long night.

'Before we get on to the reason you're here, you wouldn't have heard the news would you? It happened while you were travelling here.'

'What news are you referring to?'

'The Allies have landed in Sicily. The tide has turned,' Bill said, in a broad Glaswegian accent.

'That's the best thing I've heard in a long while. It certainly gives us a damn good excuse to celebrate.'

He refilled our glasses. 'We estimate it's only a matter of weeks before they get to the mainland and from what our sources tell us, the Italians will surrender.'

'I wouldn't be too sure of that. Mussolini will fight to the end.'

'Mussolini might, but I doubt if the people will,' Jack replied.

On hearing such news, I was elated but my euphoria didn't last. With the aid of the Resistance, we had done a good job in Greece. By fooling the Germans into believing the Allies would land somewhere in Greece, they had diverted much needed equipment from other strategic points vital to their war effort. Now I was afraid they would unleash their anger on the Greek population and things would get worse before they got better. I only hoped London would show their gratitude to the Greeks after the war was over, but I had a sinking feeling things weren't going to go as smoothly as I'd like.

'I wasn't called here to find out about Sicily, was I?' I said.

'That news would have reached me in the mountains! So what is it that Cairo couldn't transmit to me in Greece and which is deemed urgent enough to take me away from Poseidon?'

At this point, Bill went outside to join the others.

'Let's go for a walk,' said Jack. 'Somewhere where we can be alone.'

We left the house and the men on the veranda playing cards and took a stroll through the olive orchard.

'In a way your new assignment does have something to do with the Poseidon Network,' Jack said, settling himself down on the ground with his back against the trunk of a gnarled olive tree. He lit a cigarette and handed me the packet. Jack Martins could be the most jovial companion a man in SOE could have. We'd had some fun in our times, especially in Cairo, but when it came to work, especially assignments that could cost us our life at the drop of a hat, his personality changed. He was like a chameleon. Now was one of those times.

'Cairo didn't want this transmitted over the radio to Greece. The thing is, they believe Poseidon has been compromised and they sent me here to work with you. You could be in grave danger.'

I was stunned. Everything had appeared to be going well.

'I can tell by the look on your face, you find this hard to believe,' Jack said.

'You can say that again. We've lost a few men, mostly *andartes* in the line of fire, but nothing out of the ordinary. My men are still operating in the field and they haven't reported anything unusual.'

Jack put his head back on the tree, drew on his cigarette and watched the smoke curl up into the inky black night sky.

'You don't call the death of the leader of Poseidon "out of the ordinary"?' he replied, after a long pause.

I was seated firmly on the ground yet I felt a strange sensation as if the ground would give way underneath me. I threw the cigarette away and leaned forward with my head in my hands.

'Then you *do* know what I am talking about?' Jack added.

I looked at him wishing I was anywhere but here having this conversation.

'What are you saying?' I asked. 'What do you know? Why has Cairo sent you?'

The questions tumbled out, yet I knew that whatever he was about to tell me, the sickening feeling in the pit of my stomach told me I'd been duped.

'You should have told Cairo as soon as you knew the White Rose was missing, not wait until his death was formally announced. Leaving it until his widow was appointed in his place was not in your best interest. And then there's the matter of the driver — Kondoumaris — the man you suspected as a double agent.'

'How did you know about that?' I asked, lamely.

'When you asked Cairo to check out his background, which they did and reported to you that he was indeed married to a woman called Lotte, the mere fact that you put out a request alerted them to the possibility that all was not well. As I told you, I cannot divulge what I was doing, but I can tell you that at around this time, I was back to Cairo and called to Rustem Buildings for a little chat with the Colonel. He took me out to dinner at the Gezira Sporting Club. You know SOE can be stingy so when he does something like that, then you and I both know what that means. He's after information — off the record.'

'And I suppose he asked you if I knew a woman by the name of Alexis Petrakis?'

'Spot on,' Jack replied. He paused to let his words sink in. 'You see where this is leading, don't you?'

'I've a good idea, but carry on.'

'I told him that as far as I was knew, you met Miss Petrakis only twice, when in reality it was four times if you counted the time you first laid eyes on her at Shepheard's and the day you followed her through the bazaar to the Cafe Parisian. I thought it best to omit telling him about the last two. It wouldn't have looked good.'

I thanked him. By the look of things, I was in deep trouble as it was without SOE thinking I was snooping around after a woman.

'The Colonel asked if I thought you'd fallen for Miss Petrakis. I said that in my opinion, you always liked a pretty face and she would only have been one in a long line of women.'

'And he believed you?'

'Maybe. Maybe not. It's hard to tell with a man like him. Then he asked me if you knew a woman by the name of Irini Vlachou whose body was discovered in the Nile under suspicious circumstances. I did think it best to tell him that the police had been looking for you around this time but you were away in Alexandria and spoke to them on your return. I added that you knew nothing of this woman's death and it was Sir Oswald who filled you in on the details as it was on that night in the desert that you met the deceased.'

'What did he say?'

'Nothing. He just listened. No doubt he checked it out with Sir Oswald afterwards.'

'And that was all? Did you tell him I'd asked you to check Irini out?'

Jack laughed. 'I thought it better not to mention that either.'

I listened carefully to what he was saying, at the same time recalling my conversation with Maria about Irini being Theo's mistress. Whichever way I looked at the situation, my first instincts about Alexis appeared correct. All was not as it appeared and she was not a woman to be trusted. When I thought about it, the rational side of me always suspected something was not right, yet I had fooled myself into thinking that because Poseidon appeared to be operating smoothly, I was being overly suspicious. We had not had any major disasters. All the operations had gone as planned. Yet I had obviously missed something. Something so important that Cairo and London had become involved. It was bad enough that they were looking into my personal life, but it was what Jack said next that really hit me.

'Not long after you were dropped into Greece, SOE started to suspect something wrong with Poseidon's escape routes.' He indicated towards the house. 'All of those men will vouch for that. Not all the escapees have been getting through.'

'That's bound to happen,' I replied, a little too quickly. 'Sometimes things do go wrong. We can have it all worked out but there's still an element of luck. You know that.'

'Not like this. At first our agents here in Turkey might have agreed with you, but over the past few months, expected boats just didn't arrive. It got worse and they detected a pattern developing. In the beginning, the boats did get through. Then only one in two boats arrived. Now it's even worse, especially from Lesbos and Samos. Samos in particular. It didn't take them long to realise it was the boats with the men that didn't make it — Greeks and Allied soldiers. After a while, no Jews arrived at all, yet we know many left the mainland.' Jack gave me a questioning look. 'Do you know how many escapees Poseidon had on its list?

I had discussed this with Loukas on several occasions. Since I'd arrived there had been at least six hundred and seventy — and quite a few were children.

'What would you say if I told you that only a third of those made it?' Jack asked.

I felt the bile rise in my throat. 'Good God,' I stammered. 'I can't believe what I'm hearing. Why were we never alerted before?'

'Who's in charge of the escape routes for these islands?' Jack asked. 'In Poseidon, I mean.'

'The White Rose — Alexis. She wanted to continue her husband's work. He set up these routes. It's one of the reasons she took his code name. I even saw her the day she left for her last trip. I gave her money which she'd requested from Cairo. It was to facilitate bribes. She had two Jewish children with her.'

Jack was a good listener but I could tell from his eyes he felt sorry for me. He remained silent for a few minutes smoking another cigarette. I noticed he'd become a chain smoker. It wasn't a good sign.

'Larry, no Jews have arrived here in months?

'Good God,' I said again. 'This is a nightmare.'

'It gets worse. Those Jews who put their faith in Poseidon ended up in deportation camps in Poland, not here. The two children you saw never made it.'

When I pictured their frightened faces in the back of the car, I rubbed my temples hard, swearing loudly.

'Two of the original Poseidon smugglers, Stephanos and Pavlos, two fishermen from Pefkos, smelt a rat and decided to break away and conduct their own escape routes. Their boats went south towards the island of Agathonisi and then on to Akkoy. Their human cargo made it. Now you know why Cairo stepped in.' said Jack. 'This is a very sophisticated operation — carefully planned to keep you and the rest of Poseidon out of the loop.

Think carefully. Is there anything you think we should know?'

In the confusion, I wondered if he was referring to Kondoumaris's notebook. Surely not? That had only just taken place.

Jack waited a few minutes for my response. 'Fine. Let me know if you think of anything. We have a few hours up our sleeve.'

By the time we'd finished, the blackness of the night sky had been replaced by a soft dove grey and the sun was peaking out over the horizon, its golden rays already warming the land. A new day. A new chapter of my life.

'Come on,' Jack said. 'Let's get back to the others. We'll get you something to eat. You must be famished.'

I followed him through the olive trees with their dark brown twisted trunks and silvery green leaves glistening in the morning light. To the right the trees stretched up into the hills as far as the eye could see. To my left was the Aegean, sparkling like a mirror. The air was delicate, tinged with salt from a soft sea breeze. At any other time I would have savoured the serene beauty of the moment. Now I felt sick and confused. It wasn't long before we saw two Turkish women approach the house carrying baskets of food. Jack welcomed them in Turkish.

'Fatma Hanim is the wife of Ali, who owns this land. She and her daughter are superb cooks,' he said. 'They treat us like pashas.'

Fatma spread a colourful cloth on the table and started to lay out bread, olives and a soft ewe's cheese wrapped in a white cloth. Her daughter helped her, adding hard-boiled eggs, olives, cucumbers, tomatoes, and a pot of mulberry jam to the banquet. When they'd finished, they went outside to prepare Turkish coffee over the coals. The aroma of coffee wafting in from outside combined with the freshness of the food revived my appetite. Such a plentiful breakfast was not what I was used to in Greece, even in the villages where the Italians and Germans plundered everything they could lay their hands on.

Fatma Hanim returned with the coffee.

'*Sagol*, Fatma Hanim,' said Jack. 'Thank you.'

When she saw my empty plate, she pushed the cheese towards me and indicated for me to cut another piece.

'*Cok zayif*,' she said with a smile. 'You are too thin.'

The men laughed. Evidently she thought I needed fattening up. A conversation ensued about the famine that had taken place throughout the winter of 1941/42. The mortality rate was in the thousands and the country had still not recovered from it. The men told me that during this time, skeletons arrived on the boats.

'They were so malnourished, many never survived,' Ali said. 'They died as soon as they landed.'

Chapter 21

After breakfast it was back to business. As before, the men left us alone. This time Jack didn't mince his words.

'You're holding something back, Larry. I know you too well.' He didn't give me time to comment. 'You know something isn't right, don't you?'

I stared into space. A chat between old friends was beginning to seem like an interrogation. Jack waited a few minutes before continuing.

'Look, old friend. I'm trying to help you. You'd better tell me what you know. I have the authority to stop you returning and if you don't come clean, I may have to kill you. Think hard. The Colonel likes you. You're a top-notch operator and he wants you to sort this out.' He knitted his fingers together, waiting for me to speak. When he saw I was still not forthcoming, he reached into his jacket and took out a pistol. 'Don't make me use it, Larry.'

I knew he wasn't joking. SOE were capable of disposing of me without a second thought. I was not irreplaceable. One thing was certain, they were not going to let me return to Greece unless they were convinced I'd told them everything.

What I had heard over the last few hours also convinced me that somehow or another, Alexis was more involved than she let on. I owed it to everyone to get to the bottom of it.

'You win,' I replied, throwing my hands in the air. 'I confess that what you told me about the escape routes did come as a shock, but it shouldn't have. I have long suspected something was not right.'

Jack breathed a sigh of relief when he saw I was starting to open up.

'Why is that?' he asked, putting the gun away.

'Because the White Rose's actual death was kept a secret for a while. The official story about him going missing and then his ID being recovered at the scene of the accident was not true. The truth is, he died around the time I landed.'

'Go on,' Jack said, making himself comfortable in readiness for what I was about to tell him.

'When I met up with the White Rose in Athens, I had no idea it would be Alexis. That came as a great shock. That very same evening, she told me Theo, her husband, the real White Rose, had been killed returning from a meeting with three other *andartes*. They knew the men at the various checkpoints, but on that particular night, the guards at the Ekali check-point had changed. The men's papers were all in order but for some reason, the guards became suspicious and decided to search the car. Knowing there were guns and ammunition in the boot, the men made a run for it. A shoot-out ensued. Two men were killed and Theo was badly injured. The fourth man managed to help Theo and they disappeared into the woods. Unfortunately, Theo's wounds were so bad, he didn't make it and he was buried in a makeshift grave. I later found out that he was reburied in the old cemetery at the Church of the Virgin of the Swallow.'

'Who else knew? Jack asked.

'The Wolf.'

'You mean our old friend, Loukas?'

'That's right. You and I have always known him to be a trustworthy person. Alexis told him and they decided to keep it quiet in order not to disrupt the various *andartes* groups. There had been problems between ELAS and EAM and the last thing they wanted was disunity.'

Jack nodded. He understood the dynamics of Greek politics all too well.

'If Theo was killed, why concoct another story?' Jack asked. 'Why not simply tell the truth and say he was killed at a checkpoint?'

I shrugged. 'Alexis thought there could be reprisals. When I mentioned this to Loukas, he agreed so I went along with it. I had no idea what the eventual story of his death would be — or when it would be announced. I have to admit, the longer they delayed it, the more I felt uncomfortable.'

'What did the men say when they were eventually informed?'

A couple of leaders from the area where he was supposedly killed were anxious that people would blame them for his death.'

'And what about Alexis taking on his mantle and code name? Didn't they have a problem with this? Why didn't Loukas step into his shoes?'

'Knowing that the Gestapo in Athens are after him, he prefers to spend most of his time working with the *andartes* in the mountains. He also has a woman who works with him. She's young but she's clever. The two have become very close and after the death of his first wife, he doesn't want to jeopardise this. Alexis offered to take charge as she knows about Poseidon's operations from her husband. She knows all his contacts and some are in high places, as you know. Up until then, Poseidon ran an effective network. No-one wanted to rock the boat.'

'Yes, I will agree with you. Poseidon did seem to run effectively — until that point,' Jack said, handing me a cigarette. 'But you appeared worried which is why you asked Cairo to check on Kondoumaris.'

'Yes, I admit that I do have a tendency not to trust anyone who works for the Germans in any capacity.'

'Only Kondoumaris was not a double agent was he? In fact he had something urgent to tell one of the *andartes* — a man who goes by the name of Kostas.'

I looked Jack straight in the eyes. He was a smart old boy. Always had been. I had never underestimated him. Now I felt a great relief in coming clean. There was no other option. We were both laying all our cards on the table.

'How did you know that?'

Jack waved his hand in the air in circles — a very Greek expression for never mind, just get on with it, so I did.

'We had been shadowing him, but nothing out of the ordinary happened. In the end, I decided to break into his flat with a couple of my men. Dancer was one of them. I promised them that if I found nothing to indicate he was working for the Germans, my doubts were groundless and we would move on. The problem was, the night we went to his flat, he was murdered.'

Jack raised his eyebrows. 'Murdered! Who by?'

'Four men drove up to his apartment. Two got out and broke

into his flat, the other two drove near to where we were hiding and waited in the car. We saw Kondoumaris return and enter his apartment. Shortly after, the two men reappeared and left in the waiting car. When we entered the apartment we found Kondoumaris dead and his flat ransacked. He had been shot.'

'So the men were looking for something?'

At this point, I wondered if I should tell him about the notebook and decided it wiser to come clean.

'I found a small notebook hidden in his sock. Kostas had told me he kept a note of names, etc., in it. I'm sure the men were looking for that.'

'Do you have any idea who the killers were?'

This incident took place after curfew. Apparently, the neighbours suspected him of collaborating with the Germans and at first we thought it could have been Greeks out to get him. But no Greek would be doing what they did. The Greeks who kill collaborators like to leave a trademark note. This was more sophisticated. They used a silencer and were definitely looking for something — the notebook. I suspect. In the end, we decided it must have been the Germans themselves, probably the Gestapo.'

'Hmm. Did you get a look at the men or get the number plates?'

'It was too dark. We could only see their profiles. We couldn't see the number plate either, but I did notice part of the bumper bar was dented.'

'This notebook, did it contain anything important?'

Stelios found a code in it. Many of the names of people picked up by the Gestapo were there. That information had been given to Kostas. We all knew about it. What we did pick up though, was that over the past few weeks, Kondoumaris had been driving a certain top German official by the name of Franz Keller. It appears this man had been meeting a Greek woman. Whether they were having an affair is not clear but it appears likely. On the last entry — about the time he arranged to meet Kostas — Kondoumaris mentions the woman but he only gives her initials.'

'What are they?' Jack asked,

'A. T. That's all we know.'

Jack stubbed his cigarette out in the ashtray. 'And you have no idea who A.T. is?

'No. I was trying to work that out when I got the message to come here.'

I watched him get up and pace the room anxiously. 'This is serious.'

'You think I don't know this?' I answered angrily. 'I've racked my brain. At first I even thought it could be Alexis as she does know Keller.'

Jack spun around and glared at me. '*We* know who Keller is though — a very dangerous man — Gestapo with links to the Abwehr? The thing is, how does Alexis know him?'

'Alexis is friends with the Italian Ambassador, Marinetti. He has a summer residence in Kifissia — the Villa Aphrodite, not far from her home. One evening she was invited to a party. It was the night I first met her in Athens and she asked me to accompany her. I went as her cousin. Keller was there and introduced himself to us. He seemed most charmed by her.'

'It seems that Kyria Petrakis charms everyone,' Jack said with more than a hint of sarcasm. 'What else happened?'

'Nothing. He left early. His name was never mentioned again until a few weeks ago when there was a terrible massacre at Kato Hora in the mountains. The area comes under Italian jurisdiction but it was the Germans who did it. With Loukas's consent, I asked Alexis if she could smooth it over with the Italian Ambassador to ensure Germans were not sent in to wreak further havoc.'

At this point, I deliberated over what to say next as I wasn't sure Jack would fully understand but he was like a dog with a bone.

'So what has this got to do with Keller?'

'Keller happened to be visiting the Ambassador at the same time when she went to see him. The Ambassador brought him into the room and Alexis was forced to win him over too.'

'And how did she do that?' he asked, his eyes narrowing. 'By promising to sleep with him?'

When I heard these words, I felt a surge of anger.

'Yes, but in the end something happened and she didn't go through with it.'

Jack burst out laughing. 'And I suppose you came to the rescue — a shoulder to cry on — her knight in shining armour.'

I jumped out of my chair, ready to hit him. 'Sometimes you can be a bastard!' I shouted. 'You know what we have to do to win people over.'

Bill the Scot put his head round the door. 'Steady on you two!'

I put my hands up. 'Just a few harsh words between old friends,' I assured him.

When he closed the door, Jack continued. He offered me another cigarette.

'Don't lie to me, old boy. Did you fuck her?' he said in a low voice.

'Jesus Christ!' I shouted.

'I'll ask you again. Did you fuck her?'

I threw the cigarette on the dirt floor and stubbed it out, angrily.

'I knew it,' Jack replied, shaking his head. 'You're an idiot. You've fallen for the oldest trick in the book. I know you like a good-looking woman, but quite frankly, I thought you would have more sense.'

'Look,' he said, leaning closer. 'Normally, no-one gives a toss about who you screw. God knows, it's a shit life we lead and you take what you can — but Alexis Petrakis? I never thought you could be that stupid. I have no idea what she looks like but she must be a stunner for you to think of going to bed with the White Rose's wife! Sorry, let me correct that, I mean the head of the Poseidon Network

I remained silent, clenching my fist in anger and trying my best not to smash it into his smirking face.

'Tell me,' Jack continued. 'Was it worth it, because from where I am standing, you have been taken in by someone who is under suspicion of aiding the Germans — a songbird.'

I felt my head spinning. From the day I followed her in the bazaar, I knew something was wrong. I even put her out of my mind until I saw her again in Kifissia. Yet, from that very first meeting at the church, my instincts told me all was not right. Now here I was, being told something I just didn't want to believe.

'I'm sorry,' Jack said, after a while. 'I can see how hard this is for you. I'm your friend. Trust me. I know you're too clever to let anyone pull the wool over your eyes so let's see if we can't sort this out before something really bad happens.'

He told me to go outside and take a walk before we continued further. 'Go on,' he said. 'Get a breath of fresh air. Come back when you've digested all this and we'll talk more.'

I was alone for a full few hours, trying to come to terms with the fact that Poseidon was in danger of collapsing. If it did, it would certainly mean death for a few thousand of our men all over Greece. The fact that the escapees were not reaching Turkey had rocked me to the core. Alexis was in charge of these islands. She had to have known what was going on. In hindsight, I could see she was merely stalling for time when I asked to accompany her on the next trip to Samos. That trip had never eventuated. I couldn't get the image of those children's faces out of my mind. Was she knowingly taking them to their deaths? It didn't bear thinking about.

When I returned to the house, Jack was waiting patiently for me.

'Well?' he asked. 'Has the walk cleared your head?'

'I've told you everything I know, Jack. Now I think it's your turn to come clean with me.'

'Ah, but you've missed out one important fact, Larry, and it had a bearing on Cairo's decision to keep an eye on things.'

'What's that?'

'You forgot to mention that Irini was the White Rose's mistress.'

I stared at him for a moment. We were like two masters playing a skilful chess game and one was about to checkmate the other.

'I only found that out recently. Ever since Cairo, their relationship had bothered me but I had to bide my time until I could broach the subject with someone. I needed to gain their trust.

It appears that Irini wasn't the only one. From what I gather, Theo liked the women.'

Jack smiled. 'Then you and he had a lot in common.'

'That's a bit below the belt,' I replied, 'even for you.'

He laughed. 'Lighten up, Larry. Since when have you been sensitive about affairs of the heart?'

He could see I wasn't amused. 'How did you find out she was his mistress?' I asked.

'I'm coming to that. Firstly, you asked what SOE knows. Alright I'll tell you. Around the time you landed in Greece, Cairo received a coded message from the White Rose himself. It was brief, but he suspected someone had told the Germans he was a resistor and his life was in danger. He had hoped to tell you that himself, but it seems that by the time you got to Athens it was too late. So as you see, they already knew something was wrong before you asked for the check on Kondoumaris. They just didn't know what. From what you've told me, you also suspected the same thing.'

'Yes, but the network was operating smoothly,' I answered.

'After hearing nothing from the White Rose himself,' Jack continued, 'Cairo assumed all was well until you asked for the check on Kondoumaris. That's when they started to make a few enquiries of their own, starting with Alexis and Irini Vlachos. They discovered, as I did, that Irini did indeed meet up with Dimitris Papaghiotis, the German sympathiser, but it was not as it appeared to us at the time. Somehow Irini discovered Alexis had been approached by the Abwehr to spy for them. They knew she was married to a high profile businessman back in Athens and attempted to contact her at their hotel. It seems that Alexis wanted nothing to do with them, but the Germans were persistent. They told her they would make life hard for her husband and family back in Greece. Irini told Alexis to approach the foreign office and the Greek government in exile to get them off her back but she seemed too scared. They quarrelled about it.

'In the end, Irini threatened that she would get a message to Theo that his wife was being coerced by the Germans into working for them. Alexis was furious.'

'How do you know all this?' I asked.

'Because their arguments were overheard and Intelligence was tipped off. When they got wind of this, they started to tail both women. Alexis often accused Irini of trying to steal her husband. She said she would never forgive her. This was around the time you met them. When you asked me to do a bit of sleuth work, I wasn't aware of this and having discovered she visited Papaghiotis, we naturally jumped to conclusions she was a German sympathiser, but I'm afraid her visit to him may have been her undoing. Irini confronted him and told him to leave Alexis alone. By all accounts, Alexis never saw anyone thought to be connected with the Germans again. The problem was, Irini didn't believe her and that's why she made those visits to Mena House. She was not spying on the King's mistress after all. She was trying to warn the Greek family that they were in danger but no-one would listen to her. That's when she turned up dead.'

'So that's what they must have been arguing about that afternoon in The Parisian,' I said.

'Most likely.'

'We couldn't question Papaghiotis because not long after you left Cairo, he was also killed. He was in a car with one of his mistresses when someone opened fire on them. The police suspected the killers were Greeks, but it was never confirmed.'

My head was spinning. There were still many unanswered questions.

'If both women were being watched, how did Alexis get out of the country?'

Jack sighed. 'I thought you would ask that. Poseidon was in its infancy in the early days of the occupation. It was just a bunch of people who tried to resist the Italian and German occupation. After Crete, Theo worked hard to form it into a cohesive network. That's when it took on the code name, the Poseidon Network, and he became the White Rose. He approached Cairo for help. We already knew of Loukas and his attachment to the group, so it passed all the checks. Poseidon was a bona fide organisation and they wanted our help. After numerous calls between Cairo and London, SOE decided to help. That's when you and your men became involved. Theo stated that a condition of SOE and Poseidon working together was that his wife was returned to Greece. He wanted her by his side. The Colonel agreed and she was secretly flown out of Cairo via Turkey. No-one knew. Not even Sir Oswald.'

Having digested all this information, I was left with one conclusion.

'And now you suspect Alexis of being a double-agent?' I said.

Jack shrugged his shoulders. 'You tell me, Larry, because from where I am sitting, not to mention the Colonel, she cannot be disregarded. The fact that the escape routes are compromised may be just the tip of the iceberg.'

'Accusing Alexis is a dangerous thing to say without any

proof. From what you've just told me, she tried to avoid being coerced by the Germans.'

I got up and walked to the window. I needed time to think but it was clear there was no time. I had to act and I had to act quickly. Jack came over and stood by me. Fatma Hanim and her daughter were returning to the house with more food. We stepped outside while they laid the table. Jack asked the two Greeks to come over and join the discussion. We walked into the olive grove out of earshot of the others. It was there that the Greeks told me the Italians on Samos had been paid by Theo when he was alive to turn a blind eye to the escapees coming from the other islands en route to Turkey. When they told me the date things started to go wrong, I realised it was straight after his death.

'Fine,' I said after they'd finished. 'What's the plan now?'

'It's clear there's a songbird in the organisation and the Colonel wants you to sort it out. He has great faith in you. These men will get you back to Athens via a different route to the way you came. We want you to radio in every few days with an update. The code name for this operation will be Icarus. Anything transmitted with this name will tell us it has something to do with our meeting. The same goes if Cairo transmits to you using that name. Brief Dancer on this — and any others you may feel you need to involve. Stelios and Aris for instance. We'll leave it to you as to whether or not you let Loukas in on this, but remember, he's close to everyone of importance in Poseidon.'

Jack asked if there was anything I needed from him. All I really needed was a little time to figure out what I would do, but I did add that a little extra money wouldn't go astray. Paying people off was expensive. I left Turkey that night, accompanied by the two Greeks. Before I got in the boat, he handed me a wad of money.

'There you are my friend. That should keep the wolves at bay.'

We shook hands. Neither of us knowing if we would ever see each other again.

Chapter 22

I returned to Plateia Amerikis and found it unusually quiet for a warm day. Under a canopy of green trees in the centre of the plateia, the kafenia owners had set up several small wooden tables and chairs. By this time, they should have been occupied, even if there was little to serve, yet there was no-one around except for two men in smart suits who struck me as looking very much out of place. Even the kafenia themselves were empty. When I passed one, I noticed the owner standing near the doorway looking nervous and I knew immediately something was wrong. I had almost reached the apartment block when I spotted Chryssa and Yiannis hurrying towards me.

'Kapetan,' Yiannis said in a low voice. 'Don't go inside! Keep walking. Make your way to the pharmacy, but don't follow us. Whatever you do, don't go inside the apartment.'

The children kept walking and quickly disappeared around the corner. I was tired and urgently needed to catch up with Dancer, Aris and Stelios, but that had to wait. I did as Yiannis said and kept on walking past the apartment heading away in the opposite direction towards the metro. I then doubled back to Patission via another road making sure I wasn't being followed.

When I arrived at the pharmacy, the closed sign had been placed on the door. I knocked three times and pressed my nose to the glass. Yiannis slid back the bolt on the door to let me in.

'You're sure you weren't followed?' he asked, glancing up and down the street

'Quite sure.'

Maria was sitting at the kitchen table, folding bandages. She pulled herself up with difficulty and gave me a big hug. Her face was pale and drawn and her eyes red and swollen. It struck me just how gaunt she had become. In fact, all three looked as if they'd lost weight in the short time I'd been away. The other thing that struck me was the overpowering scent of candles and burning incense next to a silver-framed icon on a shelf. Beside it was a plate of *Kollyva* — food for the dead.

'We've been on the lookout for you every day for over several weeks now. As no-one heard from you, we thought something bad had happened. Are you alright? You look unkempt. You must be more careful.'

'I had an urgent assignment,' I replied.

'Of course, Kapetan. I know you can't say any more. I understand.'

'Maria, what's happened?'

'The Gestapo conducted a midnight raid on all the buildings in Plateia Amerikis a week ago.'

'Do you know why?'

'No. They wanted the names of everyone who lived there. All the apartments were searched.'

I scoured my brain to see if I'd left any incriminating evidence. Then I remembered the notebook. Thankfully, I'd had the good sense to hide it behind the mirror.

Maria continued. 'They pulled Vangelis the janitor from his bed and made him knock on all the apartment doors. When the occupants opened them, the surprised residents were confronted with a search at gunpoint.'

'*Panagia*! What happened when they got to my apartment?'

'You don't have to worry. Vangelis's wife went to warn you. When you didn't answer, she checked it before they got there. She thought the place looked too tidy and gathered you'd gone away so she quickly threw a few clothes on the floor and the bed to make it look more lived in. She left just as they reached your floor. Naturally the Gestapo wanted to know why no-one answered and ordered Vangelis to open the door. They searched your room and seeing no-one there, questioned him as to your whereabouts, but he said he had no idea where you were. Maybe you'd gone to visit relatives. They made a note of that and then ransacked the place. I don't think they found anything incriminating. If they had, they would have taken Vangelis in for questioning. After taking details of all the occupants in the building, they moved on to the next. When Vangelis called me the next day, Chryssa, Yiannis and I went there and took some of your belongings. We have no idea who they were targeting or what they were looking for — maybe guns — who knows, but it's not safe to return. I've organised another safe-house for you.'

'Does anyone else know I'm no longer there?' I asked.

'No-one. Only us. As far as Vangelis is concerned, he thinks you still occupy the apartment.'

'Maria, I have to get back into the apartment. I left something of importance there.'

She looked at me despairingly. 'You can't let anyone see you return. The Gestapo are watching the area.' She saw the look in my eyes and threw her hands up in the air. 'Okay, we'll find a way.'

I took a seat at the table while Chryssa checked the soup for her mother.

'What else is troubling you?' I asked. 'I can see you've been crying. A raid would not cause you to cry. You've been through worse.'

I looked at the candle, the hot wax already pooling around the base. Maria started to shake and tears welled up in her eyes. Yiannis put a comforting hand on his mother's shoulder but I could see he was trying hard to hold back his own tears. I noticed the table was set for four. There was a place missing.

'Where's your father? What's happened?'

At the mention of him, Maria let out a harrowing long wail. Chryssa stopped what she was doing and held her close.

'The bastards executed him,' Maria said, spittle dribbling from her mouth.

'Who?' I blurted out.

She made a futile attempt to wipe her eyes with the corner of her apron. 'The Germans of course. Ten days ago — in Kokkinia. They executed him in cold blood. An old man who never laid a finger on anyone.'

I reached for her shaking hands and held them tight. 'Tell me what happened.'

'He went to see his brother and was meant to return before curfew. For some reason, he stayed longer than usual and left it too late. In the early hours of the morning, the area was surrounded.'

'Another *blocco*?'

She nodded. This time it was worse. There was fierce retaliation. The *andartes* tried to escape by causing chaos, throwing grenades, etc., but it was useless and it only served to provoke the Germans more. They had plenty of reinforcements. Some of the men were taken away and interrogated. My father was one of them. When he told them he had no idea who the *andartes* were, he was beaten and taken to a cell. The next day, he was escorted into a walled yard along with almost two hundred men. They were kept there for hours in the hot sun. Someone came to tell me and I went there as quickly as I could, but the place was surrounded by armoured trucks and Germans with machine guns were posted around the perimeter. It was impossible to get anywhere near them. I even tried to bribe them but it didn't work. We were beaten back with guns and sticks to let more trucks pass. But I saw them,' Maria screamed. 'I saw them.'

'Saw who, Maria?'

'The masked informers. There must have been at least five. They were taken through the gates by the Germans. Someone found a place behind the wall where there was a hole big enough for us to look through and we took it in turns to see what was going on. I couldn't comprehend it. The men were split into different groups and forced to sit on the ground. Then the masked men went up and down the lines and pointed out some of the men. They were either shot on the spot by the collaborators or escorted in groups by the Germans, lined up against a wall and mowed down by machine gun. The women screamed in terror. Some fainted. The ground ran red with blood and the smell of gunshot drifted through the air with the cries of the dying. At one point, my hopes soared when I realised my father was still sitting there and I prayed to the *Panagia* to save him.' Maria started to shake again and tears streaked her cheeks. 'It was useless; the *Panagia* wasn't listening that day. A masked man with a collaborator stopped next to him and pointed. They never uttered a word. The collaborator aimed his gun at my father and shot him in the back of the head. The only thing that stopped me fainting was the thought that I would be trampled on or shot by the Germans. Only five men survived that day of horror.'

I knew no words of comfort would ease her pain and I sat in silence wondering when this would all end. After a while, Maria straightened her back, took a deep breath, and wiped her eyes.

'This is the cross we have to bear, but with bad news there is also good.'

'Do you mean Sicily?'

'Of course. The Germans have always thought the Italians never had the same fighting spirit for their motherland. Maybe that's why they are stepping up retribution. They are taking their anger out on us.'

Sadly, I thought this to be true.

'What else has happened while I've been away?' I asked, after a while.

'I've seen very little of anyone. Occasionally parcels of medicines arrived from some unknown source, but apart from that, everyone has kept a low profile. Oh yes, there is something else. I should have told you before rather than burden you with our troubles. The White Rose has been trying to reach you. It appears to be urgent. I gather she was not too happy when no-one could find you.'

At the mention of Alexis, I had a sudden feeling of anxiousness and wondered if she suspected I'd been in touch with SOE in Turkey.

'Maria, tell me something? Who else knew I lived at the apartment in Plateia Amerikis?'

She looked surprised. 'Why Kapetan, no-one except for *O Lykos*. It was he who asked me to find a place for you and he asked me not to tell anyone. Of course, Chryssa and Yiannis know — and my father knew. Why do you ask?'

'Do you think any of your customers knew? Maybe someone suspected me of not being a local.'

'Kapetan, quite a few of my customers are not locals,' Maria said, upset at my comment. 'They come from afar because word has gone out that I can help them, so a new face is something they have come to expect. We are careful. You have no need to worry. Besides, I would never put my children at risk.'

'Did the White Rose know where I lived?'

'No. I told you, the Wolf asked us not to tell anyone. If you chose to tell anyone yourself, that is your prerogative.'

'Fine, we will arrange a meeting with the White Rose, but there are things I need to do first. I must get back into the apartment as soon as possible. Can you help me?'

'Can it wait until tomorrow? It will soon be curfew. You can sleep here tonight and in the morning we will find a way. Then I will take you to your new safe-house.'

I could see her nerves were on edge and didn't want to push it any more. We ate a meal of watery soup and afterwards she showed me to my bed — the one her father slept in. After hearing of the old man's execution, and knowing what I did, I had a lousy night's sleep and woke up feeing worse than before.

When I went downstairs, Chryssa was waiting for me.

'Here,' she said, indicating to a pile of old clothes hanging over the back of the chair. 'Put them on.'

I took one look and could see they were women's clothes.

'It was my mother's idea. You are to dress up as an old lady.

Do you think you can do it? Then I will take you to the apartment. She will meet us there.'

I confess it wasn't the first time I'd assumed the role of an elderly person on a mission, but usually it was in the guise of an old man, not a woman. I shrugged my shoulders. I'd do anything to retrieve the notebook. Chryssa went into the pharmacy to join her brother while I changed. When she returned five minutes later, she burst out laughing.

'You make a fine old woman, Kapetan, but we must do something about your head.'

I had changed into a long black skirt and top and wore a pair of worn-out old shoes — the clothes of a woman in mourning, but I had nothing to cover my head. Chryssa gave me a black scarf which I tied in a knot under my chin. She stood back and surveyed me.

'No, it's not quite right. Your face is too exposed.'

She went upstairs and returned with a large black crocheted shawl. 'Try this,' she said, throwing it over my head and shoulders.

The shawl was voluminous enough to partially hide my man's figure also. Chryssa pulled it down over my forehead and stood back. Lastly she added a pair of wire-rimmed glasses. 'Much better. Now walk around the table.'

I did as I was told, but still Chryssa wasn't satisfied. She went back upstairs and this time returned with her grandfather's walking stick and one of her mother's handbags.

'Now try again. This time, stoop a little. Remember you are old and frail.'

Chryssa clapped. 'Bravo Kapetan,' she smiled. 'Now we can go.'

'I can see you've done this sort of thing before,' I remarked, hobbling out of the pharmacy.

'No. I haven't, but my mother has and I watched her,' she replied. 'I think she will approve.'

The pharmacy was already filling with customers when Chryssa and I left. Yiannis gave us a nod of approval and tried hard to stifle a boyish snigger.

The kafenia were just opening when we arrived in Plateia Amerikis. There was no sign of the smart-suited Gestapo but one could never be sure, so I took my time hobbling towards my apartment. Chryssa was by my side and I looped my arm through hers to steady myself. When we stepped into the foyer, Maria was waiting for us.

'You have five minutes,' she said, handing me the key. 'I sent Vangelis out on an errand.'

I hurried to my apartment and quickly retrieved the notebook taped to the back of the mirror. It didn't take much to see that the Gestapo had done a thorough search of the place. Some of the drawers were still open and I was thankful I'd had the foresight to hide it where I did. I slipped it under my clothes and returned downstairs.

'Did you find what you were looking for?' Maria asked, as I handed back the key.

I nodded and thanked her.

'Then it was worth going to all this trouble,' she laughed, looking me up and down.

She congratulated her daughter on doing a good job. 'I taught you well, *koritsi mou*. Although you didn't have to give him my best handbag!'

If the situation hadn't been dire, it would have been funny, but we all knew we were playing with fire. Maria leaned closer and whispered the address of my new safe-house.

'It's only a few streets away. You will have to go alone. It's too dangerous for us to accompany you. It looks like the Gestapo are back again. We will bring your belongings to you as soon as possible. Now go quickly. They are expecting you.'

I stepped outside the apartment and saw two men sitting at a table under the trees again reading newspapers. I couldn't be sure if they were the same ones as yesterday and didn't hang around to check. Number 70, Kyprou Street, was a house set back from the road by a narrow strip of garden lined with pomegranate and orange trees. It had a faded grandeur about it. The entrance was through a rusty wrought iron gate leading to the main door. To one side of the door was a life-sized statue of Aphrodite which looked quite out of character for the setting. The door was ajar and behind it was a red velvet curtain edged with elaborate silk and gold tassels. On the wall was a discreet sign in gold lettering on a black background which read "Please ring the bell for assistance". My new safe-house was a brothel.

Chapter 23

A hand dripping with gemstone-studded rings on every finger and painted fingernails drew back the curtains and a middle-aged woman in an emerald green velvet dress greeted me. The dress was fitted and low-cut, revealing her ample breasts and round figure. At the point where her cleavage met the neckline of the dress, she had pinned a corsage of silk flowers. She smelt of floral perfume, powdery and slightly overbearing.

'Kyria Rosa?' I asked.

'I've been expecting you,' she said, shaking my hand and at the same time casting a glance at my attire. 'But not like this. Kyria Maria did a good job, but your hands give you away. You must be careful.'

Having assured myself that this was indeed Rosa, I removed my shawl. She moved aside to let me pass and then closed and bolted the door. 'Come through and meet the girls.'

She led me through the hallway filled with potted plants and mirrors, into the parlour where three girls where sitting on velvet couches chatting. At the sight of me, they stood up to greet me, trying hard not to snigger.

'This is the gentleman who will be with us for a few days,'

Rosa said. 'Please make him feel at home.' She turned to me and saw the concerned look on my face. 'The girls are with us, Kapetan. You don't have to worry.'

She pulled one of them aside. 'Maroulia, take the gentleman to his room and see that he is comfortable.'

At that moment the bell rang. Rosa ushered us out of the room and down the hallway towards a back door which led to a small garden. Outside was a tiny outhouse once used for laundry and pastry-making but which had now been turned into a bedroom. It was sparse but adequate.

'This is my room,' Maroulia said. 'You can use it while you are here. I will share with one of the other girls.'

Rosa joined us carrying my bags. 'That was Chryssa. She brought these for you.' She gestured to Maroulia to return to the house. When we were alone, she asked me to sit in the only chair in the room while she sat on the bed. She wanted to talk.

'You will be quite safe here, Kapetan. We make an effort to put on a respectable front for the authorities in order not to attract the wrong attention. Many of our clients are married men and they know they can rely on our discretion. We also have a few Italian clients, but no Germans. We all work for the Resistance and make no bones about the fact that we use sex to get whatever information we can out of our clients. Some of them are collaborators. Their day of reckoning will come, but for the moment, any information which we deem will help the Resistance, we pass on. The rest of the time, we are discreet. I am sure you understand what I mean. Are you comfortable with this? If not, we will move you somewhere else immediately.'

I told her I had worked with brothels in the past and that some of the prostitutes had been extremely adept in obtaining information. She was pleased with my answer although was quick to point out that she didn't class her "girls" as prostitutes.

'We prefer not to use that word,' she said, matter-of-factly. 'I refer to my girls as "companions". It sounds a little more respectable. Wouldn't you agree?'

I shifted uncomfortably in my chair. Rosa was a formidable looking woman and, I surmised, a woman of the world. I had no idea what her background was but by the look of things, she had accumulated quite a bit of wealth. Neither she nor her girls were skinny as were most Greek women these days, leaving me to believe that they were paid handsomely by their clients, either with money or in food parcels.

I didn't judge her. In fact, I admired her. She reminded me of so many Greek women I'd encountered — tough, resilient and feisty. I never underestimated them. Throughout my career working in the Balkans, I'd always been told it was the war that made them tough. Which war, I wasn't sure. There had been so many. One thing was for sure, I was happy to have them on my side.

Then I thought of Alexis. Another tough woman who as yet, was probably the only Greek woman I had never been able to make out. That was about to change though.

Rosa continued. 'You are free to come and go. There will be no questions asked. If we have a client, please be careful. Use this back entrance and don't come into the house at all unless we invite you. You'll have to climb over the wall to leave but I'm sure that won't bother you. Underneath that dress, you strike me as a fit man. The wall backs onto the garden of a house in the next street. No-one lives there since the family died during the famine. From there you can slip past the side of the house and into the road. Fortunately, this is a quiet neighbourhood but be careful, especially on Sunday when everyone goes to church. Is there anything you wish to ask?'

I wanted to ask how many people she had helped but I already had an idea. It was quite a few. She and Maria had been friends ever since Maria moved into the neighbourhood. She was probably a good few years older than Maria and looked well for her age, especially now when most people looked unhealthy due to the dire circumstances. Knowing that Rosa and her girls were prone to sexually transmitted diseases, Maria kept an eye on their health by supplying pills, giving arsenic-based injections, or by making douching solutions late at night in her kitchen. And on more than one occasion, she had been called upon to perform an abortion, once telling me that God will forgive her sins because in wartime one is forced to do things they would otherwise walk away from. I knew what she meant. There was one question I did want to ask her about though.

'Rosa,' I said approaching the subject cautiously. 'I know you have helped evacuate Allied soldiers from Greece, but did you ever help children as well?'

'Only a few. The ones that came to me were Jewish. Some arrived here through the Wolf's contacts. From what I know, he had quite a few safe-houses for them. They were never here more than a few days. As soon as they received their new documents they were sent to the islands. From there to Turkey and on to Palestine.'

'Do you know if they ever reached their destination?'

She shrugged her shoulders. 'How can we know? Maybe after the war someone will contact us. Why do you ask?

'No reason. I just like to know if all the operations went according to plan. That's all.'

She narrowed her eyes and gave me the same look Maria gave when she knew I was fishing.

'Maria said you were a wily one. Is everything alright?'

I assured her it was just my inquisitive mind.

She got up to leave. 'Good, but you would let us know if you thought something was wrong wouldn't you? We don't want to end up looking down the barrel of a gun.'

After she left, I undressed and washed myself in cold water from a large earthenware jug, and put my own clothes back on. The midday sun was streaming through the open door onto the bed. I desperately needed to catch up on some sleep and the bed looked inviting, but there was too much to do. I went outside and peered over the wall to check my escape route. There was no time to waste and I jumped over and made my way to see Dancer.

It had been a few weeks since I last saw him and I hardly recognised him. He'd grown a beard and wore a large moustache and was sitting in the square peacefully playing backgammon and drinking mountain tea with the priest. In that moment, it was hard to believe there was a war on. When they saw me coming towards them, I knew immediately something was wrong. They stood up to greet me. The priest shook my hand and excused himself.

'What's wrong?' I asked Dancer when we were alone.

'Some bad news I'm afraid. Let's go inside.'

Once in the apartment, Dancer pulled out a chair and told me to sit down. 'You're not going to like this,' he said, sitting down next to me and rubbing his hands together nervously.

I braced myself for the worst. 'Spit it out, man!'

There was an ambush somewhere between Karpenisi and Lamia. The Wolf got word of a German munitions transport going through the area. Apparently it was headed west for Agrinio. Word was that it was to aid the Italians in the region because of the attack on Sicily. The Wolf gathered some of his men and the plan was that they lie in wait at a certain section in the mountains until the trucks passed by and then attack. When they did, they found the trucks were not filled with ammunition at all. Quite the opposite. The *andartes* fired the first shot and immediately, German machine guns opened fire from the back of the trucks covering their soldiers who poured out into the mountainside after the men. Within a few minutes, more armoured trucks arrived up the road blocking off a retreat by the *andartes*. By all accounts it was a blood bath.'

'And the Wolf?' I asked.

'He was lucky. He escaped but I believe he lost almost half his men. Some were captured alive and were brought back here to Athens.'

I swore loudly to let out my emotions. 'So it was a set-up. Do we know who the songbird was?'

Dancer shrugged his shoulder. 'I don't know any more. I believe the Wolf is here in Athens at the moment.'

It took a while for me to digest this news. In a matter of weeks, things had gone from good to bad.

'How are Aris and Stelios?' I asked. 'Do they know about all this?'

'They're fine. I believe Aris met up with the Wolf. He didn't say much though, only that a couple of the men were some of those he trained a while back when he was with Leonidas.'

'What about Cairo? Anything of importance to report?'

'Nothing out of the usual. Oh yes, there was one thing. They mentioned something about Icarus –"How is Icarus?" — Yes, that was it.'

'When are you transmitting again?'

'Tonight. After the church is closed. Are there any messages?'

'Just tell them Icarus is fine.'

'That's all?'

'That's all.'

Dancer was too good an agent to ask where I'd been and what Icarus was. He was just glad to have me back.

'I've moved by the way,' I said. 'The Germans are staking out Plateia Amerikis.'

'Do you think they're on to you?'

'Not sure. All the buildings are being watched. Maria has found me another safe-house. It's temporary. It's not a place to meet up so if you need me in a hurry, you can reach me via the pharmacy.'

*

When I met up with Loukas he looked in a bad way. The deaths of so many comrades weighed heavily on his mind, especially coming so soon after the massacre at Kato Hora. Kostas was with him and they were talking about Kondoumaris and the notebook.

'If he had been alive, we would have known what the Gestapo were doing when the *andartes* were brought here,' Kostas said. 'Maybe we could have saved some of them before they were transferred to Haidari and executed.' He paused for a moment. 'I wonder what did happen to that notebook.'

'Did you ever see it,' Loukas asked, 'or did he just tell you about it? I mean, did it ever exist? It's dangerous to keep notes when you're working for the Germans.'

'No. I never saw it, but he told me about it. Why would I doubt him? His information was always correct.'

The strain was showing on both of them and I wanted to speak up but I wasn't sure about Kostas. I still had the feeling he didn't fully trust me because I represented the British government, and, as a communist, he didn't want them to bring the monarchy back. For now, we were comrades and needed each other.

After a while, Kostas left. When we were alone I asked Loukas how Anna was.

'She's fine, thank God. The wound has almost healed and she wanted to come with us when we tried to ambush the Germans. I persuaded her to stay behind. I'm glad I did.'

'I'm sorry about what happened,' I replied. 'Do you know who set you up?'

Loukas shook his head. 'I've racked my brains, but can't be sure. Two of our men overheard the Germans talking about the transports in Larissa and reported back to us. It seemed genuine.'

'And you trust these men?' I asked.

'They've never let me down before.'

'Then maybe the Germans deliberately sent out the word knowing full well that someone would send the information back to you.'

'It seems that way.'

'Or there's a songbird amongst us.'

Loukas studied me carefully. 'That has crossed my mind. What do you think?'

I took a deep breath. Even though Jack Martins had warned

me to be careful about whom I confided in, I knew I had to have someone from Poseidon on my side to help solve this and Loukas was the obvious choice. We went back a long way. He sensed something was bothering me.

'Come on, brother. What is it?'

'Loukas, can I have your word you will not breathe a word of what I am about to tell you to anyone?'

He leaned forward and shook my hand. 'You have it.'

'You're aware I've been away. I can't say where, but I have it on authority that there is definitely a songbird amongst us — and one that knows too much.'

He lit up a cigarette and sat back in the chair. 'Go on.'

'There are two things. The first is that some of those unfortunate souls we've been sending to Turkey have not made it, especially over the past few months.'

His eyes narrowed. 'Does this include the children?'

'I'm afraid so,' I said with a heavy sigh. 'Instead of Palestine, some have ended up in Poland. For some reason, the traffic stopped. Only a few got through and that may be a ploy so that no-one would notice.'

'This is all we need.' Loukas replied, swearing angrily. 'There are quite a few escape routes. Which ones are you referring to?'

'Those around Samos'

This time his swearing evoked the Virgin. Always a bad sign when a Greek was angry. He took a deep drag on the cigarette and leaned forward, blowing a cloud of cigarette smoke out of the side of his mouth.

'You know what you're saying don't you?' I nodded. This was something that would either bond us further or tear us apart. 'It's Alexis' territory. She's in charge.'

'I know, and it doesn't sit well with me. I was told that there are two fishermen who were once with Poseidon but decided to set up their own escape route going further south. A bit of a circuitous route from what I gather but it was safer. Their human cargo made it. It makes me think they smelt a rat.'

'Who are these men?'

'Fishermen from Pefkos. Stephanos and Pavlos. That's all I know.'

Loukas had no idea who they were.

'Okay, don't let's beat around the bush,' he said after taking all this in. 'Are you suggesting Alexis has been compromised?'

'I'm not saying that. But *someone* has betrayed us. As far as I'm concerned — and Cairo — until we get to the bottom of this, everyone is under suspicion. In a short space of time we've had too many things go wrong. Maybe they're connected. Maybe not. But we cannot escape the fact that in all likelihood there *is* a songbird in our midst.'

Loukas got up and paced the room. I told him it was the last thing I wanted to burden him with, especially after another massacre in the mountains.

'You are the only person I can talk too. You and my own men. We have to get to the bottom of it, and sooner rather than later so that no more lives are lost.'

He remained silent, deep in thought.

'You said there were two things you wanted to tell me. What's the other?'

'It's about the missing notebook. I have it.'

He stopped pacing and stared at me. 'Why didn't you say so when Kostas was here?'

'I told you, you are the only one I can trust. This is not a slight against Kostas. The fewer people who know, the better. We were there on the night Kondoumaris was murdered, but like you, were surprised when he was murdered. It's not what we had expected to happen. I was with Aris, Stelios and Dancer. We knew he always arrived home late at night and were about to enter his apartment when a black car arrived. Two men got out and went inside. The car waited nearby but it was too dark to see who was in it. Then we saw Kondoumaris return — earlier than usual. Soon after, the men reappeared and left in the waiting car. When we entered the apartment, we found Kondoumaris dead. I found the notebook in one of his socks when I turned him over. It was evident that whoever killed him was looking for something. Probably the notebook. We didn't hang around and were gone by the time the neighbours were alerted.'

'Did you see Kostas arrive?' Loukas asked. 'He said he had an appointment with him.'

'No we'd left by then. It wasn't safe to hang around.'

'Why were you after him? You know he was one of us.'

'No hard feelings, Loukas, but I've been trained not to trust someone who works for both the enemy and us. I have met quite a few double agents in my time and I prefer to conduct my own checks as far as that's concerned.'

He sat down opposite me. 'The notebook. What did it have in it? Did it prove he was double-crossing us or not?'

'It was as you said. He was one of us.'

Loukas smiled. 'Then all this was a waste of time?'

'I'm afraid not. Quite the opposite. It seems that Kondoumaris had been taking Herr Franz Keller to meet a woman. She turned out to be Greek. That's probably what he wanted to tell Kostas.'

'Who was this woman? A *putana*?'

'You know as well as I do that such a man in his position would not be with a prostitute — especially a Greek. No he never actually said the name.'

I could see Loukas didn't quite understand what I was getting at.

'Most of what he wrote was of no importance, but hidden amongst the pages was a code, most likely to throw the Germans off the scent if they discovered it. It was the last few pages that were important. He named the woman by her initials — in Cyrillic.'

'What are they?' he asked with a calmness that belied the anger brewing inside him.

'A.T.'

He got up, went over to the window and stood there for a while with his back to me, taking it all in.

'*Aspro Triandafilo*,' he replied, his voice, barely a murmur. 'The White Rose.'

I would have given anything not to have heard those words.

Chapter 24

Athens, July 1943.

That same evening, we received news from Cairo that Mussolini had been toppled in a palace coup. His successor was Marshal Badoglio who was known to be less committed to the Axis cause than his predecessor. How this would play out in Greece, we had yet to find out, but the Germans were not caught napping. The atmosphere in Athens was tense. Massive German tanks thundered through the city and surrounded the Italian HQ. The Wehrmacht was out in force. Even in a city where communication was difficult, news like this travelled fast and few Athenians ventured out onto the streets, fearing an angry backlash.

I was in my bed fast asleep when Maroulia knocked on my door with my breakfast.

'Have you heard?' she said, putting the tray down on the bedside table.

'Yes, I heard. It's good news.' I answered. 'How did you find out?'

'We had Italian clients last night and they were in a

particularly good mood. When we asked what it was that made them so happy, they said we'd have good news today. We had no idea what it was but when we were alone, we tuned into the BBC and heard it. It's the beginning of the end isn't it, Kapetan?'

'Let's hope so, but you know the Germans. They will not take kindly to this and the war is a long way from over.'

She asked if I minded if she washed and changed. Without waiting for my answer, she took a few clean clothes from the cupboard and went behind a painted screen to undress. I sat on the bed to eat my dry rusks, honey and milk, while she draped her clothes over the screen and started to wash herself. My eyes fell on her lace-edged silk knickers. They were exquisite and it wasn't hard to imagine her wearing them. Maroulia was a beautiful woman.

'Hand me a towel will you?' she asked. 'There's a clean one in the chest near the door.'

I opened the large wooden chest and pulled one out from amongst a pile of exquisite hand-woven and embroidered cloths, and handed it to her over the screen. She started to hum a Greek tune as she dried herself. Moments later, she reappeared wearing her clean dress and drying her hair. I noticed she smelt of fresh orange blossom and commented on it.

'It's orange blossom cologne. Maria makes it especially for me. She's very kind you know. We were sorry to hear about her father.'

She finished drying her hair, emptied the water in the wash basin outside in the garden and picked up the tray.

'Kapetan,' she said, as she was about to leave. 'I'm not exactly sure what it is you do. All I know is that Rosa says it's important, but I want you to know that if ever you need my help, I am here for you.'

When she'd gone, I lay back on the bed thinking about the previous day's conversation with Loukas. He had found it hard to deal with the thought that Alexis could be a songbird. As for me, well I felt worse, if that was at all possible. I had missed the obvious — the White Rose. All our conversations were in Greek. *Aspro Triantafilo.* It was so obvious. Loukas's first thoughts were to confront Alexis, starting with the escape routes. "Beat the truth out of her if necessary" was how he phrased it. In the end, he calmed down and agreed with me that we had to find out for sure if she was involved. I reminded him that everyone was under suspicion until proven innocent. There was one thing we both agreed on: if A.T. did turn out to be Alexis then the matter would have to be dealt with swiftly and quietly. It wasn't in the interests of the network for this to leak out.

There was much to sort out and such a short time to do it all in. The news about Mussolini's downfall meant that this mess with Poseidon had to be sorted out as soon as possible. There wasn't a moment to spare. Since Turkey, I had mulled over again and again what to do and how to do it. I always knew that somehow or another, I had to deal with Alexis, but the latest revelations meant I had to strike quickly. I decided to pay her a visit and I was not going to give her prior warning and go through Maria. I would turn up unannounced.

*

I took the train to Kifissia. When I arrived the German presence had been intensified. My papers were thoroughly checked and

I was asked what I was doing in the area before I was allowed to leave the station. Armoured vehicles were everywhere. Knowing that Ambassador Marinetti was a follower of Il Duce, I decided to take an alternative route to the Petrakis villa; one that took me past Villa Aphrodite. I was curious to see what was going on. I needn't have bothered. The road was blocked off. There was a kiosk at the end of the road. I bought a magazine and casually asked the kiosk owner what was happening.

'Didn't you hear?' he answered. 'Mussolini has been toppled in a Palace Coup. The Germans are furious and have surrounded the Ambassador's house. He's under house arrest until they get a guarantee that the Italian army will not turn on them. No-one can get in or out. If I was you, I wouldn't hang around here.'

I decided to heed his advice, turned back and took a circuitous route to the Petrakis villa. Thankfully there was no-one around and I was conscious of the sound of my own footsteps on the cobbled road which seemed particularly loud. At this time of the year Kifissia was glorious. The trees were green, the gardens in full bloom, and the sun was beating down, highlighting the variegated colours of the leaves and flowers with an intensity only mother-nature is capable of. I took off my jacket and slung it over my shoulder and for a brief moment enjoyed the peace and tranquillity which I knew would not last.

I turned into the driveway and found Alexis's driver washing the car next to a dense hedgerow of pink and white hydrangeas. He looked surprised to see me.

'I was not informed that you had an appointment with the Kyria,' he said, dropping the rag in the water and wiping his hands. 'Otherwise I would have picked you up to save you the trouble of such a long journey, especially on such a hot day.'

I assured him it was quite alright and that this was merely a social call as I happened to be in the area. It was clear that he was not amused by answer and to my surprise, he drew out a gun and pointed it at me.

'No-one is allowed here without prior notice,' he replied, in a somewhat threatening voice. 'I am going to have to ask you to remain here while I let the Kyria know.'

This was the last thing I wanted. It would ruin the element of surprise. I always suspected the driver doubled up as a body-guard. Now I knew for sure.

'Here search the pockets,' I said, handing him my jacket. 'You'll find my gun in there.

He took it out and slipped it into the back of his trousers while I turned out my trouser pockets to further prove the point that I wasn't carrying another. Still not satisfied, he frisked me, running his hands down my body and the inside of my legs.

'Satisfied?' I asked.

'Wait here while I check with the Kyria. He turned to walk away.

I caught his arm. 'Please don't ruin the element of surprise,' I said with a wink, knowing full well he was aware of the night we spent together. 'I'm sure it will be fine. And you have my gun.'

'Alright. Go on. I will probably get a telling off for this though,' he replied with a heavy sigh.

I shook his hand and thanked him. He watched me walk all the way to the portico. I rang the bell and waited. The driver returned to washing the car. No-one came and I rang again.

After several minutes I heard heavy footsteps in the hallway. Even before the door opened, I knew who it was — Rada, and as usual, she wore her unpleasant face.

'Good day,' I said, before she could speak. 'I'm here to see Kyria Alexis.'

I didn't give her chance to reply and walked straight past her into the hallway.

Rada angrily started to call out for me to stop.

The drawing room door opened and Alexis appeared. She was wearing the same white dress she'd worn that day on the terrace at Shepheard's.

'What on earth is going on?' she asked. 'All this commotion...'

When she saw me standing in the middle of the hallway, she stopped mid-sentence.

Rada started to explain that I had barged in unannounced.

'That's enough,' Alexis said to her, gesturing to her to stop. 'Cousin Nikos doesn't need an appointment. He's family.'

'I just happened to be in the area,' I said, trying to defuse the tension. 'And I thought I'd pay you a surprise visit.'

It wasn't hard to see that Alexis was taken aback by my presence, but as ever, she put on a stellar performance. She came over and kissed my cheek.

'Dearest, Nikos. It's always a pleasure to see you. Come inside and tell me what you've been up to.'

I followed her back into the drawing room, casting a quick glace over my shoulder at Rada who threw me a look that could kill.

When we'd entered the room, I closed the door behind me and turned the key. Alexis heard the click and spun around.

'What is this...?'

Before she could finish, I grabbed her and pushed her against the wall, holding her jaw tightly to stop her screaming out.

'Look at me,' I said in a low whisper.

In that moment, she looked so fragile. Her dark brown eyes, flecked with droplets of honey, penetrated mine, and her mouth, full and inviting with just the slightest trace of red lipstick, quivered sensuously. She had a small beauty spot at the side of one of her eyebrows which I'd never noticed until now. Her skin looked smooth and inviting and I was all too aware of the swell of her breasts against the fabric of her dress. She tried to struggle but it was useless.

'Look at me,' I said again, holding her tighter.

Her lips were like a magnet, drawing me to her. I forcefully pressed my mouth over hers, wanting to taste the fullness and sensuality of that mouth again. It was delicious.

Her struggles gave way to desire. Whether it was the body or the mind that gave way first, I don't know. I didn't care. I just wanted her and she wanted me. My hand reached for her breast. Her nipples were hard which aroused me even more. I pressed my body closer to hers until eventually she threw her arms around me, moaning with desire. Every move we made only served to arouse our need for each other. I reached under her dress and pulled her knickers down. She was warm and moist with desire, and I, as hard as I have ever been. I pulled her away from the wall and lay her on to the couch, devouring every part of her body as I had done that night in the Hotel Apollo, and as I had fantasized, night after night since laying eyes on her. In that moment, nothing could have come between us. Such is the power of animal magnetism.

When we had finished, I pulled myself away from her,

fastening my pants. I picked up her knickers from the floor and handed them to her. Her smile was devoid of embarrassment.

'You took them off, you can put them back on again,' she said, with a seductive voice and at the same time moving her legs and buttocks until I had completed the task. The dark shadow of her pubic hair under the silky cream fabric looked inviting but I restrained myself from taking her again

'How about a cognac?' I said, pulling her dress down in an attempt to make her look more respectable.

'Help yourself. You know where it is.'

I went over to the cabinet where she kept an array of fine drinks and poured us both a glass.

When I turned around, she was sitting up, buttoning her dress and looking at me with a strange expression. I noticed her Beretta peeking out from under a cushion. She appeared embarrassed when she realised I'd seen it. I asked if she intended to use it on me. She smiled but never answered the question.

'Where have you been?' she asked. 'You disappeared without a trace. I was worried something had happened to you.'

I would have given anything to have believed she meant it, but I knew better. It was time to stop fooling myself. I picked up her silver cigarette case and took out two cigarettes, lit them and gave one to her.

'I had things to do. You know how it is. And you,' I asked, 'how are you?'

'It's been hectic. Quite a lot has happened since I last saw you.' She took a long drag on the cigarette and exhaled the smoke before continuing. 'I'm sure you must have heard by now that the Wolf's men walked into a trap. Too many were killed. It's taken its toll on morale.'

'Yes, I heard. Thank God Loukas wasn't killed. That would have been a disaster for us all. Do you have any idea what happened?'

We locked eyes. Her gaze was unwavering. 'No. We're still looking into it.' She changed the subject quickly. 'Anyway, at least there's good news regarding Italy.'

'I gather that Villa Aphrodite is surrounded with German armoured vehicles. How is the Ambassador taking this? As a supporter of Il Duce, he can't be too happy.'

'He's not a bad man, Larry.'

I noticed she called me Larry and not Nikos. The lovemaking had had the desired effect. She was softening.

'He's the enemy, my dear. Have you forgotten?'

'I haven't forgotten at all, but he's been very good to me — and to Theo when he was alive.'

She mentioned Theo almost as an afterthought.

'How's that?'

'From the moment he moved into Villa Aphrodite, many Greeks hated him. Not just because he was Italian, but because the villa was a royal residence. Theo and I tried to ignore that fact in order to mingle in his circle.'

'Aren't you afraid of being labelled a collaborator?' I asked.

She smiled. 'It was a risk we took, just to pick up any information. We knew who his German friends were. That's invaluable information, wouldn't you agree?'

'Most certainly. Yet if what you are saying is true, then couldn't you have found out why the guards were changed that night at Ekali when Theo was killed? Didn't it strike you as odd that happened, especially as Theo was so meticulous in his planning?'

My question touched a raw nerve

'What are you trying to say?' she asked, stubbing her cigarette out in the ashtray. 'It was just one of those things.'

'We are trained to be one step ahead of, how did you put it — one of those things.'

Her eyes flashed angrily at me. 'Anyway, why *did* you come here unannounced? I wanted to see you, but what you did was against protocol.'

'Because ever since I met you that first night in Cairo, I've thought of nothing else but you. You've consumed me, Alexis, and although you won't admit it, I know you feel the same way.' I took her hand, squeezing it tightly. 'I didn't know you were married then. You hid that well. Yet even after I found out about Theo's death, I still knew you wanted me.'

By reacting as I did, I had taken a huge gamble, and I had no idea what she would do next.'

She looked at me with those dark, exotic eyes. I was aware of her breathing, her chest rising and falling with every breath. And then, she did what I least expected. She burst out laughing.

'Oh you fool. You sweet, sweet fool!'

In that moment, I slapped her across the face, sending her head spinning sideways. She uttered a sharp cry and raised her free hand to protect herself. I hated myself for lashing out and pulled her into my arms, holding her tight. I felt her tears on my arm.

'I'm sorry. That was unforgiveable.'

She pulled away from me. 'No. *I'm* the one who should be sorry.' Her eyes glistened with tears. 'I didn't mean to laugh. It's just that... well, it's just that this is not the time to fall in love. There's too much at stake. Love makes us vulnerable and we can't afford that. Not in our position.'

'Then why did you give yourself to me as you did?' I asked.

The question was deliberately phrased to make me look like a love-sick fool, which was what I wanted her to think, and to some extent, what I had been until now.

She wiped her eyes and thought for a moment.

'Yes. It's true. I did find you attractive and maybe I did want you just as much as you said you wanted me. But don't let's fool ourselves into thinking that making love, even if it is something as beautiful as we've experienced, is love. Love is something to be avoided in war. The consequences can be too painful.'

At least that was something we both agreed on.

'And Theo? Did you love him?'

'Some things are too complicated to understand, Larry.'

'Try me.'

'In the beginning, yes, but later....'

Our conversation was interrupted by a knock on the door. It was Rada.

'Kyria Alexis. Is everything alright?'

I gestured to her to get up and answer. She smoothed down her dress and ran her fingers through her hair, unlocked the door and opened it a few inches.

'Everything's fine, Rada. Nikos and I had a slight disagreement. That's all.'

Rada peered over Alexis's shoulder, trying to catch a glimpse of me. I was sitting on the couch, one leg crossed over the other in a casual manner, sipping my cognac.

'If you say so.'

The look on her face told us she didn't quite believe us but there was little she could do about it.

Alexis closed the door and was just about to sit back down

when we heard the telephone ring in the hallway. Rada knocked on the door again.

'Whoever it is, tell them I'm not available at the moment,' Alexis called out.

'Kyria Alexis,' Rada replied. 'I think you should answer it.'

Alexis opened the door again. 'Can't you see I'm busy. Take a message.'

Rada whispered something in a low voice so that I could not hear.

Alexis told me to pour us another drink. 'I'm sorry,' she said. 'I have to take this call. I won't be long.'

She left, closing the door behind her. I got up quickly and pressed my ear to the door. I could hear her talking on the telephone but couldn't make out what she was saying. I went to the drinks cabinet to pour us another drink. On it was an assortment of framed photographs, mostly of Alexis herself. One caught my eye. It was small, barely ten centimetres square. I picked it up and hastily pulled the back apart to retrieve the photograph which I slipped into my wallet. The empty frame, I slid behind the cabinet.

A few minutes later, Alexis reappeared. She looked nervous.

'Everything alright?' I asked, handing her the cognac.

'I have to ask you to leave. Something urgent has come up.'

I rubbed the back of my hand gently up and down her arm. 'Is it that urgent? I've only just got here.'

She pulled away. 'Please, Larry.'

Larry again.

'There was another reason I came to see you,' I said.

'Can't it wait? How about I get my driver to pick you up in a couple of days. We can have lunch together.'

'No. I'm afraid it can't wait. It's important.'

She looked at her watch. 'I can give you ten minutes.'

She sat down on the couch again. 'Go on. What is it?'

'We have several people who need to be evacuated to Turkey straight away. 'Women from the prominent Athenian Jewish community.'

Her face paled and I could see her mind racing, stalling for time.

'It's not a problem is it?' I asked. 'The Gestapo are stepping up their searches for the Jews in Athens. They have a list of every single Jew in Attica and have sent out notices for them to report to the authorities. We both know what that means. Those caught hiding them will be shot. We can't risk keeping them here. Too many of our people are involved.'

'I don't know, Larry. Samos is in the hands of the Italians. With Mussolini gone, the Germans will move onto the island. They already have a large presence in Chios. It's not safe at the moment.'

'You disappoint me,' I replied, somewhat coolly. 'If you can't help me out, then I will find someone who can.'

She saw the look of displeasure on my face while I saw a look of panic on hers.

'I hadn't intended to go away again for a while. Maybe we can get them out via one of the other escape routes.'

'We've already overreached ourselves as it is. This recent crackdown has put even more pressure on us. These people have reached out to us and are prepared to pay well for this. Enough to double any bribes.'

'Who are they?'

'I can't tell you at the moment.'

I could tell she didn't take too kindly to my blunt reply.

'All I can say is that this must be done as soon as possible.'

'Alright,' she said, with a sigh. 'Let me know when you've sorted things out and I'll see what I can do.'

'Good girl. I knew I could count on you.'

'If that's all, I really do have to ask you to leave now. We can continue this discussion another time. I'll get my driver to pick you up.'

'How about we meet for lunch in Athens, rather than me come here.' I lifted her chin towards me and kissed her softly on the mouth. 'I'd like to be alone with you, even if it is only for lunch. What about the Grande Bretagne Hotel? I hear they still serve fine meals.'

I wanted to gauge her reaction.

She gave a nervous laugh. 'Are you mad? It's the Headquarters of the Third Reich. Who knows who we could bump into? Even Goering or Himmler stay there when they visit.'

Or even Herr Keller, I thought to myself.

'There's a restaurant nearby. On Stadiou — The Pavillion. It's a quiet establishment, mostly frequented by Italians. What about Saturday? Let's say 12:30 sharp. I will make a booking in the name of Xenakis.'

Alexis agreed. She offered to get her driver to take me back to Athens but I declined, saying that as it was such a lovely day, I would enjoy the walk. We shook hands, the formality hiding our earlier intimacy.

The driver was leaning on the bonnet of the car smoking a cigarette when I left. He handed me back the gun and watched me walk away without uttering a word. What was it that was so urgent that I had to leave? The telephone call had made her nervous and the fact that she had offered her driver to take me back to Athens made me think she might be expecting someone rather than going out herself. Who was it that she didn't want me to meet? I walked a short distance along the quiet leafy street and, seeing that no-one was about, concealed myself in the bushes and watched the house.

I waited there in the stifling heat for almost an hour. During that time only one car passed and it was not going to the Petrakis villa. I was on the point of considering I was wasting my time when I heard another car coming. The black car slowed down when it neared the villa and turned into the driveway. It gave me a chance to see there were two men in it. I immediately recognised the passenger from the evening of the Ambassador's party: the little Greek man with the tortoise-shell glasses. The other thing I noticed shook me to the core. The back of the bumper bar was dented. It was the same car that had arrived at Kondoumaris's apartment. It was a stiflingly hot day, yet I felt a chill run through my body.

Chapter 25

'You're quite sure it was the same car?' Dancer asked, later that evening.

'Not only that, but I recognised the passenger. A strange little man whom I met the same time that I first met up with the White Rose. He was at the Ambassador's party. I can't say I took to him and he certainly didn't want to hang around with me being there.'

'Hmm,' Aris exclaimed. 'It doesn't look good does it?

'You know what this is pointing to, don't you?' I said. 'He's involved in Kondoumaris's murder. If he's a friend of the White Rose, does this connect her in any way to the murder? At this point, we can't rule anything out.'

Aris, Stelios and Dancer remained tight-lipped. I knew them enough to know by the look on their faces they knew I was up to something.

'I have to go to see the Wolf straight away,' I said. 'There's something I need to discuss with him urgently.'

'Is there anything you want us to do in the meantime?' Stelios asked.

'Yes. Look through the notebook again. Just in case you

missed something, especially the last few entries. Aris, I want you to get in touch with the forger. I need to see him as soon as possible. Arrange a meeting for tomorrow morning.'

When I met up with Loukas that evening, he was on edge.

'What's wrong?' I asked. 'More bad news?'

Hadzigiannis the tailor has reported a couple of suspicious incidents. Two men were spotted in Ermou Street doing nothing in particular. "Window-shopping", he referred to it as. No-one "window-shops" in Ermou these days. It's too dangerous. Except for those familiar faces going about their daily business, such people attract attention.'

'The Gestapo?'

Loukas nodded. 'Looks like it. Then today, another two arrived. Different faces this time. What's more, they went into his shop inquiring after a suit. Hadzigiannis noticed that while one asked questions about the fabrics and styles etc., the other appeared to be making a mental note of the shop, including the people who worked there. It was evident that they had no intention of purchasing anything and eventually they left. That's when we were contacted. Hadzigiannis, being a fine tailor, could tell that the men's clothes were not made in Greece.'

'I also have some unsettling news,' I replied. 'I went to see Alexis today — unannounced. She wasn't too happy about it.'

Loukas raised his eyebrows. 'Did you confront her about the escape routes?'

'No. You should know me by now. I am more subtle than that,' I said, with a smile. 'I made out it was a friendly visit and that I wanted to catch up as I've been out of town.'

I didn't go into details. Loukas wouldn't have appreciated it.

'She told me about the German ambush on the *andartes* and

said she had no idea how it happened but agreed you'd walked into a trap.'

'An understatement,' Loukas remarked, sarcastically.

'I told her the reason for the visit was that because the Gestapo were conducting searches for Athenian Jews, we needed to get more out of Greece immediately and I wanted them to go via the Samian route.'

'What did she say?'

'She was hesitant at first, saying that due to the situation with the Italians, it would be difficult. I assured her that the families were willing to pay double the price which would more than cover any bribes.'

Loukas locked his hands together and thought about it. 'So you plan to set her up? Let's hope she falls for your story. Alexis is not one to be fooled easily. As for people trying to flee Greece, there's no shortage there, but I don't like the idea of sacrificing innocent people for something that could turn out to be a wild goose chase.'

'Leave it to me,' I said, with a confidence that belied the danger I was putting us all in. 'I'll think of something. For the moment I'm asking you to trust me.'

'I've trusted you in the past, my friend. Let's hope our luck doesn't run out. At this point we're not doing too well are we?'

I asked if he could do something for me.

'When the boat is ready to sail, do you think you can manage to find someone who is able to slip aboard. It's more than likely that Alexis will have a bodyguard, maybe her driver, I don't know. But I want them watched at all times, especially the people we entrust to her care. They're the ones I'm most concerned about. They will be in a vulnerable position.'

'Let me know when the departure will be and which ship. I'll do my best.'

'One more thing. You recall that I told you about the car that took the two men to Kondoumaris's apartment the night he was murdered, that it had a bent back bumper bar?'

'What about it?'

'Well I saw that car today. And guess where it was going?'

By now, I thought Loukas was ready for anything, but he wasn't ready for this. His face turned a blotched shade of deep red.

'You're absolutely sure it was the same car?' he asked,

'Not only that, but I recognised the passenger.' I clarified that statement. 'What I mean is, I saw him at the Ambassador's villa. He approached Alexis and they chatted while I fetched her coat. When I returned, he bade me a good evening and left. A peculiar man with heavy tortoise-shell glasses.'

Loukas asked for a more precise description. I did my best but he still had no idea who the man was.

'And you said he was Greek?'

'I believe so.'

'You're sure he wasn't an Italian or German with a perfect Greek accent?'

'That crossed my mind but I don't think so.'

'You know something,' Loukas said, blowing a cloud of cigarette smoke in the air. 'When you started to tell me about your suspicions of a songbird in our midst, I thought you might be just over-cautious. After all, we've worked together in the past and I know you're like a dog with a bone when you get an idea, especially when you think something's wrong. During those times, you have rarely been wrong. Where there's smoke, there's fire, was your motto. What you're telling me is unsettling. Whether it's related to the ambushes, I have yet to be convinced, but one thing is for sure, Poseidon has several hundred operatives throughout Greece. If we are brought undone, it will be a disastrous and that's putting it mildly.'

*

That evening Rosa asked me to dine with her. It was just the chance I needed to get to know her more. We dined alone in her room. She wore a mauve velvet dress with a corsage of fresh gardenias. It's perfume was heady. Like the rest of the house, the decor was ornate and overbearing. Dark wooden dressers inlaid with mirrors, a heavily upholstered couch with thick armrests and a curved back of gilded swirls, Turkish carpets and heavily fringed brocade curtains which all felt like they belonged in another era. She opened a bottle of Italian wine, a gift from a customer who freely admitted he had stolen it from the Italian Headquarters. It made a change from tsipouro and retsina. Only with Alexis, did I get to savour the finest drinks, these days.

Over a meal of horsemeat, fried courgettes, and cracked wheat, she asked how everything was. Was I happy here? Were we too rowdy during the night, etc.? I assured her that I slept like a log and rarely heard a thing, except for the music.

'The girls like to give the clients a good time,' Rosa said. 'Making love reminds them that they are human; that they still have feelings. War numbs us. It hardens the soul.'

I agreed wholeheartedly.

After we'd finished the meal, I plucked up courage to ask her a question.

'Rosa, I need your help. What I am about to ask you is extremely important. I know you work with the Resistance and that I can trust you.'

She put a cigarette in her amber cigarette holder and leaned across the table in readiness for me to light it for her. I glimpsed her ample breasts as the weight of the corsage pulled her dress away from them. For a woman of a certain age, they were still firm. In the soft light I could see she had given them a light dusting of powder which gave her skin a velvety texture. No doubt, over the years, she had perfected many tricks to keep herself as alluring as possible.

'Fire away,' she said, making herself comfortable for what I was about to ask her.

'I'm about to undertake an important mission. In fact, it's probably one of the most important since I've been here.

'And how can I be of assistance?'

'I need someone I can trust — a woman. It has to be someone who is not known to the people she will be working with. What I have in mind is dangerous, but if we succeed, we will be saving the lives of many. The woman must be cultured and know how to handle herself — and that includes the use of weapons.'

Rosa's face gave no indication of what she was thinking.

'You say *if* you succeed. Is there a likelihood you won't?'

'There is always a possibility with every mission. I would be lying to you if I said otherwise.'

'This woman, how long do you want her for and what does she have to do?'

'All I can say is that she will be given a new ID under an assumed name together with travel documents.'

Rosa queried why I stressed that the woman must be cultured.

'She must be able to mingle within the upper echelons of society. Therefore she must know how to dress, speak well, and how to comport herself. I cannot have a mere seamstress with little education.'

Rosa smiled. 'Kapetan, did you have anyone in mind?'

'Yes, and I think you already know who I am asking for.'

'Maroulia.'

'She would be perfect.'

'I don't know if she can use a gun,' Rosa replied. 'But she does know how to take care of herself. Let me speak with her. You will have your answer in the morning.'

She topped up our glasses with the last of the red wine.

'To your success, Kapetan,' she said, raising her glass towards me. 'May it shorten the war.'

The next morning there was a soft knock on my door. It was Maroulia with my breakfast.'

As was her usual custom, she disappeared behind the screen to wash herself while I ate. The room filled with the scent of orange blossom. After I'd finished eating I sat on the doorstep soaking up the morning sun. She came and sat by my side.

'Kyria Rosa came to see me last night. She said you'd like me to help you.'

'Did she also tell you it would be dangerous?'

Maroulia shrugged. 'She did, but no-one is safe these days so what's the difference?'

'The difference is that you would be knowingly putting yourself in danger. It's not a game.'

'And do you think fucking the enemy is not putting one's

self in danger?' she replied, putting me in my place. 'That's not a game either.'

She hurled her words at me in such a way that I had to smile. She was a beautiful woman who carried herself with confidence. On the one hand there was a kind of freshness and innocence about her that I found attractive, and on the other hand she was street-wise. Hearing her talk in such a blunt manner not only surprised me, it added to her attractiveness. I had always had a liking for feisty women, and had things been different, I might have taken a shine to her. As it was, women as lovers were not my top priority at the moment.

'Well do you?' she asked, waiting for my reply.

'You are right,' I answered. 'And you are not alone. We are all being fucked by the enemy.'

Now it was her turn to laugh.

'Kapetan, I told you before that I was ready to help you. What would you like me to do?'

'There's something I want to show you.'

I took the photograph of Alexis out of my wallet and handed it to her. What I was doing was a gamble but it had to be done before we could continue any further.

'Have you seen this woman before?'

She examined it closely.

'No. She's very beautiful. Who is she? She looks like a film star.'

I took the photo back and put it away, satisfied with her response.

'This mission will involve you going away for a couple of weeks,' I replied, ignoring her question. 'You will travel alone. I cannot reveal when or where until the time comes. Your job will be to befriend this woman and keep watch on her.'

'Is that all?'

'It may not seem like much, Maroulia, but you must believe me when I say this is a dangerous operation. If this person realises what you are doing, you could be killed, so think carefully. If you have any misgivings, you can pull out now.'

'I fully understand and I still want to do it. We Greeks believe in freedom or death you know. It's our motto.'

'I know and thousands have died for the cause.'

'If I die for my country, then so be it. I don't know you, Kapetan, but I trust you.' She put her hand on mine. 'You have kind eyes and I believe you are a good man. Only a good man would come from another country to help us.'

I had never thought of my work in those terms until then and her words touched me. I looked into her large brown eyes and saw a sensitivity that this damn war had not killed. Just one look like that made my work worthwhile.

'There's just one thing,' she said. 'Rosa mentioned you wanted someone who could use a gun. I have to tell you that I have never even held one, let alone fired one.'

'We will have to work on that,' I replied. 'I would hope you would never have to use it, but it's for your own safety as much as anything else.'

I asked her to give me a photograph of herself in order to make up a new ID. She went inside and pulled one out of a drawer. It was a close-up of her with another girl somewhere in Plaka.

'Will this do?'

'Perfect,' I replied. 'Now, I want you to sit tight and not breathe a word about our little chat to anyone, and that includes Kyria Rosa. Do you understand?'

'You don't have to worry,' Maroulia said. 'Now, if that's all, I will leave you to continue with your work.'

With that, she picked up the tray and left.

Chapter 26

Aris and I met up with the forger the following day. I gave him Maroulia's photograph and asked him to make her a new ID and travel documents. Aris also needed a new set as it was agreed that he would travel to Samos immediately and search out the two fishermen to see if they could throw any light on the Poseidon escape routes. In the meantime, I would contact Cairo and arrange for them to let Jack Martins know what was happening. We would need his help as getting a message to us in Athens from Samos by telephone would be all but impossible. Calls would be closely monitored, therefore we would need a radio operator and we didn't have one on the island.

The forger would have the IDs ready by the weekend. I also mentioned there would be a few more in the next few days. It crossed my mind to get a copy of Alexis's photograph for Aris but decided against it. The forger belonged to the network and it was highly likely he would recognise her. If he didn't, then it was possible someone working with him would and I couldn't take that risk. Aris would have to take the original.

By the end of the week, the wheels were set in motion with regard to the deception. There was one major problem. Loukas and I disagreed about who we would send as escapees. I wanted to send genuine escapees whilst he favoured substituting them for someone from the Resistance.

'We cannot send innocent people away knowing this is a trap,' he argued.

I on the other hand, thought Alexis was too smart and would smell a rat if the escapees were not genuine.

'They must act like people whose fate lies in the hands of someone they don't know,' I said. 'That way they will be able to show true fear. I don't like it any more than you do, but she's used to the way escapees act. She knows their fears. If we send one of our own, they won't display the same fear, not to mention that they know how to handle themselves, which will show. True fear is not an act. No, this must be done as if it is a genuine operation.'

In the end, he could see my point and gave in.

On Saturday I met Alexis at The Pavillion, as planned. She was dressed in an elegant ivory shirt with a simple, pencil-line navy skirt, belted around the waist with a wide gold belt. She wore her hair up which accentuated a pair of gold earrings. On her wrist was a matching bracelet that coiled around her wrist three times, in the design of a snake. Nothing was out of place. She was perfection itself. I got up to give her a peck on the cheek. She was wearing her perfume. How I would have given anything to turn the clock back.

'Darling Nikos, how good to see you again.'

I had chosen the restaurant because it had a discreet atmosphere. That is as discreet as a restaurant ever could be during war. Except for a few tables in the centre of the room, all the others consisted of booths divided by engraved glasswork. It was lunchtime but the atmosphere was soft and intimate. A tulip-shaped vase containing a single red rose and a small white candle in a decorative glass adorned every table.

'This is rather a special occasion isn't it?' Alexis said with a smile. 'It's the first time you and I have been alone together.' She hastened to add that she meant in public.

That fact was not lost on me.

'Even in Cairo we were not alone, were we? The Blythe Pickerings were there also.'

'And your friend — what was her name? Irini. Yes, that's it. She was there too.'

Alexis's smile faded. I had caught her off guard.

'Do you know what became of her?' I asked, innocently.

Alexis was like a chameleon. 'No,' she replied, curtly. 'Shall we order?'

She perused the wine menu for a few minutes and put it down, clearly rattled at the mention of Irini.

'So what will it be?' I asked again.

'Champagne,' she replied.

'Make that two,' I said to the sommelier, wondering how I was going to explain my extravagance to Cairo. 'Do you remember what Rommel said about champagne?' I asked.

'Didn't he say he would soon be drinking champagne in the master suite at Shepheard's?'

'Exactly. He had expected a swift victory was looking forward to it. Unfortunately, it never happened.'

'I also remember a cocktail called "The Suffering Bastard". Quite the rage if I recall. Did Joe come up with that one?'

'Yes. Joe Scialom at Shepheard's. What a character. Did you know he was a chemist before opening Joe's Bar? Worked in Sudan. I believe. Rumour has it that it was "The Suffering Bastard" that saved the Battle of El Alamein. He was asked to supply eight gallons to the front line. They said it was so lethal it gave them courage.'

'What was in it? Wasn't it Bourbon, gin and lime juice?

'And a dash of Angostura bitters topped with ginger beer,' I added.

The light-hearted banter dispensed with, Alexis wasted no time in getting down to the point of our meeting.

'These people you want me to help. Do you have any more information to give me?'

I replied that I'd spoken with the families concerned and everything was going according to plan. As soon as I had their new IDs I would let her know. She seemed on edge.

'Is everything alright?' I asked. 'I don't want to but I can always try and arrange another escape route if you've other things on.'

We finished our meal before she continued the conversation.

'I would like you to give me a few days' notice. I cannot possibly move people at a moment's notice. It's too dangerous. I need to notify my contacts and I have things to look after here too.'

I assured her that I would do as she requested and changed the subject. She was getting too nervous. The problem was, it wasn't easy to discuss many subjects with Alexis. Both of us were always on guard. She was, after all the head of Poseidon and as such had to be respected. The only time she let her guard down was when we made love, and even then I couldn't be fully sure she had entirely stepped out of that role. After all, I hadn't stepped out of mine so why should she?

Not withstanding that matter, I commented on how beautiful she looked and that I wanted to ravish her there and then.

She laughed. 'What! With all these people looking on?'

'It's the voyeur in me,' I replied with a wink. 'I like danger.'

Her smile faded. 'That's not funny.'

'I'm sorry. It was just a little joke. Anyway, I thought you might have agreed with me. Flirting with danger is something we both do well, isn't it?'

She averted her gaze from mine, clearly rattled.

It was at that point that I noticed two men enter the restaurant. They sat at the bar and ordered a drink but I couldn't help noticing that they kept staring at us through a large mirror that almost covered the entire length of the wall behind the bar. I thought I recognised them. Was it my imagination, or were they the two men I'd seen in Plateia Amerikis? I couldn't be sure. Alexis, as astute as ever, noticed a flicker in my eyes that something was amiss.

'What's wrong?' she asked.'

I looked at my watch. 'I think it's time to leave. I have things to attend to as I am sure, do you.'

I called the waiter over and asked for the bill. When I went to pick it up, Alexis, put her hand on mine.

'No. Let me. Please.'

'I asked you here and I will pay,' I replied.

'It's expensive here — champagne and chicken at black market prices. I can afford it. You can't. Cairo will have your head on a platter if they see this.'

How thoughtful she could be when you least expected it. I didn't want to create a scene and neither did I want it to be seen that the meal was being paid for by a lady, but she insisted.

'Don't make a fuss, Nikos. Not here.'

She took a handful of notes from her purse and paid. It was more than most people would earn in a month.

As we left the premises, I turned back to check on the two men. They had been watching us but turned away when they saw me look. Fearful I had walked into a trap, I couldn't wait to get away.

Alexis extended her hand. 'Thank you for a delightful lunch. Please contact me as soon as possible when the assignment is ready. I will be waiting.'

She gave me a friendly peck on the cheek. I waited with her until her driver appeared. As I had expected, he hadn't been too far away. I opened the door for Alexis to get into the back seat. He caught my eye and I gave him a friendly smile. He turned away without reciprocating. I watched them drive away and walked towards Syntagma. I had almost rounded the corner into Syntagma when I decided to stop and look in a bookshop window. The two men were standing on the doorstep of The Pavillion, scanning the street. I quickly darted inside, picked up a large book on Greek Mythology and with my face fully hidden behind its pages, watched them from the safety of the shop. Having unfortunately lost me, they retreated back into the restaurant.

Now I knew for sure. The raids in Plateia Amerikis and here were related. I was definitely being shadowed.

*

A few days later, Aris departed for Samos. He took Alexis's photograph with him, but not before I had showed it one more time to Maroulia. At the same time, I showed Aris a photo of Maroulia — he would know her as Sofia — and a photograph of Aris to Maroulia. She would know him as Athos.

'Commit it to memory,' I said to her. 'You won't see it again.'

Every time I saw her, I asked her to describe Alexis's face to me. Maroulia was observant. She remembered the smallest of details.

'Do you think I am going to forget a woman who looks like a movie star?' She laughed.

The only thing left to teach her now was how to use a gun.

Chapter 27

It was the priest in Kato Patissia who provided us with the Jews we were to send to Palestine. The Greek clergy worked closely together and had always been outspoken opponents of the persecution of the Jews. I admired them for it. They didn't hesitate to talk openly against the policy of singling Greek Jews out and deporting them. As a consequence, many worked with the Resistance to keep them in hiding.

After a secret meeting between all concerned, including Loukas, it was decided that out of ten people we would choose a mother and her two daughters. The father and two sons would remain behind. We assured them that when the women were safely on Turkish soil, the men would follow. The Kamaras family were silversmiths from Ioannina. Samuel Kamaras moved to Athens as soon as he married Esther. All the children were born in Athens and thus, had Athenian accents. Only their parents, Esther and Samuel, retained a northern accent which unfortunately made them stand out in a society already living on the razor's edge. The rest of the family were involved in the fur trade around Kastoria. Like many other Jews in that region, they had been forced from their homes and those who hadn't gone into hiding had been sent to deportation camps. At first the Kamaras family thought Athens would be safe, especially with the church on their side, but they now saw it was only a matter of time before they too were sent to deportation camps.

The two girls, Nurit and Galya, were fifteen and fourteen — pretty girls who had led a sheltered family life and they looked terrified, sobbing quietly into their handkerchiefs while we explained what would take place. Every now and again, their mother would pat them on the knee and tell them it would all be fine. They handed us their photographs and we promised to get them new IDs before the week was out. The family wanted to know if we had any idea when they would depart and on which boat. Loukas told them it was imperative everything remain secret until the day of the departure, and even then, they would have little time to say their goodbyes so they had better start doing it immediately. This caused the girls to become even more tearful but it couldn't be helped. Secrecy was vital.

After a week, Cairo passed on news from Turkey that a radio operator had been sent to Samos and was awaiting contact from Aris. It was now time to set the plan in motion. Loukas found out via the seamen working in the network that a boat would be going to the island of Syros the following Thursday. From there, they would have to change to another, smaller boat to Samos which would leave the following day. Several days later, we received the long-awaited coded message from Aris. He had located the two fishermen and they recognised the woman in the photograph although they had no idea what her name was or her importance in Poseidon. All they knew was that she was the person who was known to be helping the escapees. The transmission was cut short. We would have to wait until we were contacted again.

After discussing the situation with Loukas, it was decided to organise the escape for the following week. This time I went through the right channels and asked Maria to arrange a meeting with Alexis. Her driver picked me up at the usual place. When I got there, Alexis had prepared lunch in the garden. The setting was in full view of the house and afforded us no privacy at all. Any thoughts I might have had about being intimate quickly disappeared. It was clear she intended this meeting to be formal.

'When is to be?' she asked.

'Next week. The *Arcadia* is sailing for Syros but you will have to stay overnight in Ermoupoli and catch the next boat on the following day. The Allies have stepped up their bombing raids and more ships have been hit. The Germans have commandeered every ship they can lay their hands on.'

'How many people will I be escorting and when will I get to meet them? I like to get to know them beforehand to gauge their personalities, just in case there are any unforeseen difficulties. Some people don't cope well under pressure and it's better for them to escape using an alternate route. Then there's this Italian business. The Germans have stepped up their checks. They will be more thorough now and bribes will be higher, that's for sure.'

'Everyone has their price,' I replied. 'You've handled it well in the past. I'm sure you'll be fine this time. Don't forget the family is paying a lot for this otherwise they would have taken the circuitous route on fishing boats.'

I went on to explain that she would be accompanying three women — a mother and her two teenage daughters.

'The daughters are extremely shy and nervous, so I'm sure they'll hide in their cabin the whole time. The mother seems friendly enough.'

'And their names? I need them for the tickets.'

'You'll get them in time, don't worry. We're working on the IDs now.'

Lunch was a half-hearted affair. Neither of us had an appetite for food. Throughout it all, I could see Alexis was apprehensive and I had a sinking feeling she would pull out. When we finished eating, I looked at my watch and told her that as much as I enjoyed her company, I had other urgent things to attend to. We said goodbye with our usual handshake, but there was no peck on the cheek. As long as I'd known her, Alexis had always been self-assured. All of a sudden she seemed vulnerable — fragile even, and this time it didn't seem to be an act. It confused me. Fearful that I might weaken myself and call the whole thing off, I thanked her for the lunch and left.

Throughout the drive home, I couldn't get the look on her face out of my mind, and for the first time since Turkey, I began to have doubts. Perhaps I'd been wrong to doubt her loyalty after all.

*

That evening, I gave Maroulia a Ballisler-Molina semi-automatic, one of SOE's preferred firearms. She handled it carefully, moving it from one hand to another feeling its weight. I emptied the cartridge and showed her how to load it. After an hour or two spent in the old quarry behind Kypseli, I discovered she was a natural.

'Are you sure, you've never handled a gun before?' I asked. 'For a novice you have a great aim.'

'Well if it's a matter of life or death, then I think I'd better get it right, don't you?'

I liked her answer.

'So when will I be going on this mission?' she asked. 'I'm presuming it will be soon as you've given me the gun.'

'In the next day or two. Are you having second thoughts?'

'She shook her head, the soft curls falling around her shoulders.

'Good girl.'

That night I dined with Rosa again.

'Is it time for Maroulia to leave?' she asked, opening up another bottle of Italian wine.

'Soon.'

'She's a good girl, Kapetan. Whatever you have planned for her, you can count on her. She won't let you down.'

We spent the rest of the night in idle chatter. The wine was a good one and I welcomed the break to take my mind off the forthcoming operation. Rosa was excellent company. Well-educated and politically aware, witty and street-smart, and with a deep affection for "her girls" as she called them, I could see why she made a good madam. As soon as this operation was over, I planned to move out of Athens and I would miss her. Indeed, I would miss them all.

*

Alexis was given the new identities of the Kamaras women in order to purchase their tickets for the trip, and the evening before they were due to leave, I went to the safe-house near the church in Kato Patissia and handed over their new IDs. The family put on a brave face. The two girls no longer sobbed but their pale, drawn faces said it all. A light had been extinguished in their hearts. I had seen it all too often and it never ceased to affect me. It was one of the things that made me do what I did.

'Will we see you again Kyrie?' Kyria Kamaras asked.

'I will escort you to your departure point in Piraeus. But rest assured, when you depart, I and others will be following your movements closely. You will not be alone.'

Kyria Kamaras flung her arms around me. 'I cannot thank you enough.'

I could feel her body trembling.

Her husband pulled her away gently. 'Come, my darling, let us spend this time in prayer.'

I bid them goodbye and left to meet Dancer in the church. He was preparing to transmit to Cairo.

'You look a bit under the weather, sir. Everything alright?'

'I don't think I'll ever get used to these goodbyes,' I replied, helping him with the wire. 'This one is especially getting to me. I just hope we're not sending them to their deaths.'

'You know what you're doing. Everything's in place so all should go smoothly.'

'Everything except the fact that we haven't heard any more from Aris. I hope he reports something of substance soon. It may be too late once they've set sail.'

Dancer sat in front of his machine and looked at his watch. We had five more minutes before transmission time and they passed slowly.

'I thought that's why you've got their backs covered from the moment they leave Piraeus,' he said.

This was true. Every angle had been covered. Loukas had found someone who was able to board the ship travelling as a cabin hand. An Italian with a Greek background who'd deserted the army and joined the *andartes*. Through Loukas's contacts, he was given a fake ID making him an official representative of the Union of Greek Shipowners. He also happened to be fluent in German which was invaluable with a bigger presence of Germans everywhere. And then there was Maroulia. She was now fully briefed as to what her role was on board the ship. In fact, she saw it as an adventure, albeit a dangerous one. She was also aware of the Italian *andarte* who would communicate with her once she was on board, although she didn't know his name. All she knew was he would call her by her code name, Sofia, and mention the word Icarus. It was imperative that he mentioned both names.

Dancer started to transmit. Cairo was informed as to the time of departure of the *Arcadia* and the names the women would be travelling under, and Jack Martins was to be kept up to date with Aris's movements in Samos. Everyone was on high alert to keep their eyes open for anything out of the ordinary, especially when the boat finally docked in Samos.

Sleep was impossible that night. I tossed and turned until in the end, I got up and went outside to smoke a cigarette. I heard the door open and saw Maroulia coming towards me.

'Is it always like this before an operation?' she asked, helping herself to one of my cigarettes.

'Always,' I replied, lighting the cigarette for her.

She sat on the step and laid her head against the wall,

looking up at the night sky. 'I wonder what the future has in store for us?'

'Do we really want to know?'

'Maybe not.' She laughed. 'Otherwise I wouldn't have ended up here.'

She brought up the subject of Alexis. 'This woman I am to befriend. What can you tell me about her?'

'She's a smart lady. Not easy to fool.'

'From the look of her, I would say she has men falling at her feet.'

Alexis would meet her match with Maroulia.

'I would think you'd have the men falling at your feet also,' I replied, trying to lighten the atmosphere. 'You're not too bad looking yourself.'

'It does have advantages, as you many have gathered.' She finished her cigarette. 'Have you got anything to drink?'

'I'm not sure that's wise. You can't afford to have a hangover tomorrow.'

She ignored me and went back inside. Moments later she came out with two glasses of whisky.

'To your health, Kapetan. And to getting rid of these Nazi bastards once and for all.'

Chapter 28

Piraeus. Early September 1943

Throughout the summer the weather had been unbearably hot. Now the heavens opened and we had one of the worst storms in months. In parts of Athens and Piraeus, torrents of water flowed through the streets like rivers, tramcars stopped and cars became stuck, blocking roads and pavements. All this made it difficult to transport the Kamaras women to the port. The only thing in our favour was that it kept the Germans off the streets. When the women eventually arrived in Piraeus, they were drenched to the bone. Their fine clothes and shoes were soaked through and their carefully tended hair was a mess.

It had been agreed that we would meet Loukas at a taverna not far from the station and within walking distance to the port. He was already there.

'My God,' he exclaimed when he saw the women. 'You will catch a severe cold if you don't dry out.'

We had chosen to meet in this taverna because the owner was a friend of Loukas and worked for the Resistance. His wife came to the rescue and took the women into the back room where they could dry their clothes over the stove. The two girls, who up until now had tried so hard to put on a brave face, began crying again.

'Stop that!' the woman said. 'Stop that immediately and pull yourselves together. You will attract unwelcome attention.'

All three women were given sheets to wrap round themselves while their clothes dried. The woman left them and returned soon after with three large glasses of whisky.

'Here, drink this.'

'I'm not sure about this. We don't drink,' Esther Kamaras replied.

The woman brushed the comment aside. 'Trust me. It will do you good.'

Esther took a sip and the girls followed suit, screwing their faces up.

'Come on,' the woman said sternly, hands on hip. 'I won't leave this room until it's all finished.'

Seeing the look of determination on her face, they did as they were told.

'Now, try and get some rest. You have a couple of hours before the boat sails. By then your clothes will be well and truly dry.'

She took back the empty glasses and returned to the others.

'You've got your work cut out there,' she said to Loukas as she refilled our glasses with the rest of the whisky. 'Those three are a bag of nerves. If you ask me, it will take more than a glass of whisky to soothe them. And by the look of this weather, it's not going to be a pleasant boat ride either.'

The minutes ticked by slowly. Every now and then Loukas and I ran through what was expected to take place. I would meet up with Alexis in the same kafenio where I saw her off the last time she left for Samos. Maroulia, travelling under her new identity as Sofia, would also be there, but as a total stranger. She was there to see Alexis in the flesh. By meeting up with Alexis, I would be pointing out the woman she was to shadow. When it was time to leave, Maroulia would take over where I left off. The women, who by now had their new IDs, would be waiting for Alexis at the entrance gates to the port where Alexis would hand them their tickets. Nothing was left to chance — or so we thought.

The weather was still bad and I was worried the trip would be cancelled, but Loukas told me that was highly unlikely as they were expecting more bombing raids and it was thought that the boat would be safer at sea than as a sitting duck in the port. In the last week, the Germans had lost six ships due to Allied air attacks.

We spent the last half hour in light conversation. I asked how Anna was.

'She asks me to make sure you still carry your blue bead with you.' Loukas laughed. 'She's very superstitious, you know. All these villagers are. If they are not trying to survive, they spend their time at church, kissing icons. Me, I've lost my sense of religion. Maybe I've seen too much. Where is God when innocent people are being massacred?'

'We all have to believe in something. Blue beads, icons, what's the difference?' I looked at my watch. 'Well, I think it's time for me to leave. The rain has stopped. Let's hope it holds off until they are safely aboard the boat.'

I reached for my jacket and hat which by now were well and truly dry, and downed the last drop of whisky.

'Don't worry,' Loukas said. 'I will make sure the women will be at the gate when Alexis gets there.'

I left to meet up with Alexis with more than a little apprehension. A part of me felt a huge guilt at luring Alexis into this trap, and even now, I still hoped we'd got it wrong; that the Samos escape routes had gone wrong for some other reason. I desperately wanted to believe in her.

Just as it had been the last time I'd met her, the kafenio was filled with travellers all hoping to get on what available boats were leaving. This time there was a group of Greek musicians playing at the far end of the room. In front of them the small space reserved for dancing was already occupied by two couples dancing arm in arm. Alexis saw me and waved me over.

'What will you have to drink?' she asked, calling the waiter over.

'I'm fine, thank you. I want to keep a clear head,' I lied, already feeling the effects of the earlier drinks.

I slid the brown envelope across the table. She opened her handbag which was lying on the table and quickly slipped it inside. She placed the bag under the table, away from prying eyes.

'Anything else?' she asked.

'No. The money's all there. The women have their new identity cards with them.

After a while, she excused herself to go to the Rest Room to check the money. I looked around and saw Maroulia sitting at another table. We acknowledged each other with a slight nod. When Alexis returned, she looked satisfied and said there was more than enough money to cover any unforeseen difficulties.

Thankfully, the fact that the place was full and the musicians were playing made our conversation hard to overhear. After a few more numbers, the musicians put down their instruments and moved to a table to have a few drinks and whatever plates of food had been provided for them by grateful patrons. I glanced at Maroulia who was watching us carefully. A group of Germans came in and sat nearby. I noticed several Greeks get up and leave.

'We haven't much time left,' Alexis said. 'Would you like to dance?'

Dancing was the last thing on my mind. Without waiting for my reply, she called the waiter over and asked him if he had any Sofia Vembo records.

'"*Poso Lipame*",' she said. '"I'm So Sorry". Do have that?'

'Is that wise?' I asked. 'You know how the Germans hate her.'

'I don't care,' Alexis said, defiantly. 'She may be entertaining the Greek troops in exile, but she's a true patriot. I admire that.'

I felt a lump in my throat. Was she trying to tell me something? I couldn't be sure.'

The waiter went over to the kafenio owner to check if it was alright. Evidently, the fact that there were Germans in the room didn't bother him and he told the waiter to play it. When the first strains of the orchestra started up, followed by the unmistakable voice of the woman who had been dubbed "The Songstress of Victory", everyone stopped talking and looked around fearfully. Even Maroulia looked nervous.

Amidst a sea of nervous faces Alexis pushed her chair back and walked on to the dance floor. She picked up the side of her dress, lifted her foot off the ground to the swell of the music and with her head held by, made a spontaneous twirl. On the second twirl, her eyes locked on mine, beckoning me to join her.

"It's you I have been looking for
In a thousand dreams of mine
My lips have been searching for you.
My soul and my most profound wishes
Have been searching for you....."

Like a sailor being called by the sirens, I got up, and with our arms outstretched we moved to the rhythm of the music, brushing up against each other sensuously. Every word in the song resonated.

"How sorry I am for the years
That were spent before I met you,
That I longed for so long.
And how afraid I am
That one day I may be losing you,
Cause forgetting you would never be possible.
Lean on me closer, sweet love of mine..."

As the song drew to an end, the kafenio owner handed me a stack of plates and full of emotion, I quickly smashed them one by one. The audience erupted in cheers and started to clap. At that point the Germans got up and walked out. For one brief moment I and everyone in the room had forgotten there was a war on.

It ended all too soon. It was time to leave. People started to pick up their bags and make their way to the port. I escorted Alexis outside where her car was waiting nearby. The driver opened the passenger door for her to get in.

'I presume you are going to the port also.' Alexis said. 'Let me give you a lift.'

I got in and as the door closed, I noticed Maroulia walking ahead with her suitcase. Our eyes met briefly. When we arrived at the entrance to the port, it was chaotic. People with baggage and suitcases were crammed up against the gates, all trying to get tickets at the last minute. They didn't have a hope in the world. I scanned my eyes over the crowd and eventually saw the Kamaras women, standing in a separate line at the ticket office which was manned with submachine guns. They looked terrified.

'That's them,' I said. 'Over there.'

'How are you getting home?' Alexis asked.

'I haven't thought about it.'

'Then my driver will take you back and drop you wherever you want.'

I argued against it but she insisted. I saw him looking at me with his usual stony face.

We got out of the car. The driver handed her suitcase to her and got back in the car.

'Time to say goodbye, Larry.'

Larry. It was like rubbing salt into the wounds.

She extended a gloved hand. It's strange what goes through your mind when you think you may never see someone again. I had the strongest urge to ask her to take off the glove so that I could see her painted blood-red nails.

'You're blushing,' she said with a smile. 'Is everything alright? You're not afraid, are you?'

'Take good care of yourself.'

I brought her gloved hand to my mouth and gave it the softest of kisses. At the same time I caught a whiff of the perfume on her wrist. It overpowered the smell of gasoline and all the acrid smells that lingered in the air after the constant bombing raids.

She turned around and walked away. I stood in silence and watched her; an ethereal figure shrouded in the misty blue-tinged light that lit up the entrance. She walked straight up to the Kamaras women, introduced herself and disappeared through the gates. Behind them was Maroulia. Whatever happened next was in the lap of the Gods.

I got back in the car and we drove away.

'Where to?' the driver asked.

'The same place that you picked me up,' I replied.

We drove back in silence. He pulled up in the usual spot. I had ten minutes to get home before curfew. I got out the car and thanked him for the lift.

'Kyrie,' the driver said, winding the window down.

Unless you count the confrontation in the driveway in Kifissia in which he spoke no more than a few terse sentences, we'd never had a conversation before, and I certainly wasn't in the mood to start now.

'What is it?' I replied, gruffly. 'I'm tired. It's been a long day.'

'I just want to say something.'

'Go on, man. I haven't got all night.'

'I would like to warn you of something. It may save your life. Everything you see is not as it appears.'

With that, he wound up the window and drove away. The air-raid sirens started to wail, the rain began to pour again, and all I could do was stand there in the empty, moonlit street.

Chapter 29

The air-raids went on for longer than usual that night and I prayed the *Arcadia* got away without being hit. On top of that, I went over and over the driver's words in my mind until I thought my head would split. As usual his words were short and sweet, but what did he mean? He appeared to be trying to tell me something off the record and I had to work it out for myself. Should I confront him? Something told me that wouldn't be wise. I managed to fall asleep just before dawn but was woken up by Rosa. She wanted to know if everything had gone according to plan. I told her so far, so good. We would have to wait and see.

'Hmm! I am going to the church today. I will pray for you,' she said. 'And get some sleep. You look terrible.'

I was too tired and simply didn't have the energy to think clearly so I decided to go back to bed. It was lunchtime when I woke up and my breakfast was still on the table. After a wash I felt much better. I was still tired but at least my head had cleared and I could think straight again. It was at that moment that a thought occurred to me. Something so obvious that I could have kicked myself for missing it. The night of Theo's death, Loukas had said there were three men at the meeting yet Alexis spoke of a fourth man. The man who tried to save Theo. It didn't add up. I needed to see Loukas straight away. There was a telephone kiosk on Patission Street used by the Resistance. I headed there as fast as I could. A woman answered the phone.

'I'm sorry. The Kyrie has gone away for a few days. I have no idea when he will return. Can I take a message?'

'Damn!' I muttered to myself. 'Damn!'

'Hello!' the voice called out. 'Kyrie, are you there?'

'No message,' I replied and slammed the phone down.

It would be useless going over there, so I headed for Dancer's apartment.

'What's wrong?' he asked, nervously. 'Don't tell me something terrible has happened to those women already?'

'Something's bothering me,' I told him. 'Do you recall that Alexis said a fourth man tried to help Theo after he was shot but it was too late and he died of his injuries?'

He nodded. 'What are you saying?'

'Loukas said there were only three people at the meeting that night. Who was the fourth man? Why has he never come to our attention?'

Dancer looked perplexed. 'Maybe no-one thought to ask because hardly anyone knew Theo was dead then. And it did come as a shock, even to us.'

'You're right. It certainly was a shock. But why didn't Loukas ask more questions?'

'Maybe he did, but why should he disbelieve her? Aren't they supposed to be good friends?'

'With Theo, yes, but he didn't really know Alexis. Certainly not on a personal level.'

'So what do you intend to do about it?' Dancer asked.

'Find out who the fourth man was.'

'Can't you question Loukas again?'

'I called the safe-house. He's gone away and I have no idea when he'll be back.'

'I have a feeling Alexis's driver must know something though. Ever since I've known him, he's barely said more than a few words, but last night when he dropped me off he seemed to be giving me a warning.'

'What did he say?'

'He said everything may not be as it appears.'

Dancer shook his head. 'I don't like it. I've got a nasty feeling we're being set up. Are you going to question him?'

'Yes and I have to act now, although it will probably to be at gunpoint and that means there's no turning back.'

Later that evening, Stelios arrived for our transmission with Cairo. The news was bad. In a long coded message, I was informed that Aris had discovered that the escapees who had not made it to Turkey had been taken off the boat in Syros. The Germans already had prior knowledge as to who were on the boats and were waiting for them in Ermoupoli. My heart stopped. The transmission continued. At the same time cryptographers recently intercepted a message from the Germans that the White Rose was on the move.

Dancer jotted everything down, handed me the pad and stared at me in silence.

'What do you want me to tell them?' he asked.

'Tell them that Sofia has it under control.'

Dancer coded and tapped the message and took off his earphones. We all looked at each other in dismay.

'And do they have it under control?' Stelios asked.

'I should bloody well hope so,' I thundered.

*

Well before dawn, Dancer, Stelios and myself, arrived at the Petrakis villa. The place was in darkness. Alexis's car was parked on the far side of the driveway. Stelios went to see if it was locked while Dancer and I moved towards the portico and checked the door and windows. Our guns cocked, we silently moved towards the back of the house checking every other window on the ground floor. All were locked except for one. I shone my torch inside and saw it was a pantry or storeroom. The window was narrow, but was just wide enough for me to slip inside. Once inside, I unlocked the back door to let Dancer and Stelios in. I flashed my torch around the room and listened. An empty silence.

The plan was to take Rada and the driver by surprise. Hopefully, when faced with the barrel of a gun, they would put up little resistance. It all sounded too easy. It wasn't. When we moved into the hallway, we heard one of the upstairs doors open and footsteps walking across the landing. We pressed ourselves flat against the wall just as the light was switched on.

'Who's there?' a voice called out.

I recognised Rada's voice. The wily woman had heard us.

Another door opened. This time on the ground floor not far from where we were standing.

'What's wrong?' a man's voice shouted back.

It was the driver.

'I thought I heard something,' Rada said.

There was a long silence while they both listened. Somewhere in the hallway a clock ticked.

'You're imagining things,' the driver said, irritated at being woken up. 'Go back to bed.'

We heard him go back inside his room. The light went off and Rada returned to her room.

'Leave the driver to me,' I whispered. 'Stelios, you get Rada, but I want her alive. Dancer, keep a lookout in case there's anyone else in the house.'

By now our eyes were accustomed to the darkness. When we reached the bottom of the staircase, I covered Stelios while he went upstairs. He was as quiet as a cat burglar. When he reached Rada's room, he waved. We were to break into the rooms at the same time.

I quietly turned the door handle to the driver's room. He had locked it. I gestured to Stelios to break open Rada's door. Fortunately, it was unlocked. Her scream echoed through the house. Within seconds the driver opened the door aiming his gun towards the landing. Fortunately he didn't see me, as I had hidden myself around the nearby corner. He started to run up the stairs and stopped in his tracks when he heard my voice behind him.

'Drop the gun.' I said pointing my gun at him.

He spun around aiming his own gun at me.

'You're outnumbered,' I told him. 'Don't be foolish.'

He saw Dancer also aiming his gun at him from the other side of the hall. Slowly, he started to climb the stairs backwards, all the time aiming his gun at me.

'Throw the gun down. I just want to talk.'

In the meantime, Rada was still screaming. All of a sudden, she stopped. I had no idea what had happened. Cautiously, I moved a few steps closer to the driver.

'Throw it down,' I said again.

I was ready for a shoot-out but I wasn't ready for what came next. He turned the gun on himself and shot himself in the head. In a split second, I and the wall at the side of us was splattered in blood. A warm, viscose liquid ran down my face, momentarily blinding me. Dancer rushed forward but there was no hope of saving the driver. I wiped the blood from my face with the back of my sleeve and hurled out a string of expletives. The metallic taste of blood clung to my lips.

Quickly pulling myself together, I ran upstairs to Rada's room while Dancer searched the rest of the house. She was lying unconscious on the floor. Stelios was tearing up a sheet to tie her hands.

'She'll be fine,' he said. 'Help me get her up. She's damned heavy.'

Rada was a big woman and it took the two of us to lift her and put her on a chair. I held her upright while Stelios tied the strips of sheet around her wrists and secured her to the chair.

'She had a gun,' he said, pointing to the bedside table. ' I got to her in time before she could use it on me.'

A blue-black bruise was blooming on the left side of Rada's face. I noticed a large jug of water on a wash stand, picked it up and threw it in her face. She came to and her eyes focused on me. An evil smile spread over her thick lips.

'I always knew you were trouble,' she hissed.

At that point, Dancer appeared. With him was a young woman.

'I found her hiding in a closet,' he said, holding the gun to the back of her head.

I recognised her as Alexis's cook. I knew we were going to

have trouble with Rada and as I didn't want the cook to see what we were going to do to her, asked him to take into another room and tie her up.

I picked up Rada's gun and slipped it in the back of my trousers, pulled up a chair and straddled it, folding my arms over the back of it.

'You and I are going to have a little chat, Rada. So unless you want to end up like our friend out there, you'd better co-operate.'

Her reply was to spit at me.

Stelios smacked her hard on the right side of her face, almost knocking her over. He grabbed her hair and jerked her head back. 'If you want to save yourself, do as the man says,' he said, menacingly.

By now it was dawn and I couldn't risk anyone coming to the house. Whatever information I wanted, I had to get quickly, but Rada proved to be stubborn. I left her in Stelios's hands and went next door to see if the young woman knew anything. She was terrified. Tears ran down her cheeks and she prayed to the Virgin to save her.

'She won't help you,' I said. 'But if you co-operate, I might.'

Clearly, she knew little, but what she did say was illuminating. She remembered the little Greek man with the tortoise-shell glasses coming to the house a few times, but didn't know his name. She also recalled overhearing Rada speaking German on the phone several times. When asked what she knew about Theo, she said he and Alexis argued a lot, especially during the weeks before he was killed. I asked when that was. It was the same date Alexis had given me.

'Are you sure about this?' I asked.

'Kyrie. I know because Kyria Alexis threatened to sack me

if I mentioned it to anyone.' She started to cry again. 'Please let me go. I promise I won't say a word about all this.'

I returned to Rada who by now was in a bad state. Stelios had given her a good going over. Blood was trickling down her face from her scalp where the butt of the gun had struck her, one eye was swollen and her top lip cut. She was still defiant.

'Rada I'm giving you one last chance.'

'I believe Alexis is working for the Germans and you know about it. What do you know about the night Theo was killed?'

When she refused to answer, I aimed my gun at her thigh and shot. She screamed in pain, which in turn made the woman next door start to scream until Dancer gagged her.

'Rada,' I said, resuming my seat. 'Let's make a bargain. You tell me what I want to know and I spare your life. You will be taken back to the border and from there you can slip back into Serbia or wherever it is you came from.'

More water was thrown at her. I really thought she would die rather than talk but she surprised me.

'Kyrie Petrakis was executed,' she said eventually, spitting blood out of her mouth.

Stelios and I looked at each other, unsure of whether to believe her or not. I asked how she knew.

'Because I heard her tell someone over the phone that it had been taken care of,' she replied.

'Was Alexis working for the Germans?' I asked.

She nodded her head. 'Yes. She reported to a man called Franz Keller. The Germans put me here to keep an eye on her just before her husband's death. Kyrie Petrakis had no idea who I was but the Kyria knew. For some reason, she couldn't refuse them. All I did was to keep an eye on her and report who came to the house.'

'You mean like me?'

She lowered her head.

'And what did you tell them about me?'

'That you were her cousin — Nikos.' She paused for a moment. 'But you're not are you? Who are you?'

I wanted to burst out laughing. Could it really be true that Alexis had kept it from them that I was an agent working for the Allies?

'What do you know about Poseidon?' I asked.

'I've never heard of it. I told you, it was my job to report who she met with. Nothing else.'

'Do you know who killed Kyrie Petrakis?'

'I swear I don't know, but there's a Greek man who comes to see her occasionally. I believe he's also a friend of Herr Keller's. Perhaps it was him. I don't know his name. Kyrie Petrakis never liked him. He told the Kyria, he didn't trust him.'

I stood up walked out of the room taking Stelios with me. I called Dancer out on to the landing and after a brief discussion told them we were going to the cemetery to find out the truth for ourselves.'

'What do you have in mind?' Dancer asked.

'We're going to dig up Theo's body. This business about Theo dying after escaping is at odds with Rada saying he was executed. Stay here and keep watch. Stelios and I will go. The Church of the Virgin of the Swallow is not that far from here.'

We found the keys to the car in the driver's room and located two shovels and picks in the garden shed. By car it was a mere five minute drive away. Thankfully, it was still very early and there was no-one around. When we reached the church, we parked the car off the road out of sight, took out the shovels and picks and headed towards the churchyard.

A warm breeze was blowing as we started to dig and the air was filled with the scent of wildflowers and incense from the church. The earth was still soft and in no time at all, the fresh summer smells were replaced by a foul odour. Another few feet and we'd reach the corpse.

'The Greeks will kill us if they find out we're exhuming a dead body,' Stelios said, shovelling up mounds of earth and tossing it to one side. 'All that stuff about the soul never finding rest.'

It wasn't long before my spade hit something. We moved the rest of the earth away gently until a white cloth was exposed.

'The poor sod wasn't even put in a coffin,' Stelios said.

A ghastly overpowering stench rose up in the air making us retch. We had already covered our nose and mouth with a cloth, but it was useless against something so nauseating. It wasn't difficult to see where the head was and I took it upon myself to cut away the fabric. The corpse had already begun to deteriorate and I hoped we would find what we were looking for quickly before we succumbed to bouts of vomiting. We did. At the back of the skull was a hole — unmistakable evidence that Theo had been executed in cold blood. Any other time, we would have opened the skull and removed the bullet.

'I've seen enough,' I said. 'Enough to know that even if he had been shot and then run away, it was not his wounds he died from. It was this. I only hope he didn't see it coming.'

We started to fill in the grave and had almost finished when we saw Father Haralambos coming towards us.

'It's you again. What are you doing here?' he asked angrily. 'I've told you to keep away.'

He stopped in his tracks when I pointed my gun at him. I gestured to him to get back in the church.

'You knew didn't you?' I said, closing the church door behind us.

The priest looked terrified. 'Knew what? All I know is that this is hallowed ground and you are defiling it. God sees all and you will be punished.'

'You knew Theo Petrakis had been executed, didn't you?'

The priest turned white and stepped back bumping into the stand holding the sand and candles.

'I swear I don't know what you're talking about.'

'What happened when you buried him? I want to know every detail. And don't lie. It won't be worth it. You might be a priest, but don't think that will stop me killing you.'

It didn't take much for him to talk. He said Alexis had paid him a large amount of money to bury the body in exchange for not asking questions. He knew Theo and Alexis worked for the Resistance but had no idea in what capacity. He believed her when she said that if his death leaked out, there would be reprisals.

'Did you know the man you buried had been executed?' I asked.

He lifted his hands and cupped the side of his head in fear

'I had nothing to do with all this. The body was already wrapped when I saw it. I believed the Kyria when she said the Germans killed him.'

Strangely enough, I believed him. I knew how persuasive Alexis could be. The problem was, we couldn't let him go now.

I went outside for air. The smell of incense mixed with

the stench of death was too overpowering. Stelios came out after me.

'What are we going to do with him?' he asked.

He recognised the look in my eyes. 'You're not seriously saying we should kill him.'

'He took a bribe. He might not have known how he died but he knew something was wrong. What's more, he participated in the charade of the fake memorial, knowing full well Theo died earlier. Besides, he's seen us now.'

'He has no idea who we are. Let him go.'

I thought about it for a minute or two. 'Alright. You win. Gag him, tie him up and lock him in the church. By the time somebody finds him we'll be long gone. I'll get the car.'

The priest was praying in front of an icon with his back to the door when Stelios re-entered the church. He fully expected to be killed. Instead Stelios grabbed a narrow strip of gold embroidered cloth on which stood three icons, and tied him to a section of the wooden iconostasis. He used his own handker-chief to gag him.

We returned to the house to finish what we started. I searched through the drawers looking for anything I could lay my hands on that would incriminate Alexis, but there was nothing. Only a book by the telephone filled with names and numbers, which I pocketed.

The men were waiting for me upstairs. The young girl was still terrified and Rada was losing consciousness from loss of blood from the head and leg wounds. I took my gun out and fired. There was no other choice. The girl started screaming again.

Stelios and Dancer looked at me.

'She recognises me.' I said. 'It has to be done.'

It was Dancer who went back into her room to deliver the final shot. When he came out, he looked pale.

'I don't like it any more than you do,' I said. 'Now let's get out of here.'

*

Two nights later we received a coded message from Cairo that the package, as they referred to the three women, had been picked up by another postman and was on its way. The last part of the message was what I had dreaded. I knew then that something bad had happened to Alexis. I sat in my chair with my head in my hands.

'Get the ouzo out,' Dancer said to Stelios. 'He looks like he needs a drink.'

'Do you think the White Rose is dead?' Stelios asked.

'We will have to wait and see. I sent two people to shadow her and I am praying they are fine.'

Dancer tried to cheer me up. 'Well whatever happened, it looks as if the Jewish women are safe. At least that's something to celebrate.'

I was in no mood to celebrate anything and excused myself to go back to Rosa's and get some sleep. There was a wooden icon of the Virgin holding the Christ child in her arms on the wall above my bed. Maroulia had told me to pray to her when I felt low. I remember laughing at her at the time and she chastised me for not putting my faith in God. When I told her I kept a blue bead with me at all times for luck, she laughed.

'Kapetan, so you do believe in something.'

I gave the bead to her. At first she refused it, but I insisted, saying that this mission was dangerous and she would have more need of it than I. She put in her handkerchief and tied a knot around it so as not to lose it.

Now, here I was, for the first time in years, making the sign of the cross and praying. It was not for Alexis that I prayed, but for Maroulia. I had no idea whether she was alive or dead and I would not rest until I knew what had happened.

Chapter 30

Athens. Late September 1943

After months of secret talks between General Badoglio and the Allies, Italy finally surrendered. On the tiny island of Symi, the news was greeted with enthusiasm and shouts of *irini, irini*, peace, peace. Symi was not far from Samos, and like others, I hoped it really would herald a new peace. Everywhere, the Italians were rejoicing, selling or giving away everything from guns and ammunition to blankets and boots. The Germans reacted swiftly. On the island of Rhodes, 7,000 Germans took 40,000 Italians prisoners. On all the other islands, those who resisted were shot and their bodies dumped in the sea. Rather than face execution and imprisonment by the Germans or be sent to POW camps in Germany, thousands of Italian soldiers deserted and the ranks of the andartes swelled. Even so, large pockets of Mussolini's Fascists remained loyal, wreaking havoc on their own countrymen. Battle-hardened German troops from the Eastern Front and Yugoslavia were deployed into Greece with the intention of wiping out the *andartes*. What took place in Kato Hora was repeated throughout Greece. Things would get worse before they would get better.

After the incident at the Petrakis villa, Poseidon was put on red alert. No-one knew what took place that day at the villa apart from Loukas, who returned to Athens shortly afterwards. All the meeting places were changed and many *andartes* left Athens for a while. Hadzigiannis closed his tailor's shop overnight and the workers disappeared. Only Maria stayed where she was, dispensing medicines to all and sundry, collecting information, and passing it on to the Resistance. I could not tell her what took place that day at the villa, but knowing that she knew Theo and Alexis personally, I pleaded with her to move. She wouldn't hear of it.

'If they are coming for me, I am here,' she said defiantly.

'Think of Chryssa and Yiannis,' I argued.

They refused to leave Athens too. The best I could do would be to check on them regularly.

*

Towards the end of September, we received a message from Cairo. Icarus had been a success. What that meant, I had yet to find out, but as far as London, Cairo and Istanbul were concerned, I was to be congratulated. I was still living at Rosa's and had intended to move out, but she insisted I stay. I gladly accepted. It was comfortable and safe. Another reason I stayed was because of Maroulia. I still didn't know what had happened to her. In fact, I still had no idea what took place after the boat left Piraeus.

A few weeks later, Aris returned to Athens. Together with Dancer and Stelios, we celebrated with a bottle of whisky supplied by Rosa. I was relieved to see him, but braced myself to hear what had taken place. Aris didn't mess around. What he had to say was straight to the point. Alexis was dead. It was brutal and sobering. Even after hearing his words, it was still hard to get my head around it. What took place was even harder to comprehend.

The *Arcadia* left Piraeus shortly before the port was bombed. On board were a few civilians, the rest were German soldiers and officers being deployed to the islands. Most of the civilians were forced to share a small area in what passed for a restaurant but which now only sold drinks at prohibitive prices and no food. There were several sleeping cabins, all of which had been booked out at inflated prices. Alexis had one to herself, the Kamaras women shared another, and Maroulia had one. The rest were taken by two Greek merchants and German officers.

About an hour after the boat left Piraeus, Alexis left her room and sat in the restaurant reading a magazine. The Kamaras women stayed in their room. Maroulia sat next to her reading a book. After a while, she snapped the book shut and started a conversation with Alexis. How lucky they were to miss the bombing and how their friends and family would be so relieved to see them, etc.? At first, Alexis was reluctant to converse, but Maroulia seemed so friendly that she eventually acknowledged her. Maroulia said she had just purchased a dress shop in Kolonaki from a Jewish lady, adding that she bought it for next to nothing as the Jews would all be leaving Athens. On the surface, she appeared to give the impression that she had no sympathy for the plight of the Jews, in the hope that she might get a reaction from Alexis, but Alexis remained stone-faced.

Not to be put off, Maroulia continued chatting. She said she was looking forward to the challenge of running her own business, even though there was a war on. Eventually Alexis joined in the conversation and wanted to know where Maroulia was going. Maroulia replied that she was on her way to Chios.

'And what about yourself?' Maroulia asked. 'Are you staying in Syros or will you be going further?'

Alexis thought about it for a few moments. 'I will be staying in Syros.'

Maroulia opened her cigarette case and offered Alexis a cigarette before taking one herself. She remembered distinctly being told that Alexis would be travelling to Samos. She knew something was wrong but felt it unwise to pursue the conversation further and re-opened her book, apologising for interrupting her. Alexis went back to reading her magazine. After a while Maroulia said she was going outside to get some fresh air.

There were still several people on the deck. She stood by the rail staring out at the inky black water glistening in the moonlight when she was approached by her contact. The man introduced himself as Andreas. Maroulia did not give her name but after a minute or so, he called her Sofia. Still cautious, she waited. Then he added that if they were travelling during the day they would be able to see the sun and maybe see Icarus flying too close to the sun. Maroulia quickly understood he was using the legend of Icarus to introduce himself. He gave her the cabin numbers of Alexis and the Kamaras women. They were together for less than a couple of minutes but it was long enough for her to tell him that Alexis said she was only going as far as Syros. He told her he'd seen their luggage delivered to their cabins and they had a Samos address. Maybe the Kyria was tired and it was a slip of the tongue. Maroulia was not convinced and Andreas assured her he would look into it and report to her every hour in the same place. When she returned to the restaurant, Alexis had gone, and Maroulia presumed she'd gone back to her cabin.

An hour later, she went back on deck again. The temperature had dropped and there was a chill in the air so she returned to her cabin to get her hat and coat. About an hour before they arrived in Syros, Andreas reported some urgent news. He'd spotted Alexis talking to a man in the restaurant and busied himself cleaning the tables and sweeping the floor nearby in order to listen in to their conversation. At one point, he overheard Alexis give them the names on the women's ID's. She also told them they were not Orthodox as stated on the papers, but were in fact, Jews. From what Andreas gathered, the Gestapo would be waiting for them for them in Ermoupoli. The man thanked her, adding that Athens would show their appreciation when she returned.

Andreas went straight to the women's cabin to warn them they were in danger and took them to hide in a laundry closet. He told them not to make the slightest noise or they would be killed. He had only just locked the closet door when Alexis returned. He walked past her carrying a pile of linen. She failed to notice him as the man cleaning in the restaurant five minutes earlier.

In the event of an emergency, Maroulia had been given a separate set of IDs for the women. Now she needed to give them to them as soon as possible. That was the easy part. The hard part was Alexis. When she found the women gone, she would alert the man she'd been speaking to and, in all likelihood no-one, except for the Germans would be allowed off the boat until it had been searched.

'We have to get rid of her. There's no other way,' Andreas said. 'Which one of us is going to do it?'

'I will,' Maroulia replied, matter-of-factly.

'Are you sure?'

'Quite sure.'

'Be careful. Remember, there are German officers in those cabins too.'

Maroulia hurried back to her cabin. When she went to open the door she realised she's left it unlocked. She entered and switched on the light. Sitting on the bed was Alexis, pointing a gun at her. The gun was fitted with a silencer. On the bed was her suitcase which had been ransacked. Maroulia stood paralysed in the moment, her heart beating wildly. She told herself it was imperative she stay calm or she would end up dead.

'Why are you following me?' Alexis asked. 'Who are you?'

Maroulia gathered her wits together and attempted to brush her off with a light-hearted, friendly laugh. 'Why would I follow you? I was just trying to be friendly.'

Alexis gestured towards a cloth bag amongst the clothes that now lay scattered on the bed. 'Then why do you carry this.' She picked it up with her thumb and forefinger and let the gun slip out onto the bed.

'For the same reason you carry yours,' replied Maroulia. 'To protect myself.'

'Don't be smart. If I called someone now, you would be taken away and most likely be shot.'

'Please, Kyria, 'Maroulia replied, in a sweet voice. 'This journey has given me sea-sickness. I'm exhausted and I have to sit down.'

'Stay where you are.'

'At least let me take off my hat and coat.'

Alexis nodded her approval.

Cautiously, Maroulia took off her coat and laid it carefully over the back of the chair.

'Thank you,' she said, as she put her hands up to take off her hat.

Alexis didn't see the hatpin being drawn out from the back of the hat. It all happened in a flash. Maroulia had gauged the distance between the two of them and in a split second stabbed her in the face. Alexis's head snapped back in pain and in that moment she lost concentration. Maroulia knocked the gun out of her hand sending it flying across the room. Alexis put both hands up to her face to protect them but Maroulia was too quick. She pulled the hatpin out of her cheek and stabbed her in the throat. Alexis fell back onto the bed with Maroulia on top of her, holding the hatpin tightly in place. Alexis's eyes stared at her in utter disbelief as she lay on the bed choking on her own blood. It was over in a matter of minutes.

Maroulia had expected something bad might happen, but she had not expected it to happen like this. She had no idea who the woman she'd been shadowing really was, but she knew she was a collaborator and deserved to die. All the same, it surprised her how cold she felt at seeing how easily she'd killed her. It was as if she'd purposely numbed herself to get through it all.

She decided it was too dangerous to attempt to move the body on her own. After cleaning herself and hiding both guns, she went to look for Andreas. Thankfully, he wasn't too far away.

'What a mess.' he said when he saw the body. 'I agree, it's too dangerous to move her back into her own cabin now. We've almost arrived. Give me a hand. We'll put her in your bed and make it look as though it's you sleeping.'

That was easier said than done. Blood was seeping into the blankets.

'Let's pray no-one finds her until we've disembarked,' Andreas said, standing back to check his handiwork. The scene looked authentic but it won't take the authorities long to realise something was wrong. 'Pack your bag and go upstairs and get ready to disembark. Hurry, there's no time to waste. I'll take care of the women.'

Maroulia gave him the new IDs and quickly threw her clothes back in the suitcase. She looked out of the cabin window and saw the harbour of Ermoupoli. In the background rose the hill of Ano Syros with its white-washed buildings gleaming in the early morning sun. She picked up the suitcase, took one last look at the body under the blankets, asked God to forgive her, and left the room, locking it behind her.

The deck was already filling with people preparing to disembark. She joined the smaller group of civilians and waited. A crowd of onlookers, porters and traders, stood on the quayside waiting for the new arrivals, but before anyone could disembark, a voice over the loudspeaker announced that everyone was to have their documents ready to be checked. Half a dozen men in plain suits boarded the boat and one by one, started to examine their papers, checking and cross-checking names against a list. They were not particularly interested in the Germans soldiers and allowed them to disembark. It was clear to everyone that the men were the Gestapo. The civilians waited their turn, nervously watching on as some unfortunate soul was dragged out of the line and taken away. Maroulia was in the last group. At that moment, Andreas came on deck with the three women. Maroulia hardly recognised them. He'd given them all a change of clothes, more in keeping with those worn by villagers than the elegant city clothes they wore when they boarded the boat. Where he got them from she had no idea. He pushed them into line and walked away, busying himself with deckhand work nearby.

When it was Maroulia's turn to show her documents, her name was ticked off the list and she was told she could leave. Her heart pounded in her chest as she descended the narrow gangway, half expecting to be shot at any moment. She walked towards a group of onlookers before she stopped and looked back. Fingering her blue bead, she watched on as one by one, the civilians descended. At that moment a man approached her from behind and addressed her as Sofia. Maroulia recognised him from his photograph. It was Aris. He told her he'd already found out the Gestapo were looking for the women. The minutes ticked by until finally, they breathed a huge sigh of relief when they saw the three women start to disembark. Then she saw Andreas wave from the deck. They'd made it.

Maroulia and Aris hurried towards the women and quickly ushered them away from the crowd. They had no idea they'd been shadowed and as a consequence were terrified.

'Who are you?' Esther Kamaras asked, trying to shake herself free of Maroulia's tight grip on her arm.

'You're quite safe,' Maroulia said in a low voice. 'Please don't worry. We're in charge of you now and we have to get you away from here immediately. The Gestapo are on the lookout for you.'

The women instinctively looked back towards the deck. 'The man who saved us. Who was he? Where is he?'

'There will be time for questions later,' Aris said. 'Please do as we say. When the Gestapo realise you've slipped through their net, all hell will break loose and they'll instigate a search of the town straight away.'

Aris led the women away from the quayside and into a side street where they were bundled into a horse-drawn cart. Minutes later they left Ermoupoli for Komito on the south side of the island. There they were met by members of the Poseidon Network. A new escape route was underway.

Maroulia chose not to return to Athens with Aris.

'I think my presence will give them some sort of reassurance,' she said to him. 'But there is something you can do for me.'

'What might that be?' Aris asked.

She gave him the blue bead. 'Give this to the Kapetan. Tell him he has given me something to fight for.'

Chapter 31

I was relieved to hear Maroulia and the Kamaras women escaped, but try as I might, I could not imagine that Alexis was indeed dead, despite being given all the facts. I would leave it for Loukas to reveal the truth about her death to Poseidon. For the moment, we had to concentrate on who the Greek man with the tortoise-shell glasses was.

Since the incident at the Petrakis villa, Stelios had spent time going through Alexis's telephone book, making phone calls from various kiosks across Athens. Many numbers no longer existed. One by one, names and numbers were crossed off the list until he was left with only half a dozen. One of those was the SS Headquarters in Merlin Street. It was disguised as *Thea* Anna — Aunt Anna. At first the number looked odd, until Aris worked out it was written back to front. The call went straight through to Franz Keller's office and was answered by his secretary. Realising Alexis kept this number in code, Aris tried another number, that of *Thea* Despina — Aunt Despina. The number indicated that it was somewhere near Maroussi. A man's voice answered. Aris put the phone down. Was this the man with the tortoise-shell glasses? We discussed this with Loukas.

Like me, Loukas was still in shock about Alexis. He simply could not reconcile the woman he knew as a traitor and undertook to look into the mysterious *Thea* Despina himself. It wasn't long before he was indeed located at a villa in Maroussi. A couple of days later, I received a message to meet Loukas at an isolated farmhouse near the remains of Cadmea, the citadel of ancient Thebes. The place was surrounded by *andartes* armed to the hilt. In the centre of the kitchen was a man bound to a chair with rope. He had been severely beaten and was bleeding profusely from a head wound caused by the butt of a gun.

Loukas handed me a pair of glasses. They were tortoise-shell.

'I think this is the man you are looking for,' he said. 'We have his wife in another room.'

Thea Despina turned out to be one Manos Gatapoulos, a minor bureaucrat who worked in the office of Ambassador Marinetti. While his job might have seemed ordinary, it was anything but. Gatapoulos liaised between the Germans, Italians and Greek collaborators. It was his role to recruit Greeks by any means possible. After considerable torture by Loukas, he admitted to knowing Alexis well and recruiting her in Cairo. I asked Loukas and his men to leave us alone for a while.

'Do you know who I am?'

'Yes. Alexis's cousin — Nikos.'

Again I was surprised she had kept up this charade about me being her cousin, despite all she was involved in.

'How did you two meet?' I asked. 'How did you recruit her?'

Gatapoulos refused to talk.

'I have a lot of patience. I can wait. The problem is, time is running out for your wife. The men have decided what will happen to her if you don't talk. I don't think you'd like us to bring her body in here and show you what they did to her, do you? So if I was you, I'd talk.'

Gatapoulos knew he would not get out alive and after a while promised he would talk if we let his wife go.

'I give you my word,' I assured him.'

Over the next few hours, Gatapoulos told us everything. When the Germans discovered Alexis was in Cairo, they quickly realised she was indeed the wife of a man they suspected to be the leader of the *andartes*. Knowing this, they put pressure on her to turn informer, telling her that if she refused, her husband would certainly meet an untimely death. The Germans knew everything about Theo's relationships with other women, including Irini. They put pressure on Irini too, but she refused to turn on her former lover. It was German spies in Cairo who killed Irini, not Alexis. When Alexis found out what had happened to her, she contacted the British and offered to work for them as an agent if they could get her back to Greece. At the same time, Theo was also in contact with the British as his network was expanding.

When Alexis returned to Athens, she was again contacted by the secret police. From that moment on, she was told to report to Herr Doktor Franz Keller. She knew that if she refused, what happened to Irini would happen to them all. Again, Gatapoulos was adamant that he was simply the go-between.

'What happened the night Theo was killed and who shot him?' I asked.

This time Gatapoulos faltered. 'The Germans wanted him out of the way because Alexis said she thought Theo suspected her of spying for the Germans. They told her to kill him and she refused, even though they threatened to kill her if she didn't.

Then a deal was reached. Keller is not a man to do deals but he was besotted with her and gave in.'

'What was the deal?' I asked.

'Keller told her that if she killed Theo, he would allow her to continue to work unharmed with the *andartes* so long as she kept feeding them information. I've known him for a long time. He is ruthless, but it served him better if she continued working as a double agent. He knew from the start that she was working for the British, even though she never told him. It was her idea to give up many of those she was helping to escape. She had no choice. The Germans had too much on her. It was either that or they round everyone up. In which case hundreds would have been executed.'

Nothing would have suited me better than to think that Alexis had done this to protect Poseidon, but it wasn't as easy as that. People had died — innocent people.

'She did have a choice,' I said. 'She could have killed herself rather than give up innocent people.'

Gatapoulos forced a laugh. 'Don't you see? Keller wanted it to look like everything was fine. He will never let the *andartes* get away. With her gone, he plans to bring everyone down.'

'You didn't answer my question. Who killed Theo?'

'Keller arranged it all that night. I was there. After we'd killed the other two *andartes* at Ekali, I took Theo back to the villa to make Alexis keep her promise. She was told to shoot him herself. When she refused, I shot him. Then we buried him. The only other person who knew about her connection with the Germans was her housekeeper, the Slav — Rada. Keller made Alexis hire her in order to keep an eye on her.

'And the driver?' I asked.

'Her driver knew something was wrong. After all, he'd

worked for the family for a while, but he was warned that his entire family would be wiped out if he breathed a word.'

I went outside to get some air. It was dark by now. A silver moon hung in the sky, his face laughing down at me. I was numb. Loukas came over and I told him what had transpired.

'I'm glad she's dead,' Loukas said, 'because I would have killed her myself.'

I wasn't so sure. I wanted to tell him not to judge her too harshly; that she gave up a few for the greater good of Poseidon, but I couldn't. They didn't know her as I did. And I didn't know her either.

'What are we going to do with him?' Loukas asked.

'I think that honour goes to Kostas, don't you? For Kondoumaris.'

Loukas went to fetch him and we told him what had taken place.

Kostas took his gun out of his belt and went inside without uttering a word. Moments later, we heard a shot ring out. Gatapoulos was dead.

'What about his wife? Kostas asked, when he returned.

'No. I promised him she wouldn't be harmed if he talked. From what you've said, she knows nothing about her husband's work anyway. When this war is over, she will have to face the wrath of the people because of his collaboration with the Germans.'

'She's blindfolded and won't be able to recognise any of us,' Loukas said.

'Then take her to a spot outside a small village and leave her where she can be found by the villagers in the morning.'

*

Cairo. December 1944

It was early evening when I left my meeting with the Colonel at Rustem Buildings. He wanted to thank me personally for what I'd done in Greece. He never asked for details. Suffice to say, the matter of the songbird had been dealt with and the Poseidon Network had fought heroically against the Axis forces, and that was all that mattered. He told me to call back in a week's time when there would be a new assignment for me. For now, I was to go and enjoy myself.

'Relax, old boy,' were his exact words. 'Go and have some fun.'

It was a short walk back to Shepheard's and the atmosphere was one of merriment. British marching bands paraded through the streets and the Greeks were waving blue and white flags, celebrating the German defeat. I went to the Long Bar where Joe Scialom still reigned supreme and ordered one of his famous cocktails. During the time I'd been away, his notoriety had increased and people flocked to his bar where he regaled them with his exploits and stories about the war. Joe's outgoing and fun-loving personality belied the fact that he was one of the most trustworthy people I had ever met. Everyone entrusted him with their secrets, even secret agents.

'Ah, there you are, Mr Hadley. There's a message for you.'

Joe took a slip of paper out of his pocket and handed it to me. It was from Jack Martins saying that he would meet me on the terrace at 8:00 p.m. for drinks and afterwards supper was booked at the Gezira Sporting Club.

'What will you have to drink?' Joe asked.

'Thank you. I'll have one of your famous cocktails,' I replied. 'A Suffering Bastard. I missed them.'

I watched him pour the ingredients into an ice-filled Old-fashioned glass, add the ice and mix them together with a theatrical flourish. Lastly, he added a sprig of mint and a slice of lemon and slid it across the bar towards me.

'It's on the house,' he said with a smile.

I picked up a copy of the Egyptian Gazette and went outside to sit on the terrace. A swing band accompanied by a classy lady in a shimmering apricot coloured dress was playing a Harry James number — *You Made Me Love You*. The irony of the occasion was not lost on me. I took a sip of my cocktail and started to read the paper. Splashed across the cover were the headlines — *Violent clashes in Athens. 28 demonstrators killed.*

A voice behind me interrupted my thoughts. It was Jack Martins and it was the first time I'd seen him since Turkey.

'Messy business what's happening in Greece,' he said taking a seat and calling the waiter over. 'I'll have what he's having,' he said, 'with lots of ice.'

He pulled out a packet of cigarettes and offered me one. 'After all they've been through, this happens, poor sods. I wonder when it will all end.'

I told him I feared it would turn the country into a bloodbath. He agreed sadly.

'I have a message for you from a friend of yours — Sofia,' he said. 'She says to give you a big kiss and tell you she's never been happier. What did you do to warrant that, Larry? Charm her as you do all the other women you meet?'

'I'm glad she's fine. What's she doing now?'

'Working with Greeks in Palestine. She met someone you know — another *andarte*. They are engaged to be married.'

I was happy for her. At least someone's life had turned out well.

Jack and I had so much to talk about but for the moment it could wait. We listened to the band for a while, drowning our past in drinks.

'What was it about her that was so special?' Jack asked, after a while.

'Who — Sofia?'

He looked at me and smiled. 'You know exactly who I mean. Alexis — the White Rose.'

At the mention of her name, I looked over to the place where I'd first laid eyes on her. I could picture her as clearly as if it was yesterday — her long fingers with the painted red nails, smoothing the folds of her white dress. After she'd died, I desperately wanted to believe she'd deliberately kept my name as "Cousin Nikos" because she genuinely had feelings for me. I would never know.

I smiled. 'I don't know, Jack. I wish I did.'

He looked at me sadly. 'Oh well, at least that war in Greece is over for us now. We'll both be moving on. There are still things to do before this war ends.'

'Where do you think they're sending us, next?' I asked.

He shrugged his shoulders. 'Who knows? Anyway, old boy, finish that drink. There's a table waiting for as the Gezira Sporting Club — and two pretty girls.'

We laughed. 'Ah, Jack Martins. What would I do without you?'

*

For me that war was over. For the Greeks, the conflicts between the resistance groups in 1943 and the events of that December 1944, or *Dekemvriana,* as it would be known by the Greeks, erupted into a full-blown civil war that would last until October 1949. My old friend Loukas had taken over the Poseidon Network as the new White Rose, and in the interests of keeping the network unified, much as he and Alexis had done after Theo's death, kept the truth about Alexis's death a secret. The last I heard of him was that he and Anna had gone to fight in Epirus. Little did I know then that the Civil War was to take the lives of thousands of Greeks while thousands more were imprisoned, exiled, or executed. I fingered my blue bead and prayed for them.

Postscript

The Massacre at Komeno, which took place in Western Greece, in the summer of 1943, was the inspiration for the massacre at Kato Hora in my novel. Today, a marble monument stands in the village plateia commemorating the names of 317 villagers who died. The youngest was one-year-old Alexander Kritsima, the oldest, seventy-five-year-old Anastasia Kosta.

The village of Komeno was under the command of the Italians stationed in Arta. Since the German occupation, the villagers had been on relatively good terms with the Italian commander. On 12 August, a group of *andartes* came into the village and left their rifles propped against a tree in the centre of the plateia while they collected firewood. On that particular day, a two-man German reconnaissance team entered the village, spotted the guns, and immediately retreated to report it to the 1st Mountain Division HQ in Ioannina. After informing Athens, the Germans decided to "teach the villagers a lesson". Such flagrant conduct would not be tolerated.

The 15 August was the Feast of the Assumption and after being assured by the Italian commander that no harm would come to them, the villagers prepared for a celebration. Before dawn on the 16 August, about a hundred Germans from 12 Company entered the village and on instructions "to leave nothing standing" encircled the village and attacked, storming the houses and throwing hand-grenades into the homes while most of the villagers were sleeping.

The Germans had fully expected to confront the *andartes* and were surprised to discover there were none in the village — only old men, women, and children. Still, they continued with the attack. Most of those who tried to escape to the nearby fields and river were machine-gunned by soldiers manning the guard posts. Amid the gunfire and terrifying screams, the houses were set alight, livestock stolen, and soldiers helped themselves to booty, including carpets and jewellery. The village was a burnt-out shell, and bodies — many of them charred — lay scattered everywhere. Not even the priest was spared.

According to reports filed immediately after, the Germans noted that "the Company encountered enemy resistance and enemy losses amounted to 150".

It was one of the worst massacres to take place in Greece during WWII.

The Suffering Bastard

During World War II, Shepheard's Hotel in Cairo was frequented by British officers and the press corps. The hotel was well-known for its Long Bar, and in particular, its bartender, Joe Scialom, whose stories were said to rival anyone's, from Ernest Hemingway to Ian Fleming. Being an Egyptian-Jew, Joe spoke multiple languages and was great at remembering names, faces, and the drinks they preferred, and he quickly earned everyone's respect. In 1942, after hearing British officers complain about their hangover, Joe, who was originally trained as a Chemist, was inspired to create a hangover cure. Using ingredients that could be sourced locally, he created the Suffering Bastard. There are several versions of the recipe. One uses brandy instead of bourbon. However, over time, the bourbon version has become the most popular.

Recipe

Ingredients

- 1 oz/30 mL bourbon
- 1 oz/30mL gin

- 1 tsp. lime juice
- 1 dash of Angostura Bitters
- 4 oz/118 mL of ginger beer (chilled)

Directions

Pour unstrained ingredients into an ice-filled Old Fashioned glass. Top with ginger ale, adding more ice if needed. Garnish with a sprig of mint or an orange slice.

Also by the Author

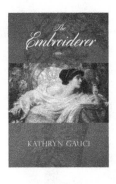

The Embroiderer

1822: During one of the bloodiest massacres of The Greek War of Independence, a child is born to a woman of legendary beauty in the Byzantine monastery of Nea Moni on the Greek island of Chios. The subsequent decades of bitter struggle between Greeks and Turks simmer to a head when the Greek army invades Turkey in 1919. During this time, Dimitra Lamartine arrives in Smyrna and gains fame and fortune as an embroiderer to the elite of Ottoman society. However it is her grand-daughter Sophia, who takes the business to great heights only to see their world come crashing down with the outbreak of The Balkan Wars, 1912-13. In 1922, Sophia begins a new life in Athens but the memory of a dire prophecy once told to her grandmother about a girl with flaming red hair begins to haunt her with devastating consequences.

1972: Eleni Stephenson is called to the bedside of her dying aunt in Athens. In a story that rips her world apart, Eleni discovers the chilling truth behind her family's dark past plunging her into the shadowy world of political intrigue, secret societies and espionage where families and friends are torn apart and where a belief in superstition simmers just below the surface.

Set against the mosques and minarets of Asia Minor and

the ruins of ancient Athens, *The Embroiderer* is a gripping saga of love and loss, hope and despair, and of the extraordinary courage of women in the face of adversity.

The Embroiderer is also available in Greek.

Seraphina's Song

"If I knew then, dear reader, what I know now, I should have turned on my heels and left. But no, instead, I stood there transfixed on the beautiful image of Seraphina. In that moment my fate was sealed."

Dionysos Mavroulis is a man without a future; a man who embraces destiny and risks everything for love.

A refugee from Asia Minor, he escapes Smyrna in 1922 disguised as an old woman. Alienated and plagued by feelings of remorse, he spirals into poverty and seeks solace in the hashish dens around Piraeus.

Hitting rock bottom, he meets Aleko, an accomplished bouzouki player. Recognising in the impoverished refugee a rare musical talent, Aleko offers to teach him the bouzouki.

Dionysos' hope for a better life is further fuelled when he meets Seraphina — the singer with the voice of a nightingale — at Papazoglou's Taverna. From the moment he lays eyes on her, his fate is sealed.

Set in Piraeus, Greece during the 1920's and 30's, *Seraphina's Song* is a haunting and compelling story of hope and despair, and of a love stronger than death.

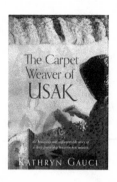

The Carpet Weaver of Usak

"Springtime and early summer are always beautiful in Anatolia. Hardy winter crocuses, blooming in their thousands, are followed by blue muscari which adorn the meadows like glorious sapphires on a silk carpet."

Set amidst the timeless landscape and remote villages of Anatolia, The Carpet Weaver of Uşak *is the haunting and unforgettable story of a deep friendship between two women, one Greek Orthodox, the other a Muslim Turk: a friendship that transcends an atmosphere of mistrust, fear and ultimate collapse, long after the wars have ended.*

Life in Stavrodromi and Pınarbaşı always moved at a slow pace. The years slipped by with the seasons and news was gathered from the camel trains passing through. The Greek and Turkish inhabitants of these two villages managed to pull together in adversity, keeping an eye out for each other. In the centre of the village stood the Fountain of the Sun and Moon. Here the locals congregated to celebrate the events in each other's life — their loves and losses, their hopes and dreams. When war broke out in a faraway place that few had heard of, a sense of foreboding crept into the village, as silently as the winter mists that heralded the onset of another long, cold winter.

1914: As the tentacles of The Great War threaten to envelop the Ottoman Empire, Uşak, the centre of the centuries-old carpet weaving industry in Turkey, prepares for war. Carpet orders are cancelled and the villagers whose lives depend on weaving, have no idea of the devastating impact the war will have on their lives.

1919: In the aftermath of the war, the tenuous peace is further destabilized when the Greek army lands in Smyrna and quickly fans out into the hinterland. Three years later, the population of Stavrodromi and Pınarbaşı are forced to take sides. Loyalties and friendships that existed for generations are now irrevocably torn apart. Their world has changed forever.

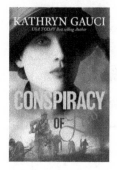

Conspiracy of Lies

A powerful account of one woman's struggle to balance her duty to her country and a love she knows will ultimately end in tragedy.

1940. With the Germans about to enter Paris, Claire Bouchard flees France for England. Two years later she is recruited by the Special Operations Executive and sent back into occupied France to work alongside the Resistance. Working undercover as a teacher in Brittany, Claire accidentally befriends the wife of the German Commandant of Rennes and the blossoming friendship is about to become a dangerous mission.

Knowing that thousands of lives depended on her actions, Claire begins a double life as a Gestapo Commandant's mistress in order to retrieve vital information for the Allied Invasion of France, but ghosts from her past make the deception more painful than she could have imagined.

Part historical, part romance and part thriller, *Conspiracy of Lies* takes us on a journey through occupied France, from the picturesque villages of rural Brittany to the glittering dinner parties of the Nazi Elite, in a story of courage, heartbreak and secrecy.

Code Name Camille

From the *USA Today* runaway bestseller, *The Darkest Hour Anthology: WWII Tales of Resistance*: *Code Name Camille*, now a standalone book.

1940: Paris under Nazi occupation. A gripping tale of resistance, suspense and love.

When the Germans invade France, twenty-one-year-old Nathalie Fontaine is living a quiet life in rural South-West France. Within months, she heads for Paris and joins the Resistance as a courier helping to organise escape routes. But Paris is fraught with danger. When several escapes are foiled by the Gestapo, the network suspects they are compromised. Nathalie suspects one person, but after a chance encounter with a stranger who provides her with an opportunity to make a little extra money by working as a model for a couturier known to be sympathetic to the Nazi cause, her suspicions are thrown into doubt. Using her work in the fashionable rue du Faubourg Saint-Honoré, she uncovers information vital to the network, but at the same time steps into a world of treachery and betrayal which threatens to bring them all undone.

Time is running out and the Gestapo is closing in.

CPSIA information can be obtained
at www.ICGtesting.com
Printed in the USA
BVHW081727230221
600893BV00002B/140

Author Biography

Kathryn Gauci was born in Leicestershire, England, and studied textile design at Loughborough College of Art and Design, and carpet design and technology at Kidderminster College of Art and Design. After graduating, Kathryn spent a year in Vienna, Austria before moving to Greece where she worked as a carpet designer in Athens for six years. There followed another brief period in New Zealand before eventually settling in Melbourne, Australia.

Before turning to writing full-time, Kathryn ran her own textile design studio in Melbourne for over fifteen years, work which she enjoyed tremendously as it allowed her the luxury of travelling worldwide, often taking her off the beaten track and exploring other cultures. *The Embroiderer* is her first novel; a culmination of those wonderful years of design and travel, and especially of those glorious years in her youth living and working in Greece.

Website: www.kathryngauci.com

Code Name Camille

From the *USA Today* runaway bestseller, *The Darkest Hour Anthology: WWII Tales of Resistance: Code Name Camille,* now a standalone book.

1940: Paris under Nazi occupation. A gripping tale of resistance, suspense and love.

When the Germans invade France, twenty-one-year-old Nathalie Fontaine is living a quiet life in rural South-West France. Within months, she heads for Paris and joins the Resistance as a courier helping to organise escape routes. But Paris is fraught with danger. When several escapes are foiled by the Gestapo, the network suspects they are compromised. Nathalie suspects one person, but after a chance encounter with a stranger who provides her with an opportunity to make a little extra money by working as a model for a couturier known to be sympathetic to the Nazi cause, her suspicions are thrown into doubt. Using her work in the fashionable rue du Faubourg Saint-Honoré, she uncovers information vital to the network, but at the same time steps into a world of treachery and betrayal which threatens to bring them all undone.

Time is running out and the Gestapo is closing in.

Author Biography

Kathryn Gauci was born in Leicestershire, England, and studied textile design at Loughborough College of Art and Design, and carpet design and technology at Kidderminster College of Art and Design. After graduating, Kathryn spent a year in Vienna, Austria before moving to Greece where she worked as a carpet designer in Athens for six years. There followed another brief period in New Zealand before eventually settling in Melbourne, Australia.

Before turning to writing full-time, Kathryn ran her own textile design studio in Melbourne for over fifteen years, work which she enjoyed tremendously as it allowed her the luxury of travelling worldwide, often taking her off the beaten track and exploring other cultures. *The Embroiderer* is her first novel; a culmination of those wonderful years of design and travel, and especially of those glorious years in her youth living and working in Greece.

Website: www.kathryngauci.com